I0702606

LORD OF GOBLINS

III

MICHIEL WERBROUCK & HADI Y. BENDAKJI

Table of Contents

GLOSSARY

Lev/Gherm: Assassinated during his victory speech. Lev was forcibly torn from his world during his moment of triumph. But death was not the end, as he finds himself in the body of a greyborn bogey named Gherm. Now in a new land, Lev must find a way to survive and—just maybe—thrive.

A white being trapped at the depths of the monster caverns had forged a contract with Lev, granting him Ainshard's key. Owing to his achievements and those of his men, he has ascended to a prominent position within Bogey society.

Ghorza: Gherm's older sister. She and Gherm are greyborns, which makes them slaves according to the bogeys' primitive society. Having lost her parents at a young age, Ghorza cares deeply for her brother, Gherm, and works hard to keep him safe and fed. She's wary of Lev and wonders how much of her brother is left. In Gherm's absence, she became close friends with a trio of peculiar greyborn girls: Abelarda, Reeza, and Lore.

Abelarda: Ghorza's friend and Volker's older sister. She is a straightforward person, unafraid to voice her opinions, and she naturally assumes the role of leader within her circle of friends. While she values her friendship with Ghorza, she is not fond of Volker's involvement with Lev. She sports a head of dyed blonde hair.

Reeza: The youngest member of Abelarda and Ghorza's circle of friends. Her kindness and calm demeanour charms children and wildlife alike. In times of tension, her presence comforts others. She has chosen to dye her hair brown.

Lore: A member of Abelarda and Ghorza's circle of friends. She comes from a family of smugglers. She has an exceptional knack for manoeuvring undetected. She is recognized by her dyed black hair.

Volker: Lev's second-in-command. He is the youngest son from a family of potters. Endlessly loyal to Lev, his honest nature and work ethic shine through despite his timid personality. He's proved himself as a capable leader and combatant who can hold his own in Lev's absence.

Rak: One of the biggest, baddest greyborn around. Even as a child, Rak was always stronger than his peers. Forced to turn to crime to save his mother, his strength, charisma, and loyalty to his men allowed him to take over the mining quarters and southern living quarters in the slums.

Hem/Hemgall: One of the few truly loyal members of Rak's gang. He likes to keep things simple and respects men who can take risks for their ambitions. Besides that, he can hold his liquor.

Vyrga: Considered to be the "Lord of Wretches" and "King of the Immoral", his actions know no bounds. He is no priest nor poet, neither a warrior nor noble. He is a greyborn, but not just any greyborn; a leader with the blood of nobles in his veins. He cares not for the consequences, as long as he gets his way.

Gelmar: Gelmar, the eldest and first child to follow Vyrga, held a unique place in his mentor's heart, serving not only as a son but also as a companion. His arrogance, coupled with his steadfast conviction that he was destined to succeed Ainshard, led to feelings of deep betrayal when Vyrga did not consider him a viable successor. Fueled by resentment, Gelmar hatched a plot to amass followers and instigate a coup. However, his plans were thwarted when Vyrga discovered his treachery and sent him into battle against Lev. Unfortunately, Gelmar met a tragic end. Defeated, he was subsequently slain by his own followers.

Heimo: Serving as one of Vyrga's trusted commanders, he holds the distinction of being the youngest among the protégés raised by Vyrga. His potential surpassed that of his comrades, hinting at a future where he could have reigned supreme. However, his somewhat unnerving demeanour made him inaccessible to others. Among Vyrga's commanders, he formed friendships only with Bolo and especially Gelmar. He harbors an intense loathing for Lev, who he perceives as having humiliated Gelmar through death. Without Vyrga's restraint, and fueled by a potent mixture of rage and a drug procured from Bodobert, he killed Oswald. During his remorseful episodes, he was manipulated by Bodobert into overthrowing the chief retainer—installed by the Jiira to govern—and his followers. His aim was to elevate the status of greyborns and bolster goblinkind's resilience against the looming threat of Brizilum. In a turn of events, he defected to the side of the Jiira who betrayed Bulgu and was on the verge of killing his other brothers, when Vyrga dealt him a fatal blow. His death was not unremarkable: due to the consumption of various potions prior to his demise, he emitted a dazzling blue light before erupting into blue flames. This was followed by a brilliant flash and a shockwave that left everyone unconscious. Upon awakening, Vyrga and the others discovered his body had vanished.

Os/Oswald: Serving as one of Vyrga's Commanders, he is also one of the children raised by Vyrga, demonstrating unparalleled loyalty among his peers. Known for his rigid, upright nature, his unwavering devotion has earned him the nickname 'Vyrga's Hound.' Given his steadfast disciplined disposition, he is considered the most probable candidate to succeed Vyrga in the unfortunate event of his passing. He was betrayed and killed by Heimo.

Ludger: One of Vyrga's adopted children and the biological elder brother of Bolo. Despite being obnoxious, quick-tempered, and generally unlikable, he harbours a deep affection for his brother and remains dutifully loyal. His flaws are mitigated to some extent by his exceptional combat skills, particularly his mastery with the spear. He carries a distinct distaste for Heimo and Gelmar. He regularly shaves his head as a response to Hemgall's childhood teasing about his 'rat tail'. Nowadays, Hemgall teases him about his short stature.

Bolo: One of Vyrga's adopted children and the younger brother of Ludger. Though his intimidating stature and assertive demeanour may suggest otherwise, he possesses a surprisingly gentle soul. Nevertheless, he won't hesitate to fight when it comes to safeguarding his kin. He is among the rare few of Vyrga's adopted children who formed a true bond with Heimo, treating him as a real brother.

Bulgu: As the expedition's leader and the youngest heir of the Jiira chief, he is recognized for his ambition rather than his leadership. His glaring flaws—notably his greed, ineptitude, and lofty aspirations—coupled with an utter disregard for others' lives, render him universally unpopular. He spearheaded the expedition with the objective of procuring a weapon believed to have been once wielded by Ainshard. He held the conviction that such an accomplishment would validate his claim to the Jiira throne. After the expedition reached the safety of the bogey caverns, he surprised everyone by saying there would be an even bigger expedition. His advisors were so upset with this decision that they decided to poison him, starting a civil war between the bogeys and goblins.

Rapha: The leader of the harem guard. She is an exile from the Ajiin, a clan renowned for its formidable warriors. Following her father's reckless deeds which resulted in his death, she and her family faced exile from their clan. Her paternal uncle, seeking to make amends for his brother's missteps, joined their exile, only to be killed in a confrontation with a Jiira warband. In the ensuing chaos, she was separated from her mother and sister, ultimately finding herself as part of Bulgu's harem guard. Yet, in spite of these adversities, she clinged to her dream of becoming a shieldmaiden one day. Her life took another twist when she was kidnapped and a spiderling crushed her left arm. Thinking her life was ending, she was offered a lifeline by Lev, who promised to heal her arm on the condition that she'd join his crew. Accepting his proposal, she pledged herself as his shieldmaiden, thereby realising her long-held dream.

Ruune: An integral part of the harem guard. She stands as Rapha's right-hand woman and closest confidant. Embodying a rowdy and boisterous spirit, she is known for her unfiltered emotional transparency, always wearing her heart on her sleeve. When Rapha was presumed dead, she temporarily stepped up to lead the harem guard. However, upon discovering that Rapha was alive, she was filled with joy and promptly returned the leadership role back to her.

Gul: A cherished childhood friend of Volker and an established member of Lev's faction. He used his persuasive abilities to coax Volker into joining their ranks, steering him away from a career as a potter. Known for his sharp wit and sarcastic humour, he carries a determined and stubborn disposition. He survived the hiveling onslaught when they attacked the bogey outpost on the second floor of the monster caverns.

Molg: One of Lev's followers. He admires Lev and is loyal to a fault. Instead of following Volker during Lev's presumed death, he went with Jem who he trusted more than Lev's protegee.

Jem: Lev's third-in-command; a seasoned, middle-aged Greyborn who has served under various groups, typically shifting allegiances whenever their leaders meet their end. His considerable experience as both a combatant and a leader is commendable, yet he opts to sidestep conflicts and adamantly declines any offers to ascend to leadership upon the death of a group's figurehead. When it was presumed that Lev had died and Volker assumed control, he decided to leave, taking half of Lev's group with him to form a temporary gang until they could find a better arrangement. Upon hearing news of Lev's return, Jem promptly reconnected with his former group.

Shahn: Born to Kafar Ramun, he is a dignified Darg hailing from the thriving state of Edoros. Despite his relative youth, he commands the Dargs under Bulgu's rule. His past is marked by a stint as a gladiator in Brizilum and, earlier still, a seafaring life that mirrored his father's own maritime beginnings. He made a deal with Vyrga to aid him in his ambitions.

Varra: One of the Dargs dispatched to participate in Bulgu's expedition. Nursing a soft spot for Volker, she makes a point to safeguard him at all costs. As is typical among mercenary Dargs, she is a proficient warrior, and her combat prowess is further enhanced by the Brizilum-crafted armour and weapons she wields. When it was believed she was the last darg alive in the expedition, Bulgu arranged for her to meet her end, ensuring she couldn't inform other dargs if she reached the surface. Fortunately, she survived. Pressured by the situation, Bulgu eventually permitted her to use a shrine to return to the surface.

Gozzag: He is the revered leader of the Deka dispatched to support Bulgu in the expedition. His age and accumulated experiences have shaped him into a wise leader who commands respect from his men. Following the expedition, he became the leader of the Dragma, a haven for all Deka and other survivors of the expedition who shared their hatred towards the Jiira. During the civil war, he struck a deal with Lev to offer assistance in the fight against Barra, the now deceased Jiira war chief.

Ban: Serving as Gozzag's right-hand man and trusted confidant, he blends a firm determination with a congenial and easy-going personality. He's a man of action, never shying away from a confrontation, be it a physical fight or a spirited drinking contest. After the expedition, he followed Gozzag.

Grasha: A strong deka, Grasha first meets Lev and the other greyborn during the expedition into the lower cavern floors. Over time, he's become a strong and reliably ally to Lev.

Thorst: A gifted green bogey. He transitioned from serving as a guard to supervising greyborn miners and is recognized as Kul's protégé. Generally exhibiting an easy-going demeanour, his attitude shifts when it involves Ghorza, for whom he harbours romantic feelings.

Kathaga: As a Priestess of Zeja, she was sought out by Lev for Zeja's blessing. Unbeknownst to Lev, Kathaga would masquerade as a mere temple servant before revealing her true identity as the priestess. Her knowledge extends beyond Lev's expectations, to the point where even his true name isn't concealed from her. Ultimately, she bestowed Zeja's blessing upon Lev's army in anticipation of their impending clash with Gelmar's forces. Operating under Zeja's direction, she masterminded Heimo's betrayal and downfall, the ascensions of both Lev and Vyrga, as well as the demise of Vyrga's father, who was the former chief retainer.

Kul: An old, pale-green bogey overseer. Once considered to be one of the best warriors of the bogey race, he fell from grace after failing to protect a noble's son during a rebellion against the Jiira. He was a good friend of Gat, Gherm, and Ghorza's father, and decided to take care of them in order to repay his debt to him.

Rogg: A bogey herbalist and witchdoctor who is neither skilled enough to treat commoner and noble bogeys, nor kind enough to charge greyborns a fair price for his services. He met his end in the bogey outpost on the second floor of the monster caverns due to an influx of hivelings swarming the upper levels. Despite his connections affording him a safer hideout, he sacrificed this advantage for his son and sole apprentice, Hermut.

Barra: Bulgu's older brother who, unbeknownst to Bulgu, assumed the role of warchief during the expedition. He shares his brother's greed and arrogance but excels on the battlefield. However, following his ambush and subsequent demise at the hands of a group of Dragma horsemen, Raban assumed the position of warchief to maintain morale among Barra's troops.

Raban: As Barra's deputy and the voice of reason during the campaign against the bogeys. This experience made him a highly skilled combatant but did not earn him much support, as mercenary work is viewed unfavourably in Jiira society. His familiarity with bogeys, gleaned from leading past cavern expeditions, also played a role in his selection. A formidable fighter and an open-minded intellectual, he holds little regard for taboos and has a distaste for Jiira traditions and customs. He empathises with other goblinoids due to his experiences. Captured by the bogeys, he negotiated a deal with Lev to secure his and his men's freedom in exchange for his service.

Maria: Raised along with Lev and Brutus in the orphanage, she's strong-willed and hard-headed. Leaving Eurasia behind at the young age of 18, she relocated to its adversary, The Empire, where she painstakingly climbed the ranks. In time, she penetrated the Empire's inner circle and reached out to Lev, promising him vital insights into the Empire's internal operations. With her assistance, Lev managed to infiltrate the Empire, becoming one of the Emperor's trusted aides. She also aided

Brutus (under the alias of Fynn) and Maik to infiltrate the Empire, helping them to secure roles as logistics managers.

Brutus: Lev's childhood best friend. Despite his large size and intimidating, scarred visage, he has a kind heart and can be shy during social gatherings. Now known as Fynn, he is part of the espionage mission into the Empire.

Maik: An imperial war veteran who served in the neutral zone. He's a spy working for Eurasia who helped Lev infiltrate the Empire.

Moritz: Moritz was a member of the bloodhounds, an order established by the imperials that is specialised in espionage. His hideout in zone five was flushed out by the Technocracy, and the Empire doesn't know he had been captured. Lev had assumed his identity to infiltrate the Empire

Bogeys: A goblinoid race known for being physically weak, but intelligent. The typical lifespan of a bogey is sixty years, and they tend to produce less offspring than other goblinoids. Within the intricate web of bogey society, the roles are colour-marked: green-skinned bogeys are categorised as commoners, blue-skinned ones hold positions akin to nobles, and unfortunately, grey-skinned bogeys are confined to the status of slaves. With the defeat of the Jiira, and the rise of many greyborn figures during the civil war, this hierarchy has been greatly diminished.

Greyborns: Bogeys born with dark grey skin, silver hair, and yellow eyes. The greyborn are slaves among slaves, as the tribe they belonged to was a victim of war between the goblin Jiira and kobold Kur. Although it was once an honour to be greyborn, a failed coup by greyborn elitists centuries ago has long besmirched their reputation.

Goblins: As the most numerous and ancient goblinoid species, they stand a tad taller than most bogeys, boasting robust resilience and adaptability to various environments. Their physical prowess is offset by their limited magical capabilities and relatively short lifespans, typically not exceeding that of bogeys. Due to their distinctive looks, aggressive disposition, and impulsiveness, they often find themselves unfairly stereotyped as violent, unintelligent brutes—a stereotype many male goblins inadvertently perpetuate. Female goblins, on the other hand, tend to display fewer of these perceived negative traits.

Dekas: A species of large red goblinoids, these individuals are distinguished by a single horn protruding from their forehead. Their impressive size, formidable strength, and intimidating appearance make them a terrifying presence on the battlefield. However, what often surprises others is their intelligence and keen logistical skills, which defy common perceptions. Additionally, they demonstrate exceptional horsemanship, with many among their ranks choosing to serve as mercenaries.

Dargs: A fascinating species of purple goblinoids, Dargs are known for their long hair and elongated ears. Despite their graceful appearances, they are formidable warriors and skilled sailors, traits that often surprise those deceived by their elegant exteriors. Primarily residing off the mainland in the prosperous state of Edoros, the Dargs experienced a substantial setback when they lost to Brizilum, subsequently becoming its vassal. This change in status led to many Dargs being subjugated as slaves and gladiators.

Burgas: Belonging to the goblinoid species, the Burgas would bear resemblance to goblins, if not for their increased size, pronounced tails, and more robust jaws. Although they may not possess the intellectual prowess of other goblinoids, they compensate for this with their exceptional senses and superior tracking skills, rendering them ideal scouts and hunters. Renowned for their outstanding honour, Burgas are exceptionally loyal; under normal circumstances, they would scarcely ever forsake their comrades.

Bugbears: A species of large, yellow goblinoids, known for their notable physical strength but less so for their intellectual capacities. Their natural aggression often overshadows their conversational skills, rendering them less appealing partners for dialogue.

Merits: Merits serve as a form of lead-based currency. Intentionally dull in appearance, they are primarily used to compensate greyborns for their work. Enforced by the upper class, this near-valueless medium of exchange was designed to limit the greyborns' access to high-quality resources and equipment.

Chosen Ones: Deemed as the reincarnations of gods or their divine champions, Chosen Ones are distinguished figures within the mortal realm. Not only do they retain their past memories, but they also command powers that exceed natural limitations. These capabilities can span from extraordinary strength to the more profound, reality-altering abilities.

Lost Souls: A reincarnated or transmigrated individual that retains their memory, but unlike a chosen one, doesn't have extraordinary abilities. Most of them die in obscurity but a few, using their past life's knowledge and experience, rise to become legends.

The Expedition: An annual event mandated by the Jiira, the expedition serves to harvest refined haze crystals and excavate treasures hailing from Ainshard's era and the age of the gods. Owing to the unique nature of this expedition, Lev and his men found themselves forced to participate, necessitating a truce with Vyrga. This year's expedition was further distinguished by the unprecedented involvement of Bulgu, a Jiira prince, who brought along with him a cadre of slaves and mercenaries from various goblinoid races. Under the ostensible leadership of Bulgu, the group confronted a relentless struggle as they battled their way to the lower floors, their journey plagued by limited opportunities for rest.

The Cycle: The cyclical process of life and death as understood in bogey mythology. The cycle is represented by four distinct facets: life, death, the afterlife, and reincarnation.

Cyfrac Oil: Cyfracs are a rare family of plants, found on the fifth floor and below, that resemble a red-coloured rye and are easily combustible. Their oil has many uses, from ceremonies to smithing, but is most valued by shamans and witch doctors because its flames spread fast and last a long time.

Bluecatcher Mushrooms: A giant, blue, carnivorous species found on or below the second floor of the monster cavern. The mushroom uses its sticky sap to catch prey before encapsulating it for digestion—the sap also works well as an adhesive for wood, leather, and cloth.

Haze Crystals: A special crystal that can store immense amounts of magical energy. This makes it a great alchemical reagent, and essential for making focus tools for shamans. Before refinement, they are highly corrosive towards creatures with low magical resistance. It is rare to find them outside of the bogey and monster caverns where they naturally grow..

The Ancient Shrines: Mystical constructions originating from the era of Ainshard, if not earlier. These shrines possess the power to teleport small bands of individuals to corresponding shrines elsewhere. Upon the Jiira's first exploration of the caverns, sacred sites above the third floor were demolished, deemed by the Jiira as symbols of heretical worship. The survival of the remaining shrines was a fortunate accident. A pioneering group from an expeditionary force rediscovered their teleportation ability when they were seeking refuge from peril while laden with treasure.

Killigs: An order of great holy warriors who served as Ainshard's elite troops. They were all the same height, about twice that of a goblin, so goblinoids eventually started measuring things relative to their height.

Corpse-eaters: A species of carnivorous, black-scaled lizards with striking emerald eyes. These creatures display a preference for scavenging on carcasses over actively hunting prey, earning them their distinct name. Characterised by their prolific reproduction, they are a ubiquitous presence across the vast expanse of the cavern.

Bogey Caverns: A section of a mysterious cavern abundant in haze crystals, artefacts from the age of the gods, and treacherous beasts. The bogey caverns are situated in the upper regions of the cavern, encompassing the entrance and first floor, which are under bogey control and serve as their living quarters.

Monster Caverns: An alternative designation for the caverns inhabited by the enslaved bogeys. This term references the lower floors, areas not under Bogey dominion. In contrast, the zones under Bogey control are referred to as the Bogey Caverns.

Hivelings: Giant, ant-like creatures that inhabit the monster caverns. They left the bogeys alone to begin with, but years of bogey invasions into hiveling territory turned the hivelings aggressive. They come in various sizes and shapes. The smallest are the workers, with the largest being the warriors.

Spiderlings: Brownish-green spider-like hivelings that dwell on the lower floors of the monster caverns. They're known to favour ambushes over direct confrontations. Their yellow blood has paralysing properties.

Ainshard: Ainshard the Great, also known as The Enlightened One, is believed to have been a goblin who conquered all the people of the forest and established a great kingdom centuries ago. The land under his control encompassed the central and western parts of the continent and was home to hundreds of tribes of bogeys, goblins, kobolds, and various other species. He's worshipped by many goblinoids, and in the eyes of the Jiira and some bogeys, he's the *only* being deserving of worship.

Jom: Revered as the father of all and the world's guardian against creatures of the void, he is a deity familiar to goblin-kind, often credited with the creation of the goblinoid races. Although his popularity has waned among most goblinoids—particularly those who lean towards Ainshard over him and his pantheon—he still commands the faith of certain races, including the bogeys. He fell victim to The Void Walker in a brutal clash, but Zeja, in an act of divine intervention, resurrected him. Under her leadership and alongside the other gods, he managed to triumph over his nemesis.

Maga: The goddess of love and fertility, she presides over her priests and priestesses who officiate marriage ceremonies and provide stress relief to followers. Naturally, such services require a generous donation.

Zeja: Born from a droplet of Jom's blood, she initially took the form of a young girl characterised by white hair and red eyes. Embarking on a quest to the underworld, she collected fragments of Jom's soul and negotiated with Dorn, the god of death, to reassemble these pieces into a singular soul, thereby resurrecting Jom. Blessed by Jom, she led the pantheon into battle against the entity known as The Void Walker, ultimately repelling it back into the abyss. This victory secured her ascension as the goddess of war.

Jorm: Zeja's son and the god of defensive wars and ranged weaponry, he may be classified as a minor deity by many, yet he enjoys significant popularity among the greyborns.

Dorn: As the god of death, he oversees the souls of the departed in the underworld. He arbitrates whether souls should be reforged for another opportunity—at life or to join the gods' table—or sent into the cycle of reincarnation for rebirth.

Tanach: As the god of slumber and dreams, he is often perceived as indolent, forever asleep. In truth, his sleep is not without purpose. He vigilantly monitors the dreams of others, purging them of any demonic influence.

Mal: The goddess of deception, she commands a following of cultists and is known for dispatching demons to possess individuals during their most vulnerable moments. Once ensnared, these victims are manipulated into committing unthinkable deeds under her influence.

The Void Walker: An enigmatic force that once sought global domination. The Void Walker clashed and overcame Jom, the father of all, and could have vanquished his kin if not for Zeja's intervention. After resurrecting Jom, Zeja marshalled her armies and ultimately brought about the demise of the Void Walker.

The State of Edoros: A once-powerful city-state that remains prosperous, situated on an island to the north-east of the continent, bordering the White Sea. It is the heartland of the Darg and their largest settlement. Despite their fall to the Brizilum, becoming a vassal state in the process, the Darg retain their pride as exceptional seamen, traders, and warriors, continuing to regard themselves as the undisputed masters of the White Sea.

Pàrras/The Frontier City: the ancient name for the ruined city that Lev and his companions uncovered. Currently, it's overrun with Kram's failed experiments: a hostile group of bird-like creatures that turn to ash upon death. The domain the city is situated in is referred to as the frontier.

The Jiira Tribe: A goblin tribe founded after Ainshard's empire collapsed. They are aggressive and arrogant, given their heritage, but their cultural and technological advantages among the goblinoids are disappearing at a steady pace. They were severely weakened after the civil war against the bogeys and Jiira traitors. Their future on the continent is now uncertain, with the Kur's superior forces ready to crush what remains of them.

The Kur Tribe: A tribe of Kobolds that fought with the Jiira for domination over the region. Not much is known about them among the bogeys.

The Brizilum Republic: A great republic situated in the eastern half of the continent. They're expansionists who seek to engulf all their rivals, converting them into vassals.

The Neutral Zone: The only unclaimed zone on Earth with resource-filled, fertile lands. It is the main theatre of war between the Eurasian and Imperial Armies.

The Technocracy of Eurasia: The Technocracy is one of the world's few superstates. The Technocracy and its United Council rule over Eurasia with an iron grip. The Technocracy is the largest continental superstate on Earth, spanning over most parts of Europe and Asia.

The Empire: The oldest nemesis of Eurasia, ruled by the 'Emperor of The West.' The Emperor's realm spans over North and Central

America. Unlike Eurasia, they're highly advanced both in civilian and military technology.

CHAPTER 1

GROUNDWORK

A sizable party of scouts, warriors, and workers from different goblinoid races milled about near the entrance to a vast forest.

"Alright, listen up," a greyborn commanded. He waited until he was sure he had the group's full attention before explaining the assignment at hand.

It was a hastily-formed party, organised for a foraging run through one of the cavern's nearby forests. They were to gather dry wood, meat, vegetables, and just about anything that looked even remotely edible. They would need many supplies for their impending hazardous trek through the mountain ranges, towards the portal that would lead them to one of Ainshard's lost vestiges.

Before the greyborn could further elaborate, however, he was interrupted by a young green bogey. "Are you sure we'll be able to find enough food on this run? It seems that we'll die of starvation before reaching the shrine."

"We'll need to be efficient. That's why Lev chose you to join this party, Hermut," the greyborn replied.

Hermut was the late witch doctor Rogg's only son and apprentice. Such was clear from the way he spoke and... looked. They were like two slices of the same mouldy bread.

Upon hearing the greyborn's words, Hermut's typically irritated countenance changed into one of smug pride and determination as he felt the group's eyes on him.

"Well, I see how it is," he said, impatiently tapping his staff. The sound intensified each time it hit the ground.

He then flung his staff upwards. The staff spun vertically in the air before cleanly landing back in his hand. "Of course Lev chose me," Hermut continued while twiddling his right ear. "My father taught me everything about poisonous plants, substances, and the like."

A chorus of relief erupted from some of the bogeys in the party.

"If it's Hermut, we'll be safe!"

"He's Rogg's blood after all!"

Hermut cleared his throat. "I'll make sure you fools don't kill yourselves before finishing this run." He slammed the bottom end of his staff into the ground, catching the group by surprise.

"Now if you'll excuse me," he declared, pointing with his staff, "I'll need you, you, you... oh, and you."

Goblinoid by goblinoid, the appointed foragers joined up with Hermut.

"That should do," Hermut said with a satisfied expression. "Now. Once we get in there, I've got some ground rules. One: grab anything you know is edible. Two: grab anything you even *suspect* is poisonous and bring it to me. Even poisonous things can be useful in the right situations." He twirled his staff before pointing it next at the forest's entrance. "Now let's go get some goodies."

On command, his small group disappeared into the lush forest, leaving Hermut behind.

"And Volker!" Hermut called out. "Don't think flattery is gonna get us any meat! Hahahaha!" He disappeared into the forest as well.

The greyborn leader, Volker, smiled in return. "Fine by me." Facing the remaining party members, he made a fist with his left hand and raised it towards the sky. "You heard him, we'll take care of hunting and gathering dry wood. Now move!"

* * *

Hermut made his way through a rough path in the forest, one that had been cleared out only a few days ago.

Volker will do anything that guy says. A promised land? Beings from Ainshard's time guiding him? He shook his head and sighed. *Lev's spiel better be true.*

Besides Hermut, several other witch doctors and shamans had been recruited to help gather and stockpile food. With their assistance, hopefully, the exodus caravan would be able to avoid cases of food poisoning. As it was, they had too many other problems to worry about, like being ambushed by stray hivelings who'd escaped the now-overrun bogey caverns.

To Volker's dismay, Hermut was the only one who showed up. To his credit, as a practised witch doctor, he could in theory handle the party's appraisal needs. In theory.

"Does this look edible, Hermut?"

"No, that's a lupo mushroom. Releases its spores within the stomach and blocks water absorption. Would kill you with dehydration in a day."

"Hermut—I mean, Doctor Hermut. I filled my basket with these red flowers, and I heard from my late aunt that they have healing properties—"

"Take one bite and you'll drop dead instantly. Didn't you hear me the other five times?!"

After a few hours had passed, Hermut had had enough. He slammed his staff on the ground. His entire group stopped to look.

"Listen, you lot. We have plenty more poison and inedible garbage than we could possibly need. Can't a single one of you reliably find food?!"

Some in the party could not resist commenting in hushed tones.

"He really takes after his old man."

"Shhh! He might hear us."

Hermut glared in their general direction. They turned away to avoid him.

"Stop wasting time!" Hermut shouted. "Find some damn food for once!"

Having exhausted himself with his shouting, Hermut found a comfortable bench of sorts in the form of a rock overgrown with moss. He sat down, then stretched and lay down. Before long, he was firmly enveloped in the warm embrace of sleep, filling the thicket with the rumbling noises of snoring.

Never had the forest been this disturbed by a single bogey, much to the party's chagrin. *If only his father could see him now!* they thought.

Even so, the forage continued. The party made sure to avoid larger predators and stray hivelings as much as possible. It was still relatively safe near the cavern grounds, but recent sightings of hiveling scouts outside the cavern indicated a growing insectoid threat.

After several hours of painstaking work, the group rendezvoused at the forest entrance. Volker surveyed the baskets, pots, and backpacks full of spoils, and finally came upon Hermut, whose red, swollen face bore splotch-like rashes. "What happened to you?" Volker asked.

The flustered witch doctor grumbled and lowered his eyes to the ground.

He didn't feel the insects biting him? Volker thought, shaking his head.

Volker grabbed a basket from Hermut's haul and inspected its contents: a few vegetables, herbs, and some fruit. It wasn't terrible, but it would have been better if Hermut had helped gather herbs himself.

Volker then glanced at the snowy mountaintops dotting most of the horizon before directing his attention to the mountain range that housed the bogey caverns. It had housed his family and so many others for generations. Its jagged six finger-like formation stretched towards the sky, as if pleading for help.

Sinner's reach. That's what the Jiira called it, and now the bogeys knew why. It was a place for those cast aside by Ainshard, cursed to live out their lives in slavery, pleading to the heavens for salvation. His eyes focussed on the rivers that flowed around three of the finger-like mountaintops. From a distant waterfall, they streamed down towards the mountain's palm where the entrance to the bogey caverns laid.

This isn't enough. Even combined with the other teams' hauls, our foodstocks will only get us as far as the shrine somewhere at the peak of sinner's reach's third finger. Volker grit his teeth. There wasn't enough time for another run. His party had to return to the main encampment tomorrow to prepare for departure.

They would have to make do.

Three days later

A group of Jiira goblins tailed Lev's group. Despite having agreed to his terms for a path to citizenship, resentment still remained. Uncertain of their futures within the new society, they looked to their pride as warriors.

"Raban! How could you accept his demands so easily? You've sold us out!" a younger goblin spat in disgust.

Others quickly joined in, throwing slurs and insults at their former leader.

Raban neither flinched nor gave any indication that their antics bothered him. Instead, he turned to face his frenzied men and spoke disarmingly. "'Sold out,' you say? Then why do we have a seat at their table and a hand in their politics? We'll be citizens in ten years!"

A taller goblin approached. Raban recognized the goblin—a berserker he had once directly commanded.

Raban straightened his back. As much as he hoped it wouldn't become necessary, he was ready to take the berserker head-on. Raban clenched his fists and rolled his shoulders as the berserker reached striking range.

The muscled goblin opened his mouth, revealing a row of rotten teeth. "We don't get a say. We're slaves now! Those promises are just bogey lies—spoken by a greyborn, no less!" the berserker yelled before slamming his right fist into the ground, leaving a noticeable crater.

"Filth that crawled under our feet for decades, nothing more." He raised his bloodied fist off the ground. "The bastards managed to pull us down into the mud this time around, but I'll make sure it won't happen again."

Raban frowned. "And how exactly will you accomplish that? With brute force?"

The berserker swung his fist in the air, causing some droplets of blood to land on Raban's face. "Damn right! It's the fastest way to show 'em that we're not scum like them!"

Raban's jaw tightened. "We number fewer. We're barehanded. We have no guarantee of any further clemency. All you're going to do is get us all killed!"

"We don't need no traitors, Raban! Your skin looks awfully grey to me today. Aren't I right, men?"

The crowd of goblins cheered. The berserker had so eloquently put their feelings into words.

"If that's how you want it," Raban snarled through gritted teeth, "then take this traitorous leader of yours head-on."

The berserker leered back. "That's a challenge I'd gladly take."

"Come on, then, lardass," Raban mocked. "Are you waiting for a cup of warm milk, or are you ready to eat the ground?"

The two goblins began circling around each other as the rest of the crowd encircled them.

A group of bogey soldiers soon noticed the commotion. Quietly but quickly, they joined the encirclement.

Raban noticed the soldiers approach from the corner of his eye. "Seems you won't have your fight," he jeered.

The berserker smiled. "Don't get your hopes up, Raban. Look again."

Raban looked around, perplexed, until he heard soldiers talking to each other, making no effort to keep their conversation quiet.

"Should we really risk our lives for a bunch of Jiira trash?" asked one. "I say we let them finish each other off. Leaves more food for us."

Another soldier, one standing with a perfectly straight back, replied, "Our orders were to preserve diplomatic relations—"

"Yeah. Protect the Jiira warchief from attacks by our guys," the first soldier interrupted. "If his own people turn against him, then what do we care? That's his problem!"

"Fair enough. This is a conflict beyond our jurisdiction. It seems we'll have to sit back and enjoy the show these halfwits will provide us."

The berserker grit his teeth and turned toward the soldiers. "What'd you call us?"

Raban spoke up right away. "They're just—"

"Not you," the berserker shot back. "*Us.*"

You poor, short-sighted fools, Raban thought bitterly. He picked up a rock with his left hand; the berserker mirrored his movement.

The two resumed circling around each other. In but a short moment, the fight began.

Raban threw his rock at the berserker to distract him and lunged.

To his surprise, his opponent ignored the rock and met his charge. In Raban's stupor, he barely avoided an incoming fist.

The berserker threw an uppercut but Raban caught it and kicked the berserker in the gut.

He didn't give up and pushed the berserker to the ground before delivering a series of punches and kicks.

Not satisfied with being reduced to a punching bag, the berserker threw Raban to the side before lunging at him.

Although the fight still blazed on, the angry mob suddenly dispersed, almost as it'd never been there.

What? What's with these guys? Raban thought as he noticed the mob's sudden retreat.

A greyborn soldier approached the scene. He was far taller and more muscular than most of his kin, with long silver hairs resting on his shoulders.

"What's happening over here?" he asked one of the soldiers.

"Oh, sir! W-Well, you see…" The soldier quickly explained the situation.

The greyborn briefly looked at the flustered group before bursting out in laughter. "Slaves? Do they see us as slavers? Don't think we're the same as your kind." His tone changed to a firmer one as he took out an intricate looking compass.

"We're almost there. You're lucky Lev didn't kill you off, or worse, leave you behind. We'd have reached the shrine sooner if it weren't for your group of pitiful warriors."

One of the goblins couldn't take it anymore. "And who are you? Lev's underling? You're worth nothing to me. We'd have won if it weren't for your filthy greyborn tricks!"

The greyborn grabbed the goblin by his neck. "Name's Rak, and you better change your tone. I serve no one but me."

After a few tense seconds, Rak loosened his grip, and the freed goblin gasped for air as he tried to regain his bearings. With crossed arms, Rak huffed at the goblin's strength, or rather, lack thereof. He'd expected more resistance from a former Jiira warrior.

Raban and his opponent exchanged a tacit look and lowered their fists before turning to watch the retreating bogeys. With wide eyes, Raban stared at the giant greyborn's back as he made his way back to the front of the caravan.

Why was Rak here? Wasn't he positioned at the forefront of the formation?

Raban inspected the greyborn's back closely. His clothing was a mess of patches, leaving much of his skin exposed to the elements. Worse yet, the greyborn's firm back was decorated with numerous scars. Most were shallow, but others looked dangerously deep. The acrid stench of his rotting wounds still lingered in the air.

Those wounds... they must've been from the civil war. Why hasn't he cleansed them? Does he feel no pain?

Raban's head drooped as he realised how much work had been put on bogey shoulders to prepare for the hazardous trek.

That can't be.

Rak had only been there a few moments, but that had been enough for Raban to understand the hardship Rak and his men had gone through to get to this point. He brushed the remainder of his questions away and focused on a more important matter.

Raban straightened his back and faced his men.

He had half-expected them to continue their murder plot, but instead found them still staring at the distant greyborn figure disappearing into the masses further ahead.

Seeing that even the berserker had joined the staring contest, Raban took the opportunity and punched the berserker in the guts with all of his strength. The muscled goblin waggled on his feet until eventually losing his balance and flipping over to the ground.

Raban grabbed the berserker by the hair and forced him to meet eye to eye.

"Your traitorous leader is still awaiting his punishment."

CHAPTER 2

EXODUS

Darkness engulfed the group of goblinoids as they trudged through the mountain range that made up the fingers of sinner's reach. The fierce and sudden cold wind brushed against the patches of leather and metal that formed their armour. They had prepared for this moment, but it was another thing entirely to actually experience such treacherous conditions.

"Lev, how far until we reach the waterfall?" Hemgall barked, packed in a knee-length fur coat. A leather strap kept the bundles of fur firmly in place as his right hand kept the hood over his head.

"These coats you had us make aren't enough to keep the cold out much longer," Rapha shouted, buried in an even more elaborate mess of fur. "Besides, how can you be so calm when we're minutes away from freezing to death?" she added with a sharp cough.

Lev briefly halted, turned around, and finally inspected the others' condition. *Even though they acclimated to the moderate temperatures at the foot of the mountain, the cold, thin air here is too fierce for them.*

Before he could return his attention to the map, he felt another consciousness join his mind.

I hope you know what you're doing, Lev. We're cave dwellers; unaccustomed to the cold. Even Rapha's struggling, and she came from a tribe of mountain dwellers.

Lev had to agree with Gherm on that front. Half of the exodus group's members, especially those who'd stayed inside the caverns during the war with the Jiira, had probably never seen a speck of snow before. Still…

Pity won't help them. I need to determine our current position.

He took out another piece of papyrus, a replica of the half-frozen, deteriorating sheet he'd been holding on to. *Damn snow. It's good the artisans prepared a batch of replicas.*

He briefly inspected the map. Lev had planned out the shortest route possible, taking as many shortcuts as he could whilst still avoiding local wildlife. According to the goblins, the animals local to the mountains were far more aggressive than their counterparts in the valley.

The wildlife he was trying to avoid reminded him of the Jiira he'd decided to spare. If given a chance they'd surely try to escape, and they'd do so in a fit of rage—like a caged animal chewing off its captor's hand before rushing out.

As much as the others had begged him to abandon those wretched souls in the depths of the cavern, many seemed reassured by the Jiira's presence. As much as they hated the goblins, co-existing with them was a far less abhorrent fate than dying in the snowy wildlands.

Lev traced his finger across the map, trying to figure out their location. *We need to keep the torches burning. As long as we're able to guide the groups with fewer shamans, we'll be fine. Though I do wish we'd had time to create more beacon staffs based on Orva's new design.*

She'd deciphered one of the runes etched on the golden staff she'd found at the bottom of the monster caverns, close to the masked gate. Upon meticulously replicating and engraving it onto other similar staffs, she discovered that light emission was greatly enhanced when magic surged the rune. This allowed them to use their staffs as powerful light beacons, hence the name.

"Lev!" Hemgall called out again. "What's the matter with you? Is the cold stopping you from answering me?"

"The snowstorm is. Is there a problem?"

"Some of our people can't go on much longer! Are we there yet?" Lev turned to Bolo, who was standing up front with Vyrga's compass.

"We're almost there," Bolo answered, earning a nod from Lev.

"You heard the man. We'll be shielded by the cavern behind the waterfall as we ascend," Lev said whilst studying his map. He turned around the map several times hoping for a spark of genius. When that failed, he settled for reconsidering alternative routes in case something went awry.

Hem gazed at the stack of torn maps in Lev's backpack. "I sure as hell hope the shrine isn't damaged after all of this," he muttered as he mended his own backpack.

After fixing the final strip of leather into place, Hem stood up and started walking back to the mid section.

"Where are you going?" Rapha asked.

"Checking on the guys in the centre, why?"

"Shouldn't you stay here with us? In case of an ambush?" Volker inquired, shielding his cold ears behind his fur hood.

"I'm sure you can handle that. I have to make sure Orva's hanging in there."

As Hem disappeared into the storm, Rak, Rapha, and Volker accompanied Lev at the front of the settler group.

"Are you doing fine, Rapha?" Volker asked. Rapha had wrapped herself in a thick blanket of animal hide, but she was still visibly shivering.

"I could ask you the same," Rapha replied. "You're shaking like a leaf."

Volker shrugged. "I doubt there's any bogey that's used to this weather. It's not like there were seasons in the cavern."

"Yeah... It used to snow like this where I'm from, so I can manage. I don't know about the others, though."

Lev looked back at Rapha. "Are the shamans not enough?"

"Look at us, Lev. We're practically minutes from death. Do you really think the shamans can support an entire group for this long?"

Lev thought about Orva's group. There couldn't be more than a few shamans left with the ability, and energy, to heal. The rest of the shamans were spread among the caravan, using their newly minted beacon staffs to light the way. This way, it was less likely for anyone to get lost and they could spare torches.

She's right, but I've got to focus on finding the waterfall first. We'll die either way if we can't find it, and once we've reached it, the mountain will shield us.

Lev grimaced before speaking. "We can't stop now. Our success depends on that shrine. Once we get there, we can regroup."

With a muffled huff, Rapha buried herself even deeper into her coat.

"Hand me an oil bottle," Rak said as he wrapped leftover pieces of cloth around a piece of wood he'd picked up hours ago. Their original stock of dry wood had almost run out. "We can't let this darkness consume our vision even more. Lev's right. We've got to find that shrine, and fast."

As the others were discussing their next plan of action, Volker scanned the abyss below him. The path they were walking on was far smaller than Lev's drawings had suggested. *Can't trust Lev's estimations,* he lamented as a frown formed on his forehead, betraying his thoughts. *Still, it's amazing how the scouts managed to scout the area this fast, especially in this weather.*

"Volker," Rak started, "you wanna go back to gathering food and materials?"

"No way. Besides, I know you hate this as much as I do," Volker smirked as he noticed Rak's discomfort. The latter's wounds hadn't healed yet, and he was struggling to catch his breath.

"What'd you say? You think I can't stand a little breeze like this?"

As the two were about to enter another pointless discussion, one stemming from boredom and cold, Lev lifted his arm in the air, swaying the torch Rak had prepared in front of him with his other hand.

"Quiet! I think we're being followed."

* * *

If not for the constant clattering of metal and weapons, along with the dim light of beacon staffs and torches, the goblinoids at the back would've lost track of the group hours ago.

Thanks to the sacrifices made by the scouting teams, a rough path had been laid out days in advance to help with the climb, guiding the caravan during their dangerous trek.

Unfortunately, their oil supply was running low, and the shamans' healing capacity was dwindling at a rapid pace due to their depleted magical energies and the diminishing supply of medicinal herbs.

"We have another one," a female shaman shouted. A group of nearby shamans followed her commands as they collectively tried to heal their newest patient. The afflicted bogey's hands and feet were pale and frigid.

A young bogey silently watched the shamans work.

"It'll be alright, kiddo," the female shaman said, reassuringly placing her hands on the kid's shoulders. "She's just a little cold right now, but we can heal her."

"Orva, we've got a problem. We don't have enough capable shamans anymore to cover the back group and we're near our end here as well," an apprentice shaman whispered into Orva's ear, a concerned expression haunting his visage.

"I'll handle her. Go to the back and help the others. We just have to hold on a bit longer, we'll be there soon," Orva answered, feigning confidence.

Once the apprentice was out of sight, Orva's shoulders sagged and she let out a deep sigh. *At least, I hope. More and more of us are barely holding on to life. I can't believe it's this cold up here, even during the spring. All the others told us the weather's great in the spring!*

"Orva, are you alright? You got to snap out of it and help me heal her. You learned how to balance your magical energy output from one of the healing masters, right?" another shaman asked.

Orva nodded, steadied her hands, and focused her magical energies on the woman's hands. A faint glow started forming around them, and soon enough, the frostbite faded away, bit by bit.

"You know we can't fully heal her here," the shaman continued. "We don't have enough—"

Orva cut the shaman off. "I've got enough for this one."

"Orva—"

Orva placed her hands on the woman's feet. "I have enough."

"You're wasting so much energy."

"I can't help it. I'm still new to healing. I just need to ease the burden on more practised healers." She looked the shaman dead in the eye. "Like you."

With a click of her tongue, the shaman placed her hands on top of Orva's. "Fine. You focus on releasing your energy and I'll guide it. Just don't exhaust yourself."

"Thank you. I'll take care of myself," Orva replied before turning her attention back to the patient.

The group moved in sections, each numbering twenty to thirty goblinoids. Bogeys, deka, burga, and even Jiira defectors had joined the settler group.

"Are we stopping again? What's this all about! I'm freezing my nuts off!" a familiar voice whined.

"Hermut, can you please shut up for a minute? We're healing as fast as we can," Orva replied with a hint of annoyance, not taking her eyes off her patient.

Hermut scoffed and crossed his arms. "Well, if only you'd listened to me. I told you this was a bad idea. Why did Lev even want to go through here? What's so special about this shrine?" He spat on the ground. "Besides, from what my old man told me from his expedition days, all of those shrines are useless anyway. They're too archaic."

The look on Orva's face was one of utter confusion. After a short moment, her eyes narrowed. "Ah, right. You've never gone on an expedition, have you?"

"In a lucky turn of events I mixed the wrong herbs and was paralyzed at the time. What does that have to do with it?"

"So you bailed out."

Hermut raised his arms in defence. "I was poisoned. It wasn't my fault."

Orva rolled her eyes. "Yeah, sure."

Hermut stomped his foot on the ground. "It wasn't!"

"Listen. The shrines above the third floor are broken. The shrines below are not."

"Let's say the shrine works. This plan is still nothing but sheer madness. Lev's crazy, Orva."

"In case you forgot, we all voted to go along with his plan. Everyone also voted for him to lead the effort."

Hermut scoffed. "That? It was a sham. Half of his 'supporters' just didn't want to be blamed if things went wrong. As for you and the others who don't see how crazy he is, I don't wanna burst your bubble, but we're all screwed."

"Shut it. He won't fail. We're alive because of him," Orva said as she formed a fist, causing the newly appointed witch doctor to stumble back in surprise.

"Sure, sure. Whatever you say," Hermut finally admitted defeat as he slinked back to his previous position.

The frostbite on the female bogey had almost completely disappeared. The other shaman gently took her hands off the patient's feet. "Alright, that should be enough for now. Orva, you can stop now."

The young bogey nervously approached the duo and placed his hand between the healed woman's before hugging her.

"Will my mom be okay?" he asked.

Orva showed a comforting smile. "Of course she will. We'll finish her treatment when we reach our destination."

The boy looked at Orva through teary eyes. "Thank you."

Orva ruffled his hair. "No problem, kid. Now, we can't keep everyone waiting so let's get going."

The sharp clanks of pebbles falling over the rough edges of the mountain's slopes were the only sounds they could hear besides the front group's constant rhythm of clattering metal. The few torchbearers and shamans that were left were situated at the front and end sections of the exodus group, leaving the centre shrouded in darkness.

The shrine. That was their final stop. An ancient Ainshardian relic hidden behind a waterfall somewhere close to the mountaintop.

"It will lead us to our salvation. One of the last vestiges of Ainshard's brief golden age is awaiting our people," an old bogey muttered as he lurched forward with the last of his strength. "Ainshard, deliver us!" he exalted before collapsing against another bogey, causing both of them to fall towards the edge.

"Help me!" the other bogey screamed in panic as he lost his balance and tripped over the path's sharp edge. He managed to barely hold on as his body hung above an abyss of darkness. The older bogey wasn't as lucky.

"What happened?"

"Who fell?"

"This is bad. Call one of the front men."

"What are you waiting for! Pull me up!" the bogey cried out again above the chatter. Despite his desperation, his fingers quickly lost their grip, and he screamed as he began to fall. His gaze never left his frozen brethren.

Just as he lost all hope, a warm feeling wound its way around his forearm. Shocked, the bogey shifted his gaze to see a tall greyborn slowly hoisting him up with both arms.

After being set back on stable ground, the bogey looked up to the greyborn, still amazed at the display of sheer strength he'd just witnessed.

"Well, are you gonna say something or just keep staring at me?" the greyborn said.

"Th-Thank you, sir. May I ask your name? I will reward you with merits, I swear!"

"Merits? Don't worry about it," the tall greyborn reassured. He placed his hand on the bogey's shoulder. "Where we're going, we won't need merits."

The bogey watched as the large greyborn left the centre and advanced to the front.

"W-Wait, what's your name? You haven't told me!"

The greyborn turned around, a giant grin plastered across his face. "The name's Hemgall, but you can call me Hem. Make sure not to trip again, and for the gods' sake, tell your friends over there to help instead of gawking like idiots next time."

That last remark struck guilt into the others who had idly stood by— they immediately rushed towards the bogey and helped him forward.

* * *

"Followed? How? It's just us and the constant howling of the wind," Volker remarked as he looked around him, trying to find what Lev was referring to.

"You're looking in the wrong direction. Look ahead, to where the path ascends."

Volker looked ahead of the path, trying to make out shapes in the wind. Then he saw it—a flicker of red scourging a white landscape. "What was that?"

Lev kneeled down, inspecting the patches of snow leading to the ascending path. "See these marks down here? What can you conclude from them?"

"They're similar to the ones we saw during the expedition."

"These dips and skids were made by something pointy. They're close together for how deep they are. There's a regular rhythm to them. They don't look like any other tracks we've seen in the snow, but they do look familiar."

"Don't tell me it's them," Gul cut in.

Volker laughed. "Still as scared as a cornered corpse-eater, aren't we?"

The blush that followed on Gul's cheeks made Volker's laugh intensify.

"Shut it Volker, you're as scared as I am!"

Volker's laugh subsided. "Well, you're right about that."

"Whoever—or whatever—left these tracks behind is large, has multiple legs, and can withstand the cold." Lev continued.

Rak squinted at the path before them. "No way. Those damn insects? They couldn't have expanded their colony this far in so little time. Right?"

Nobody answered him.

After a brief but very uncomfortable moment of silence, Lev spoke up. "We should move to the rear. If the hiveling scouts have already explored this far out, I'm not sure we'll arrive unscathed."

"How come?" Rak asked.

"If they're following us, they'll attack our rear first."

Rapha walked in closer, whilst her eyes followed the brief flickers of blazing red in front of them. "Why the rear? Those things can climb up just about anything and flank us. If the tracks are anything to go by, it doesn't seem like they mind the cold. What's to stop them from hitting us anywhere else?"

Lev kicked a rock and it fell along the cliff's edge. "The path is too narrow and slippery, not to mention that the wind's blowing hard. Hivelings are good climbers, but even they would have trouble climbing in this environment. They're much more likely to have sent out scouts when we were too preoccupied with stocking up on supplies. Warrior hivelings are probably tailing the caravan's rear."

"In that case, we shouldn't waste time." Rapha concluded, "If anything happens, let's hope Grasha and the rest of the deka notice and help defend the rear."

"I wish Gozzag and Ban had stayed with us," Volker muttered.

Rak shook his head. "Their choice makes sense."

"How so?" Volker inquired.

"Their group is small and made up of trained combatants so they'll be able to get past the hivelings and the sky devils. They also need to inform the other Dragma about what transpired and help prepare for Jiira retaliation or a Brizilum invasion. Besides, if they'd stayed, that would've put your girl in danger. Varra wouldn't have survived this trip, not in her current state."

Lev hastily stood up, frantically looked around him, and walked straight into the line of soldiers behind him.

"Five of you, follow me. Rak, you come with me as well. Gul, Bolo, Volker, and Rapha; keep moving ahead towards the shrine and set up defences with the others."

"What about my brother and Vyrga? They're in the centre," Bolo asked.

Lev shook his head. "Knowing them, they won't stand idly by. If something happens, I'll cover for them. For now, observe the hivelings' next moves. Signal me with torches if you see changes in their behaviour."

"I'm not gonna stand idle while my father is in danger, Lev," Bolo stated matter-of-factly.

Lev sighed. "Fine, come with us."

"Wouldn't it be better to use our horns?" Volker asked.

Volker saw Lev and Rapha turn towards him, annoyed.

"What?" Volker asked in a panic.

Lev pointed upwards towards the snowy mountain peak. "Avalanche," he stated matter-of-factly.

Volker followed Lev's finger, then lowered his head in response.

Lev made his way to the rear section, but felt a hand pulling him back.

"I mean no disrespect, sir, please," Volker struggled for a second before continuing, "but are you out of your mind? How in the name of the war goddess Zeja will we be able to hold back swarms of hivelings at the shrine?"

"The waterfall will help, and the entire area is surrounded by water. The shamans will prove themselves useful there."

Volker briefly pondered Lev's answer before responding. "If you're thinking of frying the hivelings, not all shamans are experts in lightning magic, sir. According to Orva, while it is simple to conjure lightning, controlling it is quite difficult."

"There's other ways to use water. They can also freeze it or manipulate it to drown the hivelings."

Volker scratched his head. "Well, I guess."

"Hivelings aren't dumb. Or at least their queen isn't. As long as we put up enough of a fight, their forces will retreat. Remember to use the ruins close by as cover. You'll manage just fine."

Volker nodded, "I hope you're right. One mistake and we'll be hiveling food."

Lev smirked, and took one step back, showing half of his face to Volker. "They're not dumb, but without their queen, they're predictable. It might have ways to order around its swarm from afar, but I doubt the queen would endanger herself and traverse through this frozen hellscape. From a distance, it can only send out simple orders, en masse.

"Besides, this isn't their natural habitat. Sure, their exoskeleton will shield them from the wind and cold, but they're larger and bulkier than us," Lev said as he pointed at the thin path leading towards the waterfall.

The wind subsided for a brief period, allowing the sound of the splashing waterfall to break through, if only for a few seconds.

"Looks like we're close after all. Now go." Lev turned and sprinted for the rear, followed by Rak and the soldiers.

In the relative safety of his mind where only the likes of Gherm might hear, Lev thought to himself. *Why would their queen order its subjects to venture out this far with such haste? At least they haven't attacked us yet. We still have time.*

The wind gained strength once again, and his friends behind him disappeared into the white blanket of frost and terror.

CHAPTER 3

WHITE DEATH

Lev kept his gaze to the ground as he tried to backtrack his way to the other groups. The tracks from the front section's carts and heavy equipment were still visible enough, despite the blizzard's best efforts.

We need to find the others quickly. These tracks won't stay here much longer. Besides, the hivelings may have already surrounded us.

He shook off that last thought. *I need to count on it that they haven't yet. The only way those insects could have reached the mountain without us noticing is if they'd gotten here days before we did. Were they waiting for us? No, they must've followed us.*

As the wind howled ever more loudly, Lev and the others continued onwards.

"Wait, do you see that?" one of the soldiers yelled.

And sure enough, Lev spotted the faint lights of torches and beacon staffs further ahead. It didn't take long for them to realise the lights were moving in a panicked fashion, swaying wildly as they seemingly drew closer.

Rak's ears twitched. He readied his sword and went into a combat stance. "They're running towards us. Something's wrong."

"Hivelings?" another soldier asked, barely keeping himself still.

"Probably warriors. Scouts must've seen enough to signal them here."

The soldiers gulped.

"Looks like the rear and centre are teaming up. I see a lot of lights grouping together."

Lev let out a deep sigh. *Seems their training paid off after all. At least they were smart enough to stick together.*

The sound of explosions and a few distant shouts became audible enough for Lev and the others to hear through the blizzard.

"Run! They're right behind us!" a panicked female voice screamed at them.

"Is that—" Rak said as he narrowed his eyes, trying to make out the female figure running into view.

"Orva," Lev affirmed.

"What are you waiting for? Run! Run, you bastards!" the voice called out again, much more clearly now.

"Yeah, that's Orva," Rak muttered before stepping towards her.

"Rak? Lev? What are you still doing here!" she said. She turned around as though to look back, but her hands twitched and she turned back around. "Never mind, just help Hem. He's further ahead, fending off the warriors."

"Where's Grasha? Weren't he and his men supposed to be in the centre? Did they head to the rear to support Hem?" Rak shouted through the howling wind.

"I don't know. I saw him on my way here, but I think he took another route."

"What other route? One wrong step and he'll fall to his death. Don't tell me the bastards deserted," Rak growled.

"I don't know." Orva's breath quickened as the sound of a distant battle echoed behind her, through the mountain range. The hand holding her staff quivered every now and then, and there seemed to be a bloody hole above her chest, but despite her ripped clothes, there were no signs of any other wounds.

"Leave it," Orva hissed to the gazing crowd. "I barely managed to heal the wound in the nick of time."

Lev cast his eye over those trailing Orva. They were largely similarly wounded.

"You should get to the waterfall, follow the tracks," Lev said.

"What? I can't just leave you. You need my support."

"You're worn out. We have the shamans in the rear. You need to move while the tracks are still visible."

"There's a large number of wounded—"

"We'll get them to the shrine, too," Lev assured her.

After a few seconds of hesitation, Orva called out to the others to follow her lead. The group following her consisted of a few soldiers, mashed together with Jiira deserters and bogeys from all ages.

Rak cracked his fists. "Those glorified ants will pay."

Lev turned his attention to the glaive. *Can you detect Grasha and the others?*

Grasha. A deka, correct? I can sense him and a few of his ilk with forty bogeys flanking the hivelings at the rear. I also detect Vyrga with them.

Vyrga? Lev mused, *I was wondering where he was.*

Master, I've also detected about a hundred vital signals, likely goblinoids, besides your group and Vyrga's. Other than goblinoids, there's another large wave of hivelings approaching the rear. If my estimations are correct, you could be facing up to a hundred and fifty hivelings within the next thirty minutes.

Other goblinoids? What do you mean?

The glaive's haze-imbued tip gave off a soft glow. *I can't make out the races this group consists of, but I do know they're approaching from a different path than the hivelings. They should arrive at our current destination within thirty-five minutes.*

Rak shook Lev's shoulder. "Lev? You awake in there?"

"I think we'll be able to pull this off after all." Lev smirked as he instinctively drew his glaive closer to his upper body.

I just hope the shrine works, Lev thought hesitantly.

The glaive's consciousness barked back. *The empire's designs never fail. Of all the inventions devised by the great Ainshard and his followers, the teleportation nodes were the magnum opus of the Empire. The shrines were built to last for aeons.*

Lev laughed. *Ainshardian fanaticism at its best.*

He felt the glaive's consciousness intensify even more, but before it, or rather she, could throw another slur of ancient rhetoric at the young greyborn, Lev quietly thanked the glaive for its optimism.

My pleasure, master, the glaive replied.

You're too easy, Gherm snickered.

Once they'd passed the group, making sure everyone passed safely, Lev and the others disappeared into the storm again.

It didn't take them long to find Hem with some of his men fighting off the giant insectoids. A silhouette of a giant greyborn slashing at hivelings and shouting cries of war wasn't hard to spot, even in a blizzard.

Hem managed to halt them at a narrow pass half a killig in size.

"Eat metal, you dirty bugs!" he shouted as he swung his axe on a warrior's head. To no avail, the warrior merely stopped attacking for a brief moment, stunned by the impact, but quickly regained its bearings and called out for more of its kind to join in on the slaughter.

Hemgall released the rune-powered mechanism keeping his axe together, splitting it into two separate heads. He ploughed each axe head into the eyes of the warrior and, in a herculean feat, threw it into the abyss.

His men's pikes kept two nearby warriors busy enough for Hem to counterattack.

Hem dug his axes into the head of the one on the left and dragged it to the ground. Before it could rebalance itself, he mauled it in a bear-like fury. It shrieked as with every chop its lifeforce left its skeletal frame.

The other warrior, in an attempt to aid its companion, leaped at Hem. As it did so, a spike blasted it in the head, knocking it back to the ground.

Hem spun around and spotted a blue-skinned shaman a few feet away. "Thanks for the save, Gerwyn," he cheered.

"Ptui. I'd do anything to make these vile insects taste half of the pain we went through on this trip."

Hem chuckled before swinging his axe into his next prey. "Don't think I don't know where your soft spots are," he mocked as he dug his axe even deeper into another hiveling's exoskeleton.

"Hemgall!" a familiar voice called out to him.

Hemgall looked behind him, still swaying his axe left and right to deter the hivelings. *Took them long enough. I must admit, these insects still hold their bite—*

"Argh!" Hem yelped as a small hiveling pierced his thigh with the sharp end of one of its legs. He lifted his axe and ploughed it straight on the culprit's head. "Death from above, you stupid ant."

Liquid sprayed out of the bug's orifices; the axe blow had crushed its internals. As it quickly lost strength, it slumped under its own weight and fell to the ground.

Hem had to kick the corpse to dislodge his axe.

A few hivelings used this chance to lunge at him, but a wall of spears held them back. Hem took advantage of this brief moment and hunched down to grab the hiveling leg still embedded in his thigh. Rather than pull it out completely, he snapped it in half right above his skin and tossed the cut half at the dead hiveling.

"Sir, are you alright?" asked one of the soldiers protecting him.

Seeing Rak and the others approaching, Hem let out a bellowing laugh. "Haven't been better. I've missed killing these things! Rak, lend me a hand, will ya?"

Rak responded by throwing his, or rather, Gelmar's bronze axe into a warrior's head. Taking advantage of its stupor, he charged towards the warrior and pulled his axe out. He and Hemgall then each grabbed one of the oversized ant's mandibles and pushed it towards a swarm of scouts near the edge. Their shrieks echoed along the mountainside as they fell to their doom.

He picked his axe off the ground before decapitating an approaching scout. "Already on the job."

Just when it seemed that the hivelings' numbers were beginning to thin, a second wave appeared to reinforce the assault.

With a twist of his foot, Rak avoided a charging warrior. Its large frame swept past him and narrowly avoided falling off the edge by successfully digging its hind legs into the ground.

Its efforts were for naught, as a heavy blow from Rak's axe sent it careening off the edge regardless. Another shrill shriek sounded as it disappeared from sight.

"Rak! There's more heading your way!" Hem roared before smashing away a scout that was aiming for his neck.

With bared teeth, Rak spun around to face the incoming threat—but none of the hivelings even came close, as they chose to ignore him in favour of attacking Hem's men. Fortunately, they were only scouts, and Rak calmly watched as Hem's men quickly dispatched them with ease.

But just as they were about to revel in their success, a gut-wrenching screech heralded throughout the battlefield. From the mist emerged a gigantic hiveling that could put all warriors to shame.

"What is that thing!" cried one of the soldiers.

Rak pulled his blunted axe off the corpse of a warrior and faced the gigantic insectoid. "Seems they finally decided to take us seriously."

Hem pretended to yawn. "If this is their idea of being serious, I'm not impressed. I bet a full bag of haze crystals that it won't take a moment to throw the big lug to his doom."

The two greyborns exchanged looks and prepared themselves.

Kicking the snow under its feet, the hiveling sped towards the two greyborns while the rest of its brood launched themselves against the soldiers' formation.

Against all odds, the hivelings' charge failed to breach the bogeys' defences, but that wasn't enough to deter the insectoid threat.

Another hiveling scout bashed its head on a shield. Unable to grab the piece of metal with its mandibles, it grabbed the edges of the shield with its front legs, and with a push of its hindlegs, brought the shield's owner down to the ground.

Try as he might, the soldier couldn't push the insect off of his shield. The weight of both the tower shield and the insect was pressing on his chest.

Wheezing for air, he looked at his brethren for aid. Some attempted to help but to no avail. Even the backline was busy preventing any of the larger hivelings with only those close to him desperately stabbing at its hard chitin. It was thanks to their efforts that it hadn't bitten his head off.

His breath grew short and his vision began to darken. The moment he had accepted his end, he felt a weight lift off his chest and heard a hiveling shriek. Before him stood a greyborn wielding an ornate glaive.

Lev bent down and offered the gasping man a hand. "Stand up and get out of here. You've done enough."

The soldier absentmindedly took his hand and stood up before being handed over to one of his compatriots. He took a look back at what happened and found the decapitated head of the hiveling lying over his shield.

Paying no mind to his rescuee, Lev swung his glaive at an approaching scout, cut off half of its head, and rallied the soldiers.

Under his command, the bogeys regained lost ground as they pushed back the hiveling swarms.

The death cries of the giant hiveling and the return of magical support cemented the battle to the bogeys' favour.

Magical energies whirled around Gerwyn before erupting from his beacon staff towards the hivelings in a fiery heat.

The immense heat caused the bugs to screech and flee in a frenzy.

A smile plastered itself on the blue bogey's face. "Yep. I've still got it. I'm still the best."

"Meh, I'm sure it's because Orva designed your staff," Hem jested, causing the blue bogey to curse under his breath.

"Sir." One of the soldiers approached Lev. "We can't stay any longer, the storm's picking up and the tracks will disappear soon."

"What are our casualties?" Lev promptly asked as he swung at another row.

"Minimal." The soldier looked in the direction of the two giant greyborns protecting the other soldiers. "If it weren't for those two, the damage would've been catastrophic."

As the two greyborns finished off the last remaining hiveling, with Hem's axe cutting away all of its legs in one smooth motion, and Rak's axe cleaving straight through its thorax, Lev blew one of his horns.

Rak turned towards Lev. "Won't more of those insects come after us?"

Before Lev could answer, a loud noise sounded from the distance. Though the constant flurries of snow limited visibility, they were able to make out a white wave tumbling down a mountain. Soon the cries of hivelings became audible as well.

"What just happened?" Hem muttered.

Lev saw a few dim lights waving in the distance.

Is that Vyrga's group? Lev asked the glaive.

Indeed. Seems he brought the stragglers along with his men.

"Perfect!" Lev said.

"What is?" Gerwyn asked.

"Watch the lights. Those are our men. They've bought us some time."

"Great," Hem chuckled despite his pain. "They deserve a reward."

Rak squinted his eyes and frowned. "You won't feel the same after I tell you who it is. Pretty sure that's Vyrga."

Hem's expression turned bleak. "Shit."

Lev laughed and turned around. He raised a torch to signal towards the arrivals before looking at his companions. "Let's not waste any time, shall we?"

The two blood-covered bogeys swung their gear clean. Gerwyn released his control over the magical energies, Hem placed his axe back over his shoulder, and Rak tucked his on his belt.

"Alright, let's move," both of the two large greyborns said in unison as they joined up with Lev before making a run for the waterfall.

CHAPTER 4

THE HIDDEN SHRINE

"We're here," Rapha said as she observed the ancient shrine before her.

It was an odd sight, especially given how hidden it was behind the waterfall. The shrine itself looked fairly intact, even if its surroundings consisted of fallen pillars, broken statues and other debris.

She, Gul, Volker, and the soldiers tasked to follow them started setting up a small field hospital for the incoming wounded.

It'd only be a matter of hours before the others all arrived. Knowing how many untrained and inexperienced bogeys had taken part in the exodus, there were bound to be many wounded among them.

Volker shook his head upon seeing everyone's sorry state.

"How are our provisions?" Volker asked Gul as he rummaged through one of the hand carts they'd taken with them when they had split from the main party.

"The front row only has repair tools, simple herbs, and water," Gul replied as he leaned against one of the shrine's pillars. "We'll have to wait until the centre gets here. They have most of the essential supplies."

Volker nodded, but noticing a strained rasp in Gul's voice, paused and looked closer.

"Are you alright?" Volker asked as he saw Gul shivering.

Gul fell to his knees. "I'm feeling... a bit sick."

"Must be from the weather. Let me find some blankets."

"No, it's something else, I think I'm—" Gul added in a weak voice before passing out.

"Gul!" Volker shouted. The other soldiers could only look on as their typically calm leader transformed into a panicking mess.

"Sir," a wounded bogey said as he limped closer, "Me and my family walked alongside him for most of the way. His strength started leaving around the time we spotted the hiveling scouts."

"Then why didn't you tell me? Why didn't you tell any of us!" Volker yelled. His vision was blurry. Blinded by tears as he held his friend's unconscious body.

"Trust me, we wanted to. It was Gul who didn't. You see he—"

"He didn't want to delay us, right?" Volker interrupted.

The green bogey nodded. "I knew something was wrong when he started wheezing, but we didn't have the time to find out. He wanted to keep the pace up."

"It was for the civilians," the bogey continued. "Last night, he saw a kid lose two fingers to frostbite. It was a terrible sight."

The bogey then made eye contact with Volker. "We took the kid to one of the healers but... after seeing that, Gul told us we couldn't slow down. Not with the promised land, with its brilliant rays of warm sunlight, almost in reach."

He then sat down, next to Volker and Gul. "You out of everyone should know that Gul is tougher than he looks. He'll live."

Volker's sobbing intensified, but not for long. "You're right. Gul will survive this. We've been through worse."

He turned his back to the other soldiers and wiped his tears.

When he turned back around, he was once again the greyborn his soldiers had grown accustomed to seeing. One who could stand tall among Lev and the like. One of the few who'd survived the expedition. The one who'd led and inspired them during the war with the Jiira.

"Move Gul closer to the shrine, where the other wounded are," he ordered calmly. "And make sure he and the other wounded teleport to safety first."

Volker took a deep breath in. *I need to collect my thoughts. What we need now are more supplies to treat the wounded and ill.*

The caravan had been organised into three sections to protect the most essential supplies from attack or loss.

The front had the most soldiers and was led by Lev, Hemgall, and Rak. Other than being responsible for protecting the front of the caravan, they also had tools and engineers to clear the path for the rest of the caravan.

The rear had the second highest number of soldiers and included the Jiira captives and most of the other non-bogey goblinoids who'd joined the exodus.

Meanwhile, the centre, which was protected from either end by the other sections, and on the sides by terrain, had the least number of soldiers. It contained the majority of the civilians and food supplies, healers, and the injured. This section was mostly protected by Vyrga and his followers, Grasha, and Orva.

"Damnit," Volker cursed under his breath. "We should've split the cargo more evenly. Our single point of failure is being chased by a herd of ravenous hivelings."

A wounded soldier stumbled forward. He chuckled, blood dripping from his lips. "Well, our so-called leader should be prepared to bring the carts himself."

Volker turned around, and walked towards the wounded soldier. "What do you mean by that? Why would Lev and the others who stayed behind be responsible for the carts? Isn't that the centre's sole purpose?"

The soldier chuckled more loudly as he straightened his back against the pillar. "Isn't he responsible for our current predicament? Whose idea was it to split the supplies like that instead of letting everyone carry their own stuff?"

Volker's face contorted in confusion and anger. "You don't know anything! Most are barely able to make the trek just by themselves—and it was decided by majority vote!"

"Majority vote, my ass," the soldier spat out. "Look what the majority vote did to your friend. He's practically dead."

Volker almost lost his cool, but allowed the soldier to continue.

"We all know that Lev calls the shots. He could've forced a change. Should've left the useless ones behind. You better hope that the centre and rear can take care of the bugs, or we're all dead meat."

Volker brandished his spear and looked down at the soldier. "You're wounded. You can barely stand. Shall we leave you behind?"

"Whatever." The soldier glanced at the shrine's platform. "Whether we get to the other side of that *thing* or not, we'll all starve without the supply carts."

The soldier tried to stand, leaning against a broken statue for support. "Lev's plan," He paused to calm his ragged breathing. "may kill us all."

The soldier hobbled away to rejoin his ailing, muttering compatriots waiting for the field hospital.

Volker's eye twitched. "Lev better fix all this," he muttered as he walked over to Rapha.

On Rapha's command, the remaining able-bodied men and women had distributed themselves around the shrine and set up a defensive barrier within the shrine's ruins. They'd carefully rolled the giant pieces of foreign stones and statues towards the waterfall's entrance, leaving one small entrance for the others.

Big enough for us, but small enough for the hivelings, Rapha recounted as she walked through the barricade's entrance. "Alright, move the wounded towards the back of the shrine. Every able man should take defensive positions along with me and Volker."

After everyone had found a spot to defend, a faint sound could be heard beside the waterfall's heavy splashing. They prepared themselves for their anthropoid adversaries. They steadied their breathing, formed a phalanx, and aimed their crossbows at the entrance point.

But before anyone could shoot or thrust, a young bogey walked through the waterfall. It didn't take long for the others to follow behind. Mothers, children, and older goblinoids hastily crashed through the waterfall and stumbled through the barricade's small entrance.

"We're finally here!" one of them exclaimed.

"Clear the shrine's platform! We're going to channel energy into it now!" Orva shouted.

The few soldiers defending the shrine's platform immediately jumped down and joined the others defending the entrance.

Orva ordered her fellow shamans to gather around the shrine. A few soldiers, along with two shamans, stood in the centre of the teleportation formation.

Orva turned to the group in the formation. "Are you all ready? This could be dangerous."

"That's why we're testing it," The oldest of the shamans answered. "From what the scouting team reported last time, we should be able to teleport back after dropping off the first soldiers. More importantly, we need to understand how many people we can send in every attempt."

"Understood. Begin the process."

At Orva's order the two shamans channelled their energy through a small pedestal at the shrine's centre. The shrine's platform lit up in a brilliant array of colours, similar to the shrine Orva had operated in Pàrras, as opposed to the measly ones found in the monster caverns' lower floors.

Once the light show was over, one of the shamans along with four soldiers had disappeared.

After a few moments, the platform lit up again and the group returned once again.

The shamans fell to their knees in exhaustion. "It works," one of them huffed.

Orva nodded and pointed at another shaman. "Let's do it again. Let's have seven people stand on the platform this time and only have one shaman activate it."

With the second experiment succeeding, more followed. In the end, Orva found out that the shrine's limit was fifty people per transfer.

"Seems like only one shaman is required to activate the shrine," Orva muttered.

"But isn't the amount teleported too low?" Volker asked.

"The shrine's less run-down than I expected, but it's still in terrible shape. It's good enough that we can send fifty at a time."

With the experiments done, they divided themselves into groups and began teleporting personnel in earnest.

There was no noticeable entry point for a staff or haze-imbued item to activate the platform, meaning the destination couldn't be altered.

Orva scanned the perimeter, checking every ruin before eventually examining the platform itself after another group disappeared into the light.

Now that I think about it, the amount of energy needed doesn't make sense. One shaman shouldn't be enough to transfer fifty people. Besides, this amount of runes isn't enough for such a complex mechanism.

She traced her hand over the pathway of the platform's connectors, hoping to figure out the mechanism behind it. *Maybe a pressure plate gets activated if enough stand on the platform and the runes connect to another set?*

Orva found no immediate evidence of a pressure plate, but continued her search regardless.

There it is!

A collection of small haze crystals lay on the platform in an intricate pattern. Large rocks were positioned around the circumference of the platform. She inspected the rocks, clearing away the dust until she could see figures embedded on their surface.

A pattern of grooves converged like spokes of a wheel in the middle, where a circular, smooth stone lay. A robed figure with a crown of spikes around its head was visible on its surface.

What's with the crown? Is it symbolism or does it do anything? Orva's eyes widened. *Is it gathering magical energies?*

"Could it be…" Orva whispered to herself.

"Could it be what?" Rapha asked, startling the shaman.

Orva whirled around in a panic. "Rapha! Weren't you protecting the entrance?"

"Yeah, but you looked confused so I wanted to check on you. Did I say something wrong?"

"It's nothing. This shrine is… it just surprised me."

"It's Lev! Lev and the others have arrived!" a chorus of voices announced.

"Where's Orva?" Lev asked as he made his way through the wall of soldiers and civilians greeting him. Now that he and the other commanders had arrived, Lev knew tensions would be higher than ever.

"Are you all gonna keep gawking like idiots or will someone give me some aid?" Hemgall barked at the crowd.

"You should control your temper," Vyrga remarked as he crossed through the waterfall. A limping Ludger leaned on his shoulder for support as Bolo followed them like a guardian giant.

"Try saying that when one of those bugs bites your leg. Oh, right. You were busy sneaking around like a corpse-eater."

"If it weren't for us, more of the foul creatures would've swarmed you. Maybe we should've let them."

"Go rot in a ditch!" Hem spat.

Orva approached the quibbling duo. "Right, what's the damage?"

Hemgall pointed at his bloodied leg. "Did you lose your edge while I was gone or is my blood invisible?"

As Orva mentally facepalmed, she approached the wounded Hemgall and started tending his wounds.

"Insolent buffoon," Vyrga spat before approaching a few other healers. The shamans wasted no time tending to him and Ludger.

Orva focused the last of her magical energy on Hem's leg. "Don't those bugs know when to give up?"

"Doesn't seem like it. Thanks to that cocky bastard, we've held them off for now. But we can't stay long. Something's brewing."

The light faded away as Orva gave herself a moment before continuing her efforts. "Brewing?"

"They're trying to wear us out. The bugs got smart and are increasing their assault force before sending another wave of warriors."

Orva wiped the sweat off her forehead and shifted her attention from Hem's leg. "It *has* been eerily quiet here. Was that Lev's theory?"

Hem raised an eyebrow, then grunted as he propped himself off his back to meet Orva's kneeled height. "They stopped following us when we got to the waterfall. They're building their numbers. You don't have to be as smart as Lev to see what they're doing."

Orva stayed silent, waiting for Hem to continue. When she heard no immediate response, she cleared her throat and met eyes with Hemgall, whose raised brows suggested impatience. She quickly looked back down at his leg and continued her healing efforts.

Hemgall relaxed his shoulder, falling flat on the ground underneath. "Anyway, they'll be here soon. We don't have much time to waste." He glanced at the platform, a weak grin appearing on his face. "I see you've started the next stage of the exodus."

Orva looked back at the shrine in time to see another group disappear into the light.

"Yeah, I've assigned a shaman to each group. I've made sure to keep enough around for you and the others."

"Good. That's good," Hemgall said as he closed his eyes.

Orva's heartbeat quickened. "I need help. He's losing too much blood!"

A few other shamans approached and kept the wound closed with fur and cloth from their tunics.

"He isn't gonna make it if this bleeding doesn't stop," Orva blurted out.

"He will," another voice said.

Orva looked behind her. She saw Lev approaching her as he cleaned his glaive. "He'll be fine. Trust me."

"Trust you?" one of Orva's shamans snorted. "How can we trust you when we don't even know if those creatures will be waiting for us at the other end? They might be waiting for us to gather on the other side."

"They're not."

Another soul intruded upon Lev's mind. *Lev!*

What, Gherm? Now isn't the time.

Gherm paused, but quickly took up the pace once again. *She's right, how can you be sure?*

The hivelings are leading us here, Lev responded. He could feel Gherm's confusion intensifying with a mix of anger.

Leading us? Gherm's soul boomed within Lev's mind.

Another consciousness quickly entered their debate.

Master is right. The hivelings are tainted by the mark of a powerful being. The culprit's magical residue is familiar to that of Ainshard's court. You know them as the guides.

Lev froze. The shaman, once indignant, now stood silent, perplexed at Lev's behaviour.

He'd theorised that the hivelings were looking to claim the valley and mountains for themselves, and were driving out the goblinoids by any means necessary for this purpose but this…

They're being led by one of the guides? Lev finally responded to the glaive.

I'm afraid so, and this one has a familiar scent. From the frontier lands where you found me, master.

Lev bit his upper lip. *Kram!*

CHAPTER 5

SILENT OBSERVERS

As the last goblinoids finally crossed through the waterfall and arrived in the cave, a group of newcomer goblins unassociated with the Jiira stood in a corner of the cavern, speaking with Lev about their intentions. They'd heard of his plan, and after witnessing the platform at work, they wanted to join the exodus group instead of staying behind in these increasingly-hazardous lands.

Are these all of the goblins you identified earlier? We won't find another band of goblins waiting on the other side of the waterfall, right? Lev asked the glaive.

Correct, she stated matter-of-factly.

A squad of soldiers pushed two heavy marble pillars stationed near the waterfall's mouth until they tipped over, blocking what remained of the waterfall entrance.

With the hiveling menace still lurking around, many bogeys and goblins volunteered to fortify the blocked entrance with granite chunks and smaller shattered stones from the ruins surrounding the shrine.

Raban watched the berserker who had threatened him carry a large barrel of supplies and head towards the shrine's platform. "You seem unusually eager for someone who hates his leadership," Raban remarked to the berserker.

The giant goblin shot a glare at his commander without stopping. "Well, I hate dying to giant bugs even more. Besides, the first batch we'll send to the other side are supplies."

Raban laughed. "Fair enough. I'll let you continue carrying bogey supplies undisturbed."

Hem groaned as he saw the light of the platform shine for the umpteenth time. He was sitting on the ground while a shaman tended to his injuries. "This is taking too long," he muttered. He turned towards the other shamans. "Can't you do this any faster? I'm missing all the action."

All Hem got was a few judging stares. Whenever the shamans weren't busy working the shrine, they were tending to other wounded; they had no time for pestering idiots.

Just as Hem was about to loudly express his impatience once more, a searing pain traced stripes around his body as his wounds closed at a ridiculous pace. The pain quickly faded, leaving a peculiar itch.

"There. I'm pretty good, aren't I?" Gerwyn gloated. The shaman previously tending to Hemgall could only stare in shock as the wound fully closed, leaving only a few scars behind.

"The pain says otherwise," Hem grumbled.

Gerwyn waved his hands in the air. "Toughen up, greyborn."

"We've been working together since the start of the exodus. Isn't it about time you stop being an ass and call me by my name?"

"Hah, I don't feel like it. Just be happy you can swing that fancy axe of yours again ." The blue-skinned shaman glanced at the other greyborns. "Your compatriots aren't so lucky."

"What are you on about?" Hem answered, annoyed.

"They're about to crack. The priests and the elders tried to keep everyone calm, but if you guys hadn't arrived with the supplies and civilians, they'd have given up and chosen to become insect food long ago."

Hem laughed and pushed his chest out. "We're greyborns. We've seen worse."

Gerwyn's eyes narrowed. "Don't let that confidence send your men awry."

"Be glad our precious leaders didn't hear you say that," Grasha chimed in.

He took a peek through the waterfall from the gaps between the pillars. It was dusk already. "Well, our leaders have to see us through this first. It's getting dark already."

"I'm not sure about Vyrga, but Lev will." Hem stretched his previously injured leg.

"Perhaps," Gerwyn responded after nodding sagely. "Your ragtag bunch might be all we have left to defend against the horrors of this world. Had it been my choice, I would have hired professionals."

Hem, who had locked eyes continuously with Gerwyn, spontaneously burst out in more laughter. "No wonder you're still friendless in your thirties."

"Heheh. Says the former lackey." After speaking, something caught Gerwyn's eye; his expression suddenly soured.

Hem leaned forward with wide eyes. "What? Did something happen?"

"Yes. Something I hate with every fibre of my being. More importantly, now that you're fully recovered, I have other matters to attend to."

Gerwyn didn't even wait for a reply from Hem and marched straight towards a few younger shamans playfully moving medicinal supplies towards the platform. All three shamans froze under his searing gaze.

"Having fun, aren't we?" the senior shaman said through gritted teeth.

"W-We were just taking a break, sir," the oldest youth replied.

Gerwyn clenched his fists. The exaggerated smile on his face as he tried to remain calm caught the attention of nearby soldiers. "A break," he finally spat out. "That's wonderful."

"Sir!" said another young shaman. She stumbled backwards trying to stand at attention. "Sir, we were awaiting further orders, and there was nothing to do, so we decided to take a—"

The youth swallowed his words once Gerwyn started pacing around her like a predator waiting for its prey to snap. "We all need a break every now and then to handle the stress. Don't we?"

"Yes, sir."

"Especially in these trying times," Gerwyn said as he watched the younglings' body language.

All three of them quickly nodded.

Gerwyn brought his hand to his chin and gazed at the ceiling. "So, how long have you been on break?"

The youth who had spoken first paused. "I-I-I—M-M-Maybe—"

"Hiveling got your tongue? *Speak*!" Gerwyn yelled.

As bystanders gathered to watch, the youths began shivering. The youngest among them was about to break down in tears.

Gerwyn let out an exhausted sigh. "I won't escalate this further. For now, focus your attention on the task at hand. Our very lives are at stake here. Don't forget it."

After a few seconds of hesitation, the shamans moved back to the other soldiers near the ruins.

He shook his head in disappointment. *Damn lessers. Even the greyborns aren't slacking off.*

Gerwyn felt eyes boring into his back. He clicked his tongue and turned around to tend to the wounded from the back section.

"I've always hated that strict buffoon," Orva grumbled to Lev. "By the way, you look ticked off. Something wrong?"

"He's a piece of work," Lev admitted, "but we need all the hands we can get." He placed a hand on his forehead. "His strict nature is the least of our worries right now."

Both Rapha and Orva took a step back.

"What do you mean?" Rapha started. "The field hospitals are treating the wounded, and the shrine works."

"Not amazingly well, mind you," Orva cut in, "but everything's going as you expected, isn't it?"

"Not everything," Lev answered darkly. "It appears that we were lured here."

"Lured? By whom?" Orva said with crossed arms. "Those insects are smart for what they are, but they're not capable of much more than attacking and retreating together."

Lev's expression darkened further. "They're being influenced."

Rapha took a step towards Lev. "Who could possibly influence them?"

"Kram and the white being."

Both Rapha and Orva glanced sideways.

Rapha broke the silence first. "Why would two beings, two beings only *you* seem to have had contact with, use *them* to lure use here?"

"They haven't told me anything, but I have my suspicions."

Orva looked at the waterfall. The translucent, liquid barrier, even with the makeshift barricade behind it, wouldn't shield them from a hiveling assault. They were trapped.

"But didn't they promise us Pàrras, the ruined city we found in the frontier lands? Didn't they ask you to bring us here?" She started to fear for the worst.

"All I know is that they gave me Ainshard's key, the power to change things, by signing their contract. However, they're also making something else clear."

"Which is?"

"We're not welcome in these lands anymore," Lev said.

He turned his sight to the shrine. The ancient patterns on its surface told a foreboding tale about its past. It reminded him of the expedition's strange sightings. *Could the crowned figure be Kram? He was the lord of Pàrras and the frontier after all.*

The ambience of the waterfall abruptly halted, the typical splashing of water against rock replaced by the endless clicking of mandibles.

Hivelings feelers pierced through the water and surveyed the ground beyond before withdrawing. Once most of the feelers had retracted, several hivelings pushed another into the waterfall. Its exoskeleton smashed against a nearby pillar. After regaining its balance, it rejoined its kind behind the waterfall.

Lev looked at the entrance. *They found us already? I thought we'd have a bit more time.*

"Stay sharp, men!" he yelled at the soldiers stationed behind the barricade of fallen pillars close to the waterfall. But before he could order his men to push back the hivelings, he and the soldiers noticed the hivelings' strange behaviour.

Despite having arrived on the scene, instead of frenziedly attacking as they usually did, the hivelings remained motionless on their side of the waterfall.

"Sir, they're not engaging us. What do we do?" one of the soldiers yelled, unsure if he should take this opportunity to stab his spear into one of the idling hivelings.

All eyes were on Lev now. "Stay where you are, spears at the ready. We need to be prepared if they decide to charge. Crossbowmen, be ready to fire."

He turned back to Orva and Rapha, who were still in shock. No one had expected the hivelings to arrive this soon. Even as the atmosphere in the cavern changed from a hopeful one to an icy haze of impending doom, the unexpected visitors continued to hold their ground, simply observing the goblinoids.

"Believe me now?" Lev asked.

"Hivelings are simple-minded creatures, easy to manipulate and plentiful in supply. No better divine messengers exist," he continued.

"You're awfully calm about this, Lev," Rapha said. The force in her voice drew the attention of the goblinoids in the teleportation queue, causing some to glance in their direction.

"The hivelings are tainted by another power," Lev mumbled. "It's hard to explain."

A flurry of panicked murmurs at the shrine's queue caught Lev's attention. A burly greyborn was pushing and shoving those in front of him to clear a path for himself. "Get out of my way," he snarled at the frozen goblinoids still entranced by the docile hivelings.

The greyborn's intentions became clear as he swiftly approached the shrine. Soon enough, other goblinoids began pushing their way through the line.

"Run towards the shrine!" a blue bogey yelled. "This is our last chance! Who knows how long they'll stay back!"

It didn't take long for the remaining goblinoids to follow his advice in a frenzy.

A curious warrior hiveling peered through, surveying the insides of the waterfall's cavern. Its beady eyes observed the cacophony of violence among bogeys, briefly pausing to face the shrine. After a tense moment, it slowly moved back until even its blade disappeared behind the waterfall.

"What's it doing?" a goblin yelped.

"Is it retreating?"

"Perhaps it's waiting for reinforcements?"

"Shut up!" the earlier greyborn shouted. "Don't be stupid, it's waiting for its countless siblings to arrive for the feast."

The greyborn grabbed a shaman by the neck, then drew a crude bronze knife from his pocket and pointed it at him. "You! You'll help me get out of here."

But before he could demand anything else from the frightened shaman, another voice intervened. "Or what?"

"L-Lord Vyrga! I advise you to join me and get to safety. Most of the supplies have been transported to the frontier already."

"Safety? All I see is one of my own men trying to flee like a coward. I expected more."

As Vyrga advanced toward him, the burly greyborn stumbled backwards until he lost his balance and fell. His knife slipped out of his hand and skidded out of reach.

"I was just trying to—"

"Run," Vyrga interrupted.

"Does it matter?" Lev interrupted, approaching the two. "We're safe for now."

"Safe?!" Vryga yelled. He'd been composed until now, but. Lev's words finally snapped something.

"There are hivelings gathering in front of the waterfall, mere feet away from us, and you think we're safe. Even when the expeditionary force went through the deeper floors of the cavern, I never saw the insects this organised."

Vyrga fell silent, uncharacteristically struggling to find the words he needed. "It feels like... they're being... directed."

Lev chuckled. "It's because they are."

Even Vyrga was suprised at Lev's words. He straightened his back and loosened his expression. "You seem to know a great deal about the current situation. Care to explain?"

"They're being controlled by one of the beings I met when we visited the frontier. Actually, we even saw a copy of his likeness."

Vyrga thought back to the events that happened in the ruined city. His eyes widened. "It can't be... Kram the Wise? You told us he'd been gone from the frontier for centuries. Only that shallow replica of light remained, and even that is fading into oblivion, if it hasn't fully already."

A mix of emotions coursed through Vyrga. How could a dead god—a false god—influence hivelings? "That's simply impossible. If what you said about the contract was true, then that white being, along with Kram, are still trapped. There's no way they could control the hivelings."

"Then how would you explain our current predicament, Vyrga?"

"We've seen murals of hivelings in the city. There must be some active ancient relic closeby acting as a deterrence mechanism."

"That's also plausible," Orva muttered.

Vyrga smiled towards her. "Indeed, it is. Now let's not waste our time. Whether they're observing us or waiting for reinforcements, we should make haste and increase the shrine's teleportation capacity somehow." He turned back and took a few steps towards the shrine. "Orva, you're the expert."

Orva shook her head. "You flatter me. Neither I nor the rest of the shamans know enough about the shrine to alter its function. It's too enigmatic."

"Couldn't you modify it using your staff like you did last time?"

"How?" Lev questioned. "There isn't any form of relic or device for Orva to use to control this archaic technology."

When did you become an expert in such subjects? Vyrga was about to argue, but one look at Orva confirmed Lev's statement.

Vyrga shrugged. "Thought you magic-inclined shamans might know a thing or two more than I do."

"I hate to say it, but Lev's right," Orva said. "It's impossible to change the shrine's parameters. It's already a miracle we're able to operate it as is without the need for any special controllers."

Vyrga issued no response.

"So," Orva continued, "are you and your cronies going to abandon us now?"

Vryga's shoulders shuddered, first in fury but then in pain. Vyrga felt a constriction in his chest that strengthened by the second. Only a few noticed him fix his posture and clench his hands. "Only a fool would believe he can survive the unknown alone. Numbers are one of the few weapons we have to overtake the masked wretches festering in the city."

"Numbers are important," Lev agreed, "but leaving obstacles behind would only yield issues in the short-term, wouldn't it?"

"Try not to muddle your mind in your conspiracies. I don't believe in beings of bygone times influencing a collective as centralised as the hivelings'."

Vyrga had turned to leave when Lev placed his hand on his shoulder.

"Collective?" Lev shook his head. "How would any signals from the queen reach them all the way out here?"

Vyrga tensed his shoulders. "You should stop while you still can, Lev."

Lev lifted his hands from Vyrga's shoulder. "Sure. I just wanted to make sure you understood our situation."

Away from Lev's sight, Vyrga's face contorted in anger. *This brat. If you don't reign in your arrogance...*

He glanced over his shoulder at the young greyborn who had brought so much change to his world. *And yet, I feel like he may be right about this. Perhaps I should investigate those ancient beings further.*

As more hivelings gathered in front of the waterfall, the tensions within the remainder of the settlers skyrocketed.

"Can't you channel your energy faster?"

"Take my children first! I'll join another group!"

The line of goblinoids defending the waterfall quickly thinned as more left the barricade in panic and fled towards the shrine.

Volker hurried as many of the remaining refugees towards the shrine as he could. *We can't force them to hold the line much longer*, he thought. *The hivelings will bring reinforcements soon.*

"They would rebel if we forced them, wouldn't they?"

Volker's heart jumped as he heard a familiar voice completing his thoughts.

"Lev?"

"Don't worry, I'm thinking along the same lines. I don't think the soldiers will turn on us even if we force them to stay. We'll remain until the last group has gone through."

Vyrga briskly paced towards the platform with four of his men. He exchanged glances with Lev before the light engulfed him, leaving nothing behind.

"Are you sure you should stay here, sir? What if whoever's behind the hivelings is after you?"

Lev let out a soft chuckle. "I'd be the last one on their blacklist. I'm still useful to them."

"Useful?" Volker whispered.

"The contracts still binds me—and them. They can't touch me."

* * *

"Lev!" Orva yelled.

Both Volker and Lev turned towards Orva. They'd been too focused on the hivelings to notice that the last groups had already vanished through the light.

"We're last. I'll activate the shrine."

"Well, isn't that great. Would you mind carrying old me over there?" Hem said as he motioned at his leg.

As Rak helped Hem to his feet, Gerwyn and Lev kept eyes on the hivelings. Their numbers had drastically increased, and they pushed and shoved each other as they watched the retreating goblinoids. It was as if the exodus were a spectacle, or perhaps a circus.

Even so, none of them crossed the boundary. Their blurred shapes were all that Lev and the last group could make out through the water.

"Looks like you were right," Gerwyn said as he centred himself in the centre of the shrine's intricate platform. "Anyway, it's about time we leave these accursed lands behind us. Now, shall we?"

Rak slowly lowered Hem onto the platform. "Lev, what are you waiting for? An invitation?" he yelled.

Lev snapped out of his daze and trudged his way towards the shrine.

"Orva, I'll activate it this time," said Gerwyn. "You're too exhausted to operate it anyway."

"I can manage just fi—" Orva slumped towards the ground.

"See? Now gather close, towards the centre."

The platform let out an exceptionally bright burst of light from its haze crystals.

"Whoa, what's this?" Volker yelped.

Lev's eyes traced the thin cracks spreading throughout the crystals. "Seems like this thing's also at its limit."

The light travelled through each groove in the platform, lighting each haze crystal on its surface until the crowned figure, too, was lit. Cracks formed in the figure's crown as the crystals turned brighter one by one.

"I can feel it! It's overcharging its energy!" Gerwyn shouted. A ringing sound intensified to painful volume.

"We're its last cargo. Let's make it count," Orva said as she regained her bearings.

Their bodies were engulfed by the bright light, and they too, were transported to another land. Just as they lost their vision of the waterfall, their observers rapidly entered it. The last thing Lev felt was a hiveling feeler gliding over his forehead.

No matter. They were on their way to a land with untold mysteries, both dangerous and beneficial. The frontier lands awaited their new inhabitants—their new custodians.

CHAPTER 6

THE FRONTIER

Following the flash of bright light from the platform, the world turned still. There were no sounds, no smells, and no sights other than a crushing black void and two spheres of light, one below his feet and one above, each about a hundred killigs away.

This is... different. What is this place? And where are the others? Lev asked.

Lev moved his arms, then his legs. *Seems I can move my body.* He tried touching the void outside of the lower sphere but was repelled by some kind of barrier. *Seems I can't get out. Not that I'd want to. The last thing I need is to be stranded by myself.*

The sphere below him glowed brighter, and a sense of weightlessness surrounded his body. He began floating towards the second sphere above him.

The closer he got to the upper sphere, the brighter it glowed and the faster he floated until he stopped midway.

Lev's eyes opened wide. *What's going on? Why did I stop?*

The lower sphere glowed brighter and brighter, then suddenly collapsed on itself.

Dread filled his heart as a bright wall of light emerged from below him. It sped towards him and flattened him on its surface like a pancake before racing towards the upper sphere at a stupendous speed.

With gritted teeth Lev closed his eyes and braced himself for impact.

Instead of slamming into the sphere, the sensation of the wall pressing against his body disappeared. After a brief moment of nothingness, Lev felt the soft impact of soil on his newly-returned corporeal body.

The first thing Lev noticed was the absence of cold. The blizzard, which had haunted them ever since they had reached the upper regions of sinner's reach, had left in favour of a gentle breeze.

He stood up and massaged the back of his head. "Never again," he hissed.

Lev tried opening his eyes but they were still sensitive from gazing at the blazing sphere. He rubbed his eyes as he heard a thud from behind him, followed by a groan.

"What... What was that? Am I still alive?" Lev heard a young, masculine voice mutter.

Lev tried opening his eyes again, but the brilliant rays of light blinded him once again. "Volker? Is that you?"

"Yes, sir. Where are you?"

Lev's hands touched the ground near him in search of something solid in an attempt to get a grasp on the situation. *Grass.* He swept his hands around farther away from his body until he felt branches. *Looks like we've arrived.*

"We're here," Lev finally announced.

It didn't take long for his eyes to adjust to the warm light of the morning sun. A small forest clearing greeted the party, with only a tall shrine covered in moss and a small platform on their left as a testimony of sentient intervention.

Seems Ainshard's people at least took into account that no one wants to smash their head on a cobblestone floor once they arrive, Lev mentally observed.

Volker rubbed his eyes. "It's dawn, but it was still dark at the shrine. How's that possible?"

"This trip felt different. It wasn't like this last time we were transported," Lev answered. "I'm no expert, but I think we should be more careful when using half-destroyed shrines in the future."

"Fair enough. Do you think we're far enough from the cavern for those insects to give up?" Volker said as he got up.

"We should be," a feminine voice answered.

Both Lev and Volker turned towards the shrine. There they found Orva gently scraping moss off the shrine with a bronze knife, inspecting the runes underneath. Gerwyn was also nearby, inspecting the platform.

Orva turned to the two greyborns. "Took you long enough. Everyone else is lazing around."

"Isn't that dangerous?" Volker asked. He pointed at a wooded area in the distance. "What about the creatures roaming the forest?"

"I heard from the scouts. It's mostly deer around here, with a few wolves keeping their distance. Those four-legs won't leave the cover of trees. They must be shocked from seeing goblinoids for the first time in a long while, so should be safe as long as we keep our distance," Orva answered.

Lev nodded. As his vision cleared, he surveyed his surroundings and found Hem sitting on a nearby boulder.

"What are you looking at?" Lev asked, catching the giant greyborn by surprise.

After a moment of surprise, Hem's expression softened. "You made it. I was just thinking." Hem stared into the distance. *Nothing but small trees. We're surrounded by a wall of vegetation and mountains.* "Where are the other groups? The ones who passed through earlier?"

Lev pointed at an obelisk on a hill peaking above the forest line close by. "Probably over there."

Goblinoid footprints and wagon tracks led towards the strange landmark.

"Most likely," Orva replied. "Now that you're here, can we get a move on?" She hurriedly stuffed her fur coat into her satchel in favour of something more weather-appropriate.

Volker turned to Hem. "Do you think they left someone there to meet us?"

Lev advanced in the direction of the strange relic. "Let's find out."

At Lev's behest, Hem whistled to gather everyone near the shrine.

"Can't we stay for a while longer?" Gerwyn pleaded. His eyes kept darting towards the shrine, clearly entranced by its mysteries.

"We need to rendezvous with the others before it gets too dark. You can come back here when we're not in danger," Rapha replied.

"That'd take months," Orva grumbled.

"It's that or nothing. My men are waiting for orders," Rak replied.

The two shamans groaned as they shuffled their feet towards the party.

As they approached the monument, Hem noticed a piece of cloth stuck to a branch. "They *were* here after all."

He took a look at the obelisk and admired its design. Throughout the ages it'd stood in this spot. Unyielding, unbroken. It bathed in the sun's light, standing about a killig tall. Even over the centuries it had stood, its granite surface had only eroded marginally in these forgotten lands.

Orva was the first to approach the obelisk close enough to make out rough shapes and runes on its surface. "There's Ainshardian writing on it."

"Can you translate it?" Gerwyn asked.

"Can't you? Aren't all noble shamans taught Ainshardian?" Orva asked.

Gerwyn fidgeted in his place. A few moments later, he coughed and fessed up, "Ainshard's language was never my strong suit. I cared more about refining the arts of the present than playing with the relics of the dead."

Hearing his answer, Orva groaned and turned back towards the obelisk. *I guess those lessons with Vyrga came in handy.*

"It's really worn." Her eyes tried to discern each rune. "Wait. There's something else written below it."

The group gathered around the relic.

Hem examined the white scratches. "Looks fresh."

"That's because it is," Gerwyn replied. "Look." He grabbed a piece of flint left behind near the obelisk.

Orva read the white markings aloud. "Head north until you see smoke."

"Why would there be smoke in the north? I thought we were supposed to lay low. We don't know what's lurking out here," Volker remarked.

Lev pointed north. "Doesn't look like we need to." There in the distance, behind a few small hills, a skinny plume of smoke slowly drifted higher. "They probably made these scratches last night. We really took our sweet time up there."

"We sure did," Hem said with a grin on his face, "and it's a good thing we did, or they wouldn't have had the time to get so comfy at a campfire or scribble on rocks."

Whether due to exhaustion, stress, or the influence of higher beings, Hem's joke brought a smile to everyone's face.

"A campfire would be nice," Rapha muttered with closed eyes as she imagined the smell of roasted nuts.

As they set their course northwards, the once-distant plume became larger and larger. They heard laughter once they reached the top of the hills.

"They're really partying!" Hem shouted.

The group at the campfire looked up, dumbfounded.

"It's Hem!"

"Hemgall and the others are here!"

"Lev's here too!"

Warm voices welcomed them, as one by one they were hailed as heroes.

"Damn right it's me!" Hem bragged. "Now. Where's that mead we stashed?"

Gerwyn groaned. "Is that all you care about? Alcohol?"

"Look who's talking. Aren't you the one who hugs a bottle of red darg wine every time you sleep?"

Gerwyn didn't answer. He lowered his head to hide his embarrassment and quietly made his way down the hill.

"Serves him right," Orva commented between chuckles. She proceeded down the hill, followed by Rapha and the others.

"Hey, Hem!" yelled one of the men at the campfire. He plopped down a large wooden barrel with a cheeky grin on his face. "Looky what we have here!"

Volker couldn't help but sigh after seeing the jovial giant comically running down the hill towards the mead kegs. "There goes the last of our mead supply. It'll take a while before we can plant hops and find honey. What will we do until then, sir?"

Lev did not respond.

Volker approached more closely. "Lev. You alright?"

Lev had been standing still on the hilltop.

"Let's join the others, sir. It's time we rested." Volker took a step closer. "You, too, sir."

"We're finally free, Volker," Lev said. His eyes did not leave the tents and campfires below.

"We are, sir."

"Now we can start anew," Lev said, voice faltering on the last syllable.

In the distance, the light of the sun high in the sky bounced off the surface of a gleaming construction. It was so bright, so reflective, so *promising*, that Volker found it difficult to stare too long at its strange architecture. He snuck a peek at his leader's face and saw a tear refract the sunlight at him. "What are you looking at, sir?"

"Our new home."

* * *

As Volker and Lev walked through the encampment, they noticed a similar stench. One they'd encountered all too often both inside and outside of the caverns.

The smell of death, and the dying.

"Toss him out. He's in Dorn's hands now," a shaman said from inside of a healing tent.

The pair walked closer until they reached the tent's flaps. Before Lev could lift them, a shaman stormed out, carrying a body covered by a bloodied cloth.

"Wait!" Volker shouted.

"I need to dispose of this body. Orders from Kathaga."

She's running the healers as well now? What other ambitions do you have, Priestess of Zeja? Lev made a mental note of the old lady's actions.

"Alright, but before you do, can we check the body? Might be one of ours," Lev asked.

With a deep sigh, the shaman allowed the two to look at the body. What the shaman did not expect, however, was for both of them to turn pale mere moments after.

The sight of Molg's face, frozen in a flurry of fear, pain, and anger, along with the gory collection of holes in his abdomen, would haunt them for years to come. Even though his allegiance to their cause had become questionable after Lev's presumed death during the expedition, Lev and Volker still respected him for his service during the expedition and subsequent war with the Jiira.

"This is horrible," Volker said in a weak voice.

Lev placed the cloth back. "Tell me about it."

"Healer, is there a Gul or Jem among the injured here?"

"Don't know about a Gul, but we do have a Jem. Although he'll be leaving the mortal realm soon as well."

Lev bit his lip. "Volker, search for Gul. I'll check on Jem."

"I will, sir."

After seeing Volker enter a different healing tent, Lev entered the one before him, burdened with a responsibility he'd experienced far too many times. That of seeing and comforting a compatriot for the last time.

It took a while for Lev to find Jem among the injured. Some missed limbs, some screamed, and others remained silent. Jem was among the silent.

He'd noticed Lev when he entered, and had been smirking since. This had made spotting Jem possible for Lev, if not easy.

Lev kneeled next to Jem. "Looks like you're the only one here who can still do something other than mourn," he remarked.

"Heh, I've done my time. All that awaits me now are Zeja's grand banquets behind Jom's gates. If she doesn't want me, then at least the pain'll leave me when I join the cycle."

Lev lowered his head, ashamed of the men he'd forgotten about. If only he had an extra pair of eyes... "Listen. I'm sorry, but Molg's..."

"I know. Poor bastard died soon after the hiveling ambush at the rear. Got surrounded by a few scouts," Jem paused to take a deep breath. "I still hear his screams, the pain he must've endured. I still wonder if his body was able to decide which hurt most. His frostbitten limbs or his abdomen."

Jem grunted as he pushed himself up. "As for me, the shamans told me I angered the gods."

"What?" Lev looked behind his shoulder at one of the shamans tending the wounded.

"You know, they don't call it sinner's reach for nothing. I must've been too big a sinner."

"Jem, tell me what really happened. The gods be damned for incurring their wrath on a good man," Lev said in a lower tone.

"Well, from what I can remember, the first thing I noticed was the difficulty to breathe. It worsened when we started ascending higher into sinner's reach. Soon after, I felt nauseous."

Lev nodded. *Altitude sickness, I should've known.* He scrutinised Jem for more ailments, and found multiple infections on his arms and limbs. *The healers could only do so much. If only we had the means to treat frostbite properly, he would've made it without the infections.*

Jem wheezed before continuing. "Well, after the hiveling ambush, I lost all strength in my body and collapsed. That's when the others carried me and Molg to the shrine's field hospital."

"What about Gul? Did you see him?"

A moment of silence followed as Molg recounted the events. "Volker made sure they transported him here with the first group. Me and the others followed after."

"Makes sense, Gul's still Volker's best friend. I bet they got even closer after all the things they endured."

"Listen, Lev. I need some peace right now. Collect my thoughts and pray for whatever sins I committed."

Lev stood up. "Good luck on the other side, my friend. I'll make sure your family is well taken care of. Give the gods my regards, and tell them to sit back in their ethereal chairs and enjoy the show."

The other injured looked at Jem with dumbfounded expressions as he laughed between sickening coughs. "I'll add a piece of my mind as well."

The two made eye contact one last time.

"Show them what greyborns are capable of, liberator."

CHAPTER 7

THE SPEECH

"Alright, pack up. We're moving," a soldier yelled at a group of bogeys still slumbering in their tents.

"Now? Why the hurry?"

The soldier grabbed one of the tents' wooden reinforcements and yanked it out of the ground, causing the tent to collapse on its occupants. "Because one of our leaders says so."

Slowly, but surely, the goblinoids gathered near the centre of the camping grounds. Different branches of the goblinoid race were neatly lined up in front of a makeshift pedestal consisting of two small boulders with a wooden plank fixed on top of it.

Some squabbled over the horrors they'd encountered in the mountain ranges. Others contemplated leaving or following their favorite commanders into other lands, hoping to build a settlement away from Lev, Rak, and Vyrga's control.

"What's this all about?"

"Is Lev going to speak?"

"I hope Vyrga knows what we'll do now."

"I'm sure some of the blues have gotten their act together. Maybe that Gerwyn fellow? Meinrad is also a fine speaker."

"Nah, the old hierarchy is gone. They're all on the same level now. I'd follow Rak anywhere."

"Speaking of following, those damn bugs couldn't have followed us here... right?"

"Hem and Rak would kick their scaly asses back where they came from."

"Silence," a loud voice announced. "Vyrga will speak now." One of Vyrga's men had made his way to the pedestal unnoticed by the others. The goblinoids waited with anticipation as they watched a greyborn emerge from one of Vyrga's tents.

"It's Vyrga!" a couple of greyborns whispered.

Vyrga noticed that many of the previously enslaved greyborns were glaring at him. It was apparent that years of squeezing them dry for his protection racket had damaged his reputation. Bringing in the heads and treasures of the deserters, including those of his father, Reingard, had done well for his public appeal, but sadly not as much as he'd hoped and expected.

Nevertheless, Vyrga calmly observed the crowd and prepared to speak. "Prosperity under strong leadership is what we all seek."

The crowd fell silent.

At the back, where Rak's men had organised their tents, another familiar face listened attentively.

"Rak, are you sure about this? You could've given a speech instead of Vyrga," Hem asked the entranced greyborn next to him. "Hey, do you hear me?"

"Be quiet for once, Hem. Vyrga had time to prepare. Besides, I need to know what's coming for us."

"Coming for us? We just finished off those hivelings and we still have to take care of those masked freaks. Why would Vyrga turn on us now?"

Rak sighed deeply. "He's thinking ahead. The city's not that far from here. We'll need stable leadership once we take it. Don't forget we made a deal with the bastard—no interference between our gangs."

"He wants to rule, doesn't he?" another voice joined in.

"Lev," Rak replied, still focused on Vyrga. "Glad you're here."

"Pàrras, our new home, is awaiting our arrival," Vyrga announced with his right fist placed on his chest as if he were rounding up his men for a raid.

The crowd listened attentively. Vyrga slowly turned his head towards the distant buildings bathing in the sunlight. "Unfortunately, the vermin who have desecrated its walls and turned it into their nest feel differently."

"He's talking about those avian monstrosities, isn't he?" Volker thought aloud. Hem and Lev side-eyed him before giving him their full attention.

Hem was the first to break the silence. "What happened, kid? Why are your hands covered in blood!?"

I'd know that look anywhere. Lev thought to himself.

Volker's face was ashen and tear marks stained his cheeks. One look at Volker's soulless eyes was all the evidence Lev needed to confirm his suspicions.

"I'm sorry for your loss, Volker."

"It was the will of the gods, sir. There's nothing that could've been done," Volker softly replied.

"Indeed. Fate is a cruel mistress. All we can do is make sure that Gul won't be forgotten and his loved ones will be taken care of."

"His mother died during childbirth, so he was raised by his father, who died two expeditions ago. He had no loved ones, sir."

Lev placed a hand on Volker's shoulder. "I wouldn't say that. You were by his side. His memory lives on with you. From what I see, you already have an amulet of the dreaming god on you. Was Tanach his favourite?"

Volker nodded. "Most bogeys swarmed to Ainshard, Jom, or Zeja, but not Gul. Tanach was the one he liked. Gul... understood him, and unpopular as Tanach is, Gul was always grateful toward him. You know, for protecting everyone's dreams, and helping him meet with his parents in his sleep. Perhaps Tanach will take him in as one of his own, or help him rejoin the cycle in peace."

"I'm sure he will. For now, go rest," Lev advised.

Volker frowned. "Why? I am fine, sir."

"Lev's right, kid. This is the time to grief and clear your mind," Rak instructed.

"I said I am fine."

Noticing Volker's irritation, Lev sighed.

"Volker, you won't be part of the operation in the city."

"But sir—!"

"That's an order! After the speech, I need you to take care of funeral rights for our dead and help maintain order till we're back."

A deafening silence ensued among the four.

Volker grit his teeth and nodded.

"...Yes, sir." He turned on his heel and left.

"He'll thank you later," Rak muttered as he turned his attention back to Vyrga's speech. Lev and Hem followed.

"The primitive beasts infested what was once a beacon of culture and prosperity and morphed it into a shell of its former grandeur. It is our responsibility, our duty to drive out the pests and restore the city to its true form."

Vyrga shook his head. "There will be those who'll oppose us. We're foreign elements in new lands, and if its denizens happen to be hostile, we should be prepared for conquest by force."

Lev couldn't help but let out a soft chuckle. *It'll be more of a bloody slog than a conquest. Forget about foreign powers, if those hostiles are as numerous as we think, we might be dead before any of us can claim the city. If Vyrga is this confident, there must be something he's hiding from the public.* Lev clicked his tongue. *And from me.*

"And so, we will find our civilization in the last remains of Ainshard's golden age," Vyrga announced. He then halted his speech to let the crowd process what he'd said so far.

A wave of murmurs caught Lev's attention. The mention of the ancient ruler's name had riled the Jiira captives. *The goblins seem anxious about conquering one of their idol's cities.*

"The cradle of our past is ours for the taking, to rebuild and to prosper."

"And you're the one who'll lead us," Rak scoffed, turning to Lev. "Can you believe his spiel? If the odds weren't in Vyrga's favour, he'd plunge us into another civil war just to try and even them out."

"It's a game to him, Rak," Lev stated, trying to calm Rak down.

"A game? We're refugees with nowhere to go but that dreaded husk of a city," Rak said, more loudly than he had intended.

Hem patted Rak's back. "We'll have to endure this for now." He looked at Vyrga's remaining officers and could only recognize a few. "He's not looking to take over just yet. This is just a stop along the way."

Rak turned to Hem with narrowed eyes. "Then what is he trying to pull off here?"

Hem threw his arms wide, as if to announce some ancient god's gospel. "Can't you tell? A chief with a tribe too small is nothing but a hoodlum. He's recruiting."

Without interrupting his speech, Vyrga's eyes surveyed Rak's group. He deftly motioned for one of his officers, then surreptitiously gestured toward Rak's group.

Lev chuckled to himself. Vyrga was clearly sending someone to eavesdrop on their conversation. Unfortunately for him, Lev was well accustomed to such petty tricks.

Vyrga continued his speech. "We should depart at dusk, when most of the creatures roaming these lands are slumbering."

At dusk? Lev thought back to what he'd seen in the city. *Do those creatures even sleep? And what about nocturnal predators?*

"Yeah! We should leave and rebuild as soon as possible!" a middle-aged greyborn near the pedestal shouted. Lev noticed a fancy pouch tied to his rope belt.

After noticing that detail, it wasn't hard for Lev to find a couple more. He grimaced. *Seems Vyrga learned from the best.*

Others quickly joined the middle-aged greyborn. Some youngsters approached Vyrga as he climbed down the pedestal. Lev couldn't hear their words, but it was likely they were asking to join Vyrga's ranks.

Vyrga shook his head, placed his hand on one of the youngster's shoulders and gave a warm, albeit unsettling, smile.

Lev turned around and started walking towards his tent. *The fox hasn't lost his cunning.*

Rak clenched his fists so hard that they turned white. Out of the corner of his eye, he noticed a robed figure shuffling closer to them from amongst the crowd. He growled. "I can't take this anymore. I'm leaving."

"Take care, Lev," Hem muttered before following Rak.

The robed figure paused, then turned back through the crowd to find his master, who had struck up a conversation with a group of bogeys. "Vyrga, sorry to interrupt," he whispered, "but we were unable to reach them in time. Rak and the others left just as your speech concluded."

Vyrga's tight-lipped smile and narrowed eyes told Ludger he wasn't pleased. He whispered his reply in Ludger's ear. "We'll find out what they're plotting later. For now, join Bolo and the others." Vyrga turned back to the bogeys.

Without replying, Ludger briskly turned and walked away. As much as he disliked taking blind orders, now was not the time to question Vyrga. The group of fresh recruits followed him, playfully marching towards Vyrga's section of the encampment.

Ludger frowned, a deep crease forming in his forehead. *This doesn't feel right. This isn't how Vyrga typically operates.*

* * *

As the goblinoids approached the broken remains of the city's southern gates, the sound of wind howling through the desolate carcasses of a once densely populated residential area caused some to halt in their tracks.

"Move aside!" a voice called out. "We need to make sure the city doesn't have any nasty surprises before we settle."

It was Bolo and, alongside him, Vyrga and a few of the fresh recruits. "Form groups of three and take a turn at each intersection."

The poorly-armed amateurs nodded and entered through the gates.

Their nervous faces almost broke Bolo's façade. "Are you sure about this?" he asked Vyrga. "They have nothing to protect themselves if those masked creatures pop out of the ruins."

Vyrga responded with a mirthless chuckle.

"What's so funny?"

"They'll be fine."

Vyrga's cannon fodder weren't the only ones scouting the city. Lev, with Orva at his side, led a small group of shamans through the western gates.

As if losing Jem and Molg wasn't bad enough, fate can't seem to help but fuck with me and my men, Lev cursed.

Lev took a deep breath before focusing on the task at hand.

They'd entered what Lev surmised to be the former administrative sector of the ancient city. The offices, filled with decaying, leather-bound books and scrolls containing, according to Orva and the shamans, numerical records and logistics reports, confirmed his suspicions.

There were three objectives he wished to complete during this scouting trip. The first, which had already been completed, was to find a good place to establish an administration building from which they could effectively process the hurdles that came with establishing a settlement.

The second was to make sure that there weren't any creatures waiting in or around the city, ready to massacre the settler group upon entry or during the hours of darkness.

Lastly, he wanted to find and research the anomalies they'd seen during their previous visit. The first anomaly, the magnificence of the orb, seemingly capable of projecting its power over the entire city, had been ingrained in his mind since he'd last seen it. The second was K-35, the city's manager whom they had encountered in the city's presumed armoury. If the holographic image of Kram was truly capable of managing the city, they'd be able to unearth more Ainshardian secrets.

"It sure is quiet here," Orva said as she kicked the remains of a bronze bucket.

Lev eyeballed a building farther down the street. "Would you rather those abominations hunt us down like cattle?"

"I would rather not run into them," Orva conceded. "But I'd also like to know they're dead."

"Then let's turn left here. Judging by the pretentious architecture and statue remains, that should be where the noble and affluent lived. It'll take a while for us to comb through all the buildings, but it'll be safer than searching through the slums with Vyrga. The countless alleyways there present a greater risk of ambush."

Orva turned towards Lev, confusion written on her face. "That was the slums? How could you tell? It looked like fine housing to me."

Maybe it's because I'm too used to the view, but I can recognize a slum from miles away, Lev thought. Even after all this time, he could not forget the slums of Neue Berlin. "They're fine, but it was still the shoddiest," he answered.

Orva smirked. "Still leagues better than we're used to. Slums they might be, but we've been living in filth as long as we can remember. Anything here is better than the cavern system."

"Can't argue with that."

Orva took a deep breath of the fresh night air. "At least I can breathe properly here. The air smells nicer and isn't stale."

The roads narrowed closer to the ruins of the city's inner walls. "Looks like we're here," Lev declared.

The tall ruin of a building towered above Lev's small group. Two lonely pillars, each topped with a statue of a warrior, still flanked the building's entrance. One was a beastfolk warrior wearing a bear's hide and brandishing an axe. The other may have been a goblinoid holding a piece of parchment in its left hand, though the lack of a head made it difficult to tell.

The building's scale and ornamentation reminded Lev that although he had encountered mostly goblinoids thus far, other sentient races had inhabited Ainshard's kingdom. There were even statues resembling humans among the rubble.

Orva gasped. She approached the beastfolk statue and studied its features. "It looks a little different from the kur, but could this be a kobold? Never knew any of them served under Ainshard."

Lev approached the broken statue. "Who knows? This could have been an exception rather than the rule."

The group entered the building. Rays of light poured in from the glassless windows, casting a beautiful yet eerie glow on the weathered interior. The steady drumming of water dripping through cracks in the roof above them signified that the ancient building had long lost its battle with the elements. Despite this, the structural integrity of the framework was a marvel of engineering that Lev's party had never encountered before.

"How many people lived here?" Rapha asked, wide-eyed.

"Lived? I bet they worked here," Lev answered, somewhat hiding his own eagerness to explore the other parts of the city.

"Well, looks like those creatures aren't here either, and we'd hear Vyrga's men screaming if they'd encountered any near the south gate," Hemgall concluded

"This place is quite fascinating." One of Orva's shamans he marvelled at a lavishly decorated altar. In its centre was another statue of the beastfolk, but its arm was broken and its weapon was lying on the floor.

Soon the shaman's fascination turned to confusion. He walked behind the altar. "Weird. Why are there waterways near the altar?"

Hemgall recoiled in disgust at the grimey ooze in the waterways. "I never thought water could get so dirty. How did that happen?"

"The drains must've been blocked by some underground debris," Lev answered. He paused in his steps.

"Is something wrong?" Hem asked.

Lev's eyes went wide in shock as he came to a realisation. *Could they be in the—*

"Wait, Lev! Where are you going!?" Hem yelled.

Lev ran outside the building and frantically searched for any sign of large sewage drains or manholes.

Hem quickly joined him outside, with Orva right on his heels.

"Lev." Orva gasped for breath. "Looks like you beat me to it. Something's different about this city."

Lev turned to Orva. "What do you mean?"

"Isn't that why you ran out? You were the first to notice the creatures last time, so I took a page from your book and found something's off. There haven't been any vibrations this time. Remember last time? It was everywhere in the city. Try and sense the energies around us."

His eyes widened. "You're right, something's different—" Lev's heart skipped a beat. "The orb!"

Both turned and sprinted for the plaza. As they turned the last corners, they expected to see the orb floating in the centre, calling out to them, to Lev. To their surprise, however, there was no orb to be seen.

"I could've sworn… it was here… last time," Lev gasped.

"I don't sense the manager's aura either. I guess K-35 left with it," Orva added.

Hemgall chuckled behind them. "Last time you couldn't sense K-35 at all!"

"I'm sure the orb's still there!" he declared somewhat smugly.

With a prompt *hmph*, Orva wildly flailed her arms in the direction of the plaza. "Well, then where is it?"

Hemgall and the others entered the plaza from behind the two. Where the orb had almost consumed him in its beauty before, all that remained was an empty plaza surrounded by rubble.

Hemgall stepped forward, somewhat caught in a daze. "W-Where is it?"

"It's gone, and so are those creatures," a familiar voice said from around the corner. The sounds of wagon wheels squeaking and goblinoid clamour swiftly displaced the eerie silence of the plaza.

"Vyrga. What do you think you're doing?" Lev accused. "The masses can't enter the city yet. Those masked creatures could be lurking in the sewers!"

"You think we haven't checked?" Vyrga sneered. "We've explored enough of that labyrinth. We saw no signs. But we still sealed all the entrances just for you, my dear Lev."

Lev pondered with furrowed brows. "That's peculiar, if not troubling."

Vyrga nonchalantly waved his hand. "Fact of the matter is that they're gone, at least for now." He turned to the masses. "This is a great opportunity to rebuild. Let's reinforce the perimeter."

* * *

Tents lit the dark plaza. Lev lay on his bedroll, unable to sleep. He couldn't shake the thought of those creatures hiding below his very feet. *How could Vyrga be so sure about their absence, and the orb? He couldn't have hidden it. The orb's too big to easily hide. Maybe he just noticed the lack of magical energy, too. He's a greyborn too, after all.*

Lev sighed. *It's going to be a long night.*

He wasn't the only sleepless bogey that night.

Volker had taken it upon himself to fulfil his orders to the utmost of his abilities and handle the funeral rights. For his closest friend, and the rest of their comrades.

Many souls wept for those who were lost, but others took the night to prepare for the future.

In Lev's, Rak's and Vyrga's tents, decisions were made, plans drafted. A power struggle was brewing from within the remaining ranks of the bogey tribe—a tribe that would soon evolve into something far bigger.

CHAPTER 8

SHOW OF HANDS

The sound of clashing swords echoed through the forest clearing. Two warriors faced each other: a young fellow, and an older lass. Despite her opponent's superior height and physique, the female warrior easily forced him to backpedal.

Clang! The force of their blades colliding rang through their arms and chipped their swords' edges, but neither cared. The younger warrior had messed up his stance by putting too much force behind his blow, forcing him to swing wide. This allowed the older warrior to dodge the attack and hit her inexperienced compatriot in the abdomen with the hilt of her sword.

The younger warrior gasped in pain. After a few deep inhales, he found his bearings again and positioned his battered sword in front of him.

The older warrior didn't return this gesture. Instead, she lowered her sword and sighed deeply, wiping the sweat off her forehead. "Don't bother. With how sloppy you've been today, it's clear your mind is elsewhere."

Volker tightened his grip on his blade. "How was I sloppy?"

Rapha frowned and shook her head. "Besides swinging like a brute? You continuously fell for obvious feints, and you were barely capable of blocking my attacks in time. Don't even get me started on your posture. I think we should end it for today."

Volker slightly angled his feet and tried to redistribute his weight evenly. "Let me try again. I'll get serious!"

Rapha loosened her shoulders, re-sheathed her sword, and turned to leave.

Just as Volker opened his mouth to protest, Rapha turned back around and locked eyes with him. "Let's just call it here. The farmers need our help." She started on her way back to her tent, but spared Volker a few more words. "I know what you're feeling; the need to let out all of that anger and frustration. I felt the same when I lost my family and became a harem guard."

"Then what should I do?"

Rapha shrugged. "That's up to you. Befriending Ruune and taking on a leadership role helped me. You already have people in need of your help, and your family's alive. Use that to find your answer. Lashing out won't fix anything, and this isn't the time for brooding."

Volker massaged his forehead and groaned. He knew all too well that Rapha was right. She was just as concerned about the city's recent political volatility as he was. After collecting his thoughts, he lowered his sword and went to change into farming clothes.

Lev had tasked the two of them with establishing a new farming settlement along the eastern perimeter of Pàrras and preparing it for the warmer seasons. Before they left, Lev had asked some goblin farmers to teach the two their techniques, such as how to rotate crops and set up perimeters around their fields to keep wild animals away.

He sent me here to sort things out, Volker reflected as he gazed upon the fields of tree stumps and untilled land that surrounded the small settlement. *Knowing him, he likely paired Rapha with me to prepare me for his plans.*

As usual, they and most other bogeys had been greatly surprised by Lev's ideas. Even the goblins, whose tribes had lived on the surface for centuries, took a keen eye to his innovations.

Unfortunately, progress had been slow. Although greyborns were familiar with the patches of light from sky holes that allowed mushrooms and underground flora to grow in the caverns, none of them had ever lived above the surface. As such, none of them knew the first thing about soil, watering, or nutrients.

Even so, Volker enjoyed the beauty of nature and fresh air for their own sakes—the associated morale boost was a mere bonus. *I wish you could see this, Gul. The days of scavenging for food to scrape by will soon be gone.*

Unless, of course, something were to destroy their serenity.

During their trip to the farming settlement, the entourage's long-incessant complaining had made it clear that though the city's underground ruins were connected to the bottom of the monster cavern, they had settled in a land far, far away from the hivelings, so he wasn't concerned about something dangerous having followed them from their old home.

I just wish the corpse-eaters hadn't hitched a ride amongst our supplies. The little bastards are trying to infest the city.

Volker also knew, however, that the entourage had, for a time, followed an old, overgrown path that extended deep into the woods. It was, after all, far easier to follow an existing road than to try to blaze a new path.

Hopefully he was just being paranoid, but Volker and Rapha had both overheard some of the farmers' conversations during their trip. Their stories, particularly those of the newest arrivals, were rather worrying. They spoke of hearing clicking sounds from the forest and finding clawed footprints on the ground.

Despite Lev and the others assuring everyone that the hivelings couldn't access the underground ruins, there still might be another passage for hivelings and other monstrosities to sneak through.

Volker shook his head to clear his thoughts, then changed his clothes, stored his gear, and met Rapha outside with a calm smile.

Rapha clicked her tongue. Volker wasn't fooling anyone.

"You want to talk to me about Lev, right?" Rapha asked, grabbing two ploughs from one of the storage rooms and throwing one towards Volker.

Volker struck his plough to the ground. "It would be better if we focused on the fields first. We neither have horses nor dekas here to help us with removing the stumps—"

Rapha turned up the soil with her plough. "You'll feel better if you talk about it."

Volker had to agree with her. Although Lev and Vyrga had joined forces to fend off the hivelings and Jiira, without a common enemy, the two were at loggerheads once more.

To resolve the power struggle without spilling a drop of blood, Lev had used his connections to convince those with power and influence among the settlers of the frontier city to hold an election for its next leader.

At first, there'd been chaos. Gang leaders, overseers, elders, and nobles who'd fallen from grace after the revolution, quarrelled over their legitimacy in the new order. After much discussion, and some forceful persuasion with the more obstinate of the bunch, Lev had managed to formulate a plan that everyone, begrudgingly or not, accepted.

It'd seemed like a solid plan at the time. Despite fielding several unpopular policies, such as creating a system for the Jiira captives to obtain citizenship, Lev had developed a wide circle of influence and the respect of many. He was the obvious chalk bet to win the election.

Sure, Vyrga had spent great effort in recent times to improve his reputation, but was still largely hated by the greyborn populace for his and his gang's activities back in the cavern.

It should have been an easy victory.

So how had it gone so wrong?

* * *

"How could this happen?" Lev muttered. He was sitting by himself in his new house, subconsciously tapping the table.

Lev had believed in the certainty of his electoral victory.

An earlier attempt at elections had ended in a tie with Vyrga; this had almost sparked a fight between the factions. As it was, the council had been forced to repeat the elections. There could only be one High Chief.

Unfortunately, the tied vote and increasing polarisation between Lev and Vyrga's forces had inspired three new adversaries to announce their candidacies. Not that they'd stood any chance of winning.

Lev released a breath he hadn't realised he'd been holding. With a frustrated groan, he reclined into his seat and, with closed eyes, thought back to what had transpired.

* * *

Over the rancour, Rak yawned as he observed from his seat in the back row. If it were up to him, he'd rather delve into the depths of the cavern again than listen to the clamour. He nudged Lev, who was waiting for the council to finish their discussion and cast their votes.

"They're not going to screw us over, right?" Rak asked. Because of time restrictions, a lack of literacy, and the immediate need for a leader, the first election was to be decided orally through a simple majority vote via the council members.

"You worry too much," Lev replied. "I've already… *persuaded* a few electors to make the right choice."

Rak stared at Lev and clenched his jaw.

"Don't look at me like that. I haven't fallen so low as to cheat," Lev huffed.

"Oh, really?" Rak snarkily inquired. Although everyone had consented to Lev's voting system, albeit with some compromises, Lev was the one who had written its ins and outs.

Lev stuck his tongue out. "At least I didn't come here wearing a full set of armour."

"Of course I did. After the last election, I'm surprised you didn't," Rak countered.

"Well," Lev started as he closely inspected Rak's excessive protection, "Don't pillage all of the city's armouries just yet, we need to study them so we can produce similar designs."

As Rak was about to complain, the voting bell rang. It was finally time.

An old blue bogey named Meinrad stood on the pedestal in the centre of the grand hall. The light coming down on the pedestal made Meinrad look quite regal.

Lev's eyes lit up. The grand hall itself was nothing as short of a miracle. They had arrived to find the building situated quite centrally in the ruins and better preserved than the neighbouring edifices. The grand hall had needed some patching up, but its history as the pinnacle of the lost civilization had been apparent from the moment they'd first stepped foot inside, and it was all the grander at that present moment.

Meinrad cast a deep gaze towards the fifteen electoral seats. Finding that quorum had been reached, the corners of his mouth twitched upwards before he cleared his throat.

There were a total of five factions with each of them having appointed three electors and a candidate. Born out of the common struggles they faced in the frontier lands, the factions were a microcosm of the city at large. Bogeys, goblins, deka, and a few others had united along racial lines for the first time in centuries. Yet, it was abundantly clear that there was still a long way to go.

Soon after the initial settler group arrived and took control of the city, some neighbours living south-east of Pàrras had taken note. Thankfully they spoke the same language, albeit with a thicker, but still comprehensible dialect. After hearing of the greyborn rebellion, the hiveling attacks, and subsequent exodus, many surveyed the city to see for themselves whether the previous inhabitants had truly disappeared.

With their absence confirmed, many left behind their hamlets and villages for the ancient city.

Lev had long expected there to be at least three main factions, powers he knew would rise above the rest since their goals aligned with a substantial slice of the frontier's population.

The large influx of migrants hasn't affected his predictions; instead, it solidified them. New factions continued to open and fold as more goblinoid races and tribes joined the city, but most newcomers found themselves swayed by the influence of the major factions. Even after the smaller factions eventually united in an attempt to consolidate power, their power and influence still paled in comparison to the big three.

A quick look at the factions was all it took to see that old resentments remained. The members representing the goblins had been part of a subgroup within the Jiira. These goblins had not personally slain and pillaged in the Jiira's conquests, but had kept the Jiira invaders alive and fed. This alone alienated them from most of the population and limited their influence. To have a voice, they'd thrown their support behind the minority faction, a collection of deka, burga, and other goblinoids who didn't feel represented by the big three.

The minority faction had wanted Shahn to be their leader but against their expectations, he'd declined and even refused to join the political establishment, as had Grasha.

Lev took a glance at Raban. The grizzled goblin stood with a straight back and a high chin, his expression solemn and proud despite the hateful stares upon him.

He wasn't here to vote, nor was he a candidate of the minority faction. As an active participant of the Jiira's war, until his service was over, the most he could do was watch over the future of his kind from the side.

After comparing the former mercenary and Jiira commander to the shivering refugees making up half of the minority faction, Lev couldn't help but sigh. *We need to find a way to cut his sentence to a few years. Someone needs to kick these goblins back into shape.*

He turned his sight back to his surroundings and basked in the grandeur of the hall with a smile blooming on his lips.

A medley of rich colour dotted the background of the hall. Each candidate sat before their faction's flag—two of which represented greyborns, specifically. Given historical relations, most greyborns didn't feel well represented by the other two bogey factions and found themselves divided between Lev and Vyrga's factions instead.

I'm sure that it won't be long before the other factions divide among themselves, Lev thought.

As he'd expected, the once-united bogey faction, the previous biggest faction after Lev and Vyrga's, had split into two camps, the Loyalists and the Renegades, just days before the second elections due to irreconcilable differences. Despite their differences, however, the two factions would surely still be lockstep when it came to keeping Lev and Vyrga in check.

If only that.

While he waited for the elections to begin, Lev's eyes traced the flags.

His faction had the simplest one: solid black background with the crimson eye of the war goddess, Zeja, on top. After all, he'd been given the title "the liberator" by Kathaga, the high priestess of Zeja, and wanted to use Zeja's renown to garner support. Its simplicity contrasted heavily against Vyrga's, which was a solid yellow flag with two detailed black wolf heads facing the east and the west.

At long last, Meinrad began to speak. "We've gathered here today to achieve an important milestone in the building of our great nation. About a year ago, we broke the chains that bound our kin for decades, if not centuries. We have only now started to shape our new home, Pàrras—a city dating from the golden age of Ainshard."

Some electors smiled, reflecting on Ainshard's accomplishments of old. Some of them even felt like Ainshard for a moment. Uniting the goblinoids was surely one of the most impressive feats Ainshard had accomplished in his storied lifetime.

For goblins and many other goblinoids, the mere mention of his legend fostered a sense of unity. Others, amongst them Kathaga and the other head priests of the bogey gods, however, did not feel the same. Some considered him a false god. Others dismissed accounts of his exploits as Jiira propaganda.

Still, many found inspiration in his legacy, real or not, and all those present held hope and optimism for their newfound nation, born in the ruins Ainshard had left behind.

Meinrad cleared his throat once again. "Though we have established ourselves in these unknown lands and rebuilt many parts of this mighty city, we still lack two important aspects needed for any proper society."

Meinrad paused for a moment, trying to find the right words.

"A proper system of governance, and a wise leader," he finally said.

Meinrad had thought it impossible for the now deprecated ruling class and its followers to consent to Lev's proposal: a system where a single authority commanded a handful of lower authorities. It was almost identical to the system they had all fled, except instead of nobles wielding power, they now had "elected chiefs."

But to his surprise, there had been little discord. Including him, many were even enthusiastic that there was to be a semblance of normalcy in the new order. Those that did protest had been quickly swayed by Lev's persuasive words.

The audience quietly waited for Meinrad to continue. The nobles now running for office, opposing the individuals they had once considered "property," bowed their heads.

"We've made progress with the system, and it is now time for us to choose its leader. We have five great candidates worthy of leading us, and it is up to us to determine who among them is most fit for the task."

Meinrad paused, expecting protest once again, but none occurred. After a moment, he raised two fingers and continued. "In this pursuit, two facts bear repeating."

He produced a rolled-up piece of parchment from under the pedestal and read it aloud. "First—all you who have been granted the privilege to vote—know that your constituencies are counting on you to advance their interests, not just your own."

He lowered the parchment and planted his feet firmly on the pedestal.

"You represent the will of your people."

He raised the parchment again and continued his dictation.

"Second, remember that your choices affect not just yourselves and your constituencies, but also our entire society."

Still the audience showed no reaction.

"Know that you shall answer to the *people* if you make the wrong choices."

This caused the candidates to grin—all except for two; the greyborn candidates.

While Meinrad continued his speech, Vyrga glanced at Lev. "You seem agitated."

Lev gestured at the faint scratch marks on Vyrga's chair. "I could say the same for you."

"Let's just be glad we didn't have to pacify our men. It doesn't appear we will be thrown out today."

Lev chuckled.

"In such a scenario, everything you've worked for would have been for naught. Especially the part where you become High Chief. Unless..."

"'Unless'?" Lev asked, involuntarily raising one of his eyebrows.

Vyrga turned his gaze back towards the old blue bogey in the centre of the hall. "Nothing."

Lev also turned back to Meinrad, who took a swig from his wineskin before wiping his beard with a cloth.

Meinrad continued. "Now, it's time to cast your votes. Let's begin with our first contender, Gerwyn from the Loyalist bogey faction."

A blue, middle-aged bogey rose from his seat and nodded towards Meinrad.

"Gerwyn was born an Albrecht, one of the oldest and most prestigious families among the blue bogeys. His accomplishments in the realm of magic are admirable, and he demonstrated courage and leadership during our journey from the cavern to Pàrras. Who here chooses Gerwyn?"

Only two electors raised their hands. Lev almost smirked when he saw that the first was an elector of the minor faction, while the other was a Loyalist blue bogey who happened to bear a resemblance to Gerwyn.

Rak boisterously laughed next to them.

"He's having fun," Vyrga commented.

"Not anymore," Lev added as Rak started a shouting match across the room with Gerwyn before the latter could even sit back down. His fellow electors pacified the situation.

Lev shook his head. *Looks like Gerwyn is really full of himself. He's not even among the best magic users, and what qualities does he bring as a leader?*

At least he got what he deserved. He and the other candidates shouldn't have forced us to allow factions to vote for their own candidates . Did he really think he'd stand a better chance with that rule change? In the end, he still failed to garner more than two votes.

"Two voted, and thirteen remain. Now, the second candidate, Hiltrude of the Renegade faction."

A green bogey rose from her seat with a flourish. Lev caught a few other bogeys exchanging looks before they nudged their electors, two green bogeys, to raise their hands.

"I haven't even listed her accomplishments!" Meinrad snapped. The offending electors averted their gazes.

Meinrad grumbled under his breath before beginning again. "Without Hiltrude, we would have lost many more of our brethren during our pilgrimage. With her expert oversight, our craftsmen and builders were able to assemble numerous carriages at a moment's notice, allowing us to bring along much-needed food and supplies. She also assisted in securing supplies for the convoy. During the journey itself, she proved herself a capable fighter, as she helped to defend the convoys from the hivelings."

"If only that were true," Lev whispered.

Hiltrude's supporters fidgeted in place. Meinrad sighed and muttered under a few unheard curses before allowing the electors to vote. She ended with two votes from the electors in her faction.

"The 'dissidents' are at work, it seems. These elections of yours are a joke," Vyrga mumbled.

Lev shrugged. "Factions are inevitable in any functioning society."

"So it seems. You have Gerwyn and his small lot of fools who still don't accept that things have changed. We have Hiltrude and her band of cowering weasels who pose as rebels, still foolishly defiant against their previous blue overlords. There's also the desperate mess calling itself a minority faction. A pitiful group of outcasts and ex-mercenaries stuck together on a sinking raft in a sea of bogeys. And then there's us, only one of whom will become the High Chief. But who will it be?"

Vyrga's gleeful look gave Lev a tightening feeling in his chest. After trying to examine Vyrga's face for tells, Lev shook his head and turned back toward the hall, waiting for the next candidate to take the stage.

"Well, that was unorthodox," Meinrad grumbled.

After that rose the candidate of the minority faction. It was an unassuming darg dressed in a fur cloak who Lev had never met or heard about before. Meinrad introduced him as a well off merchant who'd taken the frontier market by storm with luxurious clothing and spices from Brizilum. The blue bogey waxed eloquent about the economic prosperity the darg would bring if he were able to reform trading policies, which would allow for the city's leaders to draw more funds for the construction and maintenance of infrastructure.

Strange, Lev mused. *Even without Shahn, I'm sure the minority faction had better options than some outsider. Something tells me I should better keep a closer eye on their party.*

Other than the shock of the candidate getting the vote of a loyalist and the amusing sight of a fuming Gerwyn, the voting process was anticlimatic. The candidate had gotten two votes. Those of the aforementioned blue bogey Loyalist and a bugbear from the minority faction.

When Meinrad turned towards him, Lev proudly stood up.

The old, blue bogey spoke again. "It's time for our fourth candidate, Lev. He led the charge against the Jiira. As if he was the champion of Zeja, he crushed the foes who shackled us and invaded our borders, causing the damn gob—" Meinrad quickly changed his wording. "—the enemy to flee with their tails between their legs. And when the hivelings broke through our defences and assaulted our homes, it was he who rallied his men and led us to our new home."

"You paid him well, didn't you?" Vyrga spat.

"Beyond his impressive combat prowess, his ideas and policies have been instrumental in binding our fledgling society together and helping us overcome so much. He's achieved so much more than anyone could have thought possible, especially for a greyborn. I could continue, but we shouldn't take longer than necessary. Who here chooses Lev to become our new High Chief?"

After Meinrad finished his speech, four hands were raised.

Three of them were greyborns of Lev's faction, including Rak, and the last vote was from a deka of the minority faction.

Vyrga's eyes twitched. He'd made contact with the deka earlier, and with the right incentives, the deka had vowed that he'd vote for him . "Well played, Lev," he muttered, "Well played."

Lev grinned. Based on his count, from both his original band of supporters and the additional voter he had persuaded with the help of Grasha, he'd already won the elections. While his men had been unsuccessful in their attempts to infiltrate Vyrga's party, they'd still managed to keep an eye on their activities. As far as he knew, Vyrga hadn't made contact with the two remaining electors outside of his faction yet. The remainder belong to the Loyalists and Renegades, and likely wouldn't vote for a greyborn.

"And now for the fifth candidate. Despite his... *colourful* past, he played an important role in fending off the Jiira and hivelings. But that's not all! He and his men have played a crucial role in helping maintain order and rebuild the city. Who here chooses the greyborn Vyrga?"

A brief moment passed as those present counted the hands in the air—but it didn't take long for everyone to realise what was happening.

The crowd gasped. All five remaining electors had their hands raised in the air.

Nearly everyone in attendance, even Vyrga, turned their attention to Lev. Even Gerwyn and Hiltrude seemed shocked at this turn of events. They eyed each other before returning their gaze towards the murmuring crowd.

Before long, cries of outrage and insults broke out between Lev's and Vyrga's factions. One of Lev's members deftly leapt from his seat and tore Vyrga's flag from its pole. It didn't take long for the other factions' members to follow suit, scrambling and jumping about to desecrate their rivals' flags. A Renegade bogey threw a clay flask towards the Loyalist seats. They in turn replied with a volley of assorted items. Soon fruit, more flasks, cups, plates, vases, and even furniture could be seen spreading their wings across the grand hall.

A cup to the head knocked Gerwyn down. Hiltrude, meanwhile, hid behind a column to avoid a flying chair.

Meinrad had seen enough. "Silence! Guards! *Guards*!" he yelled.

The quarrel ended quickly as soldiers flooded into the court and unceremoniously pinned down the more aggressive troublemakers, including Rak, who had been ready to throw his chair at Ludger.

With the crowd subdued, healers arrived to treat the injured.

Meinrad was livid as he returned to his feet. "We travelled so far and lost so much to get here, but even now, in the only home we have left, you lot can't even behave yourselves!"

Only the sounds of ragged breathing filled the air. As if by previous agreement, Lev and Vyrga exchanged glances and silently nodded.

Lev stood up and performed a slight bow to Meinrad. "You are correct. Our actions were not befitting of leaders, let alone adults. I apologise for the actions of my supporters."

Vyrga also stood up. "As do I. It is as Meinrad says. We should strive to better our society, not fight amongst ourselves."

Lev offered his hand, and Vyrga shook it. An awkward silence filled the air before some members of the quorum began to clap in spite of the lingering tension.

I fear for the nation where its people are so easily swayed by their leaders and their personal vendettas, Meinrad thought as he dismissively shook his head. "Are you both ready? Vyrga, are you ready for your inauguration? And Lev, do you accept the outcome?"

Lev's eyes glinted. "I will. For the sake of bogeykind and all goblinoids."

"And I am ready to accept the role and responsibilities of High Chief," Vyrga responded.

Meinrad displayed a shallow smile. "Perfect. The ceremony will be held in a week's time." He then returned to the pedestal and addressed the hall. "This concludes the first election of the frontier. I sincerely hope the next one will be more civil. Now everyone, get out!" he bellowed.

Later that day it was announced to the public that Vyrga had won the elections. This caused a fair amount of confusion and a few violent outbursts from those he had victimised in the past, but Lev's apparent acceptance of the election results pacified them quickly enough.

The following week passed quickly. Vyrga became High Chief and swiftly appointed Lev as Chief of Commerce, due to his experience in the market tunnel back when he was still working under Rak..

And so, Lev sat in his office, silently speaking to Gherm, whom he had ignored during the elections. "You were right. I shouldn't have only focused on Vyrga's faction."

Of course. After all, you two weren't the only candidates. I thought you'd be more cautious, Gherm admonished.

"You really know how to brighten my day, don't you, Gherm?"

Don't block me off next time. Then maybe I'll care about how you feel. I'm not some tool you can just throw away whenever you want, Lev.

Lev sighed. "I know. But I had to focus on the elections and you were distracting me."

Maybe if you'd listened to my "distractions," you might've noticed that Gerwyn and Hiltrude were targeting you, Gherm reprimanded. *I told you to avoid rushing your experiments. You scared votes away instead of impressing them.*

Lev's brows furrowed. "How was I supposed to know that we can't make gunpowder here? I followed the process to the letter, yet nothing happened!"

There were previous records by Ainshard and the inventors and alchemists under him. Beyond that, remember that no matter how similar your world and mine may be, not everything will work the same.

"Thanks a lot for explaining that," Lev almost spat out loud. "Our only saving grace is that we managed to find an efficient method to cultivate the land. At least we won't be starving anytime soon."

Lev got up from his chair and ambled towards the closet. "Well, although I'm not the High Chief, I'm still an elected official."

Yeah? Gherm replied, apprehensive.

Lev's hands fumbled around inside the closet. "I thought of eliminating the competition, but that would be stupid. We'd lose capable personnel and I'd lose public favour. So, I have a better idea."

Which is...?

Lev pulled out a large rolled-up piece of parchment—a scroll—and set it down on the table. "I just need to assure my victory in the next term. That much can be easily done."

He unfurled the scroll, displaying a freshly made map. It was extremely detailed, filled with all the information his scouts had gathered about the region. Many had contributed to it, particularly migrants from the city's neighbouring villages, and Orva, who'd spent countless days and nights poring over the records that remained of the city's old library.

Lev traced his finger along the map. Using the twin mountains in the northeast as a landmark, he pointed at a crossroad connecting the frontier to two other cities. "I just need to do my job—improve the city and handle trade."

CHAPTER 9

THE FOREIGNER

The sound of heavy breathing echoed throughout the forest, quickly followed by the clattering of armour and weapons.

A slaver tiredly trudged up the hill and surveyed his surroundings, squinting in an attempt to see through the darkness. His dog barked violently towards something in the distance. After raising his torch and taking another look, the slaver spotted the backside of his fleeing target. "Found him!"

The captain should never have bought him, even if he looked like a bargain, the slaver reflected. *He must be a noble's bastard or from some fallen house.*

His thoughts of the man's origins were interrupted by the twang of a bow.

"Don't shoot!" the slaver growled. "We need to capture this bastard alive and unharmed!"

"Fine, fine. Just know you're making this harder than it's supposed to be," the archer argued after lowering his bow.

"Boss's orders," the slaver grumbled.

Mud and dirt collected itself on the slave's already-exhausted body as he manoeuvred through the forest. His path had been fairly straight so far. The area was not densely wooded; his battered, bruised feet could manage the wet, flat ground below him.

He could still hear the faint shouts of his pursuers and barking of dogs behind him. Judging from the volume of their voices and the soft glow of their torches, they were slowly closing in on him.

To his surprise, however, the noise behind him soon subsided, and even the approaching light seemed to slow.

They're anticipating something.

As he continued to run forward he soon saw, and heard, water. A river snaked through the forest to impede his path. Worse yet, mere feet before him, it flowed down a sheer cliff to form a waterfall. If he hadn't had his wits about him, he might have fallen over the edge, into the continuation of the river below.

Or if he were unlucky, he might have landed on jagged stones—such a fall would have killed him instantly.

The slavers know the layout of this forest.

As he contemplated his options, he heard footsteps closing in on him. He turned and looked into the eyes of his pursuers. He was deathly exhausted, barely clinging onto his last vestiges of strength, but his pursuers seemed far better off, with only a few out of breath.

The look of exhaustion on the slave's face caused some of the slavers to grin.

The highest-ranked slaver scoffed. "It's over. Don't try anything funny now."

The slave looked down towards the turbulent river. For a moment, the laughter of the guards faded into the darkness of the night.

As the slavers' dogs reared on their hind legs, ready to attack at a moment's notice, the slave's expression contorted from desperation to determination.

This change in the slave's behaviour made the slavers hesitate. One raised his left hand and closed his fist, ordering the men to stay alert.

They slowly approached the slave, surrounding him.

"Go on. Jump. We'll catch you either way," taunted the highest-ranked slaver.

"Better off dead than alive with you," the slave spat back. He took a few steps towards the edge and peeked over the cliff.

The water crashed and rumbled.

Before the slavers could grab him, he closed his eyes and threw himself down the waterfall.

The slavers stood there, dumbfounded, before one of them looked below.

"Did he just really jump?" he asked.

"Crazy bastard. I can't believe he set fire to the boss's tent, released the other slaves, and started a rebellion. Imagine calling yourself 'Eleric the Innocent' without any irony. You can't make this shit up," the leader lamented. "Then he led us on a damn goose-chase all the way from Brizilum to here, deep in the gods-forsaken lands of those accursed long-ears. Now he jumps down a waterfall? When can we catch a damn break!?"

"Must be somethin' in his blood. Guy's tall, with fair skin and that gold-brown hair. Must be special."

"Just marry him."

"I'm just commenting on his looks! He clearly wasn't a commoner."

"Gee, ya think? If he were, we'd have killed him on sight just now!" The slaver cleared his throat. "If anyone asks, I didn't dare him to do shit. Let's hope the other squad catches him down there."

At that moment another slaver arrived, panting as he struggled to restrain one of his dogs. "Sorry to break it to you, but we lost track a while ago."

The leader of the group sat down on a nearby trunk and sighed deeply. "What do we tell the boss?"

"Guess we'll have to pick twigs. He's a goner for sure. It's the middle of the night and that's a long fall. We'll probably find his corpse near the shoreline in the morning," the slaver looking over the waterfall replied.

* * *

Eleric tried to catch his breath, but the rapids colliding with his fragile frame prevented him from surfacing.

He'd used up most of his strength fleeing; there was barely enough left to keep himself afloat, let alone swim against the current.

He flailed wildly for something to grab onto. Just as his body was ready to give out, a drifting log passed by. Eleric desperately wrapped his body around the log and held on for dear life.

With every collision, with rocks or otherwise, Eleric readied himself for death. Eventually night turned to day, and the rapids sweeping him downstream slowed to a gentler flow.

Eleric felt little but the water flowing across his body and the threat of countless slavers chasing him. Just as the hazy figures in his mind were about to catch him, he heard a loud crash and opened his eyes. His precious log was caught in the shallow riverbank. With what remained of his strength, he pushed himself off the log and face-first onto the sand and gravel.

Finally, Eric muttered, or perhaps thought. His vision briefly flickered before going blank.

Sometime later, he felt something cold poking him in his sides. His eyes shot wide open, and he instinctively turned himself around, facing the sky. Two grey figures slowly entered his vision, and as his eyes adjusted to the bright sun above him, it soon became clear to him that they were some sort of... goblins.

He had never seen anyone, or anything, like them. Some had pleasing features, similar to the Bereke he'd heard of. Though, he'd never expected to associate elves with goblinoids. Their golden yellow eyes scrutinised him.

What in the hells are these things?

Eleric glimpsed at the creatures' equipment.

Bronze.

The two grey-skins exchanged a glance before pointing their weapons towards Eleric.

The older-looking of the two calmly spoke to Eleric, but he couldn't understand what he was being told.

"I don't know your language," Eleric said in a dry tone. In response, the goblin, or rather goblinoid, raised an eyebrow and babbled about something else.

Eleric attempted a disarming smile. "Sorry, I still can't understand you. You wouldn't happen to know Edoria, the language of Brizilum?"

The two goblinoids looked at each other and exchanged some words.

"Can I at least get up? My legs are getting cramped," Eleric said as he slowly stood up. Once upright, he towered over the two grey-skins. The taller and younger-looking of the two barely reached his chest.

The two grey-skins' eyes widened as Eleric straightened his back. When he reached full height, the shorter one stumbled and fell backwards.

Well, he thought, *if I can't reason with them, at least I can probably overpower them. Maybe if I—*

Eleric's thoughts were disturbed by a shout in the distance. He and the two grey-skins turned in unison as a mixed group of uglier goblin-like creatures, led by another grey-skin, came within shouting distance.

There goes that idea.

The older-looking goblinoid waved his hand towards the newcomers as they cautiously approached.

The goblin newcomers spoke in a tongue almost as strange as the one used prior, but luckily Eleric could decipher some words as ones he had heard from darg sailors back in Brizilum.

After a short while, the creatures seemed to relax. Some of them sat down on the sand and leaned back.

The younger grey goblinoid looked back at Eleric and beckoned for him to come with them. He complied, only to see a length of rope appear in one of the goblinoids' hands.

Eleric presented his hands. The creature tied his hands in front of him, palms facing outwards. *From one captor to another,* he quietly complained.

When his new captors pulled him forward, he matched their pace. After an hour of arduous trekking, Eleric finally laid eyes on his new captors' "settlement". He couldn't help but whistle aloud. The goblinoids laughed. Eleric hoped that their treatment of prisoners would be as decent as their city looked.

Not long after, Eleric crossed the gates at the tugging of his captors. He tried to suppress the uneasiness swelling within him, but being surrounded by goblinoids of various colours did little to quell his nerves.

Most of them had green skin, but there were a fair amount of grey-skinned goblinoids. Once the bustling streets gave way to quiet sheets, he figured his captors were leading him to their masters.

Eleric smiled once he recognized the purple skin of a darg walking toward him. The darg sported a fur coat, much like the fashionable Brizilum merchants who traded in the western parts of the republic.

The darg's appearance proved to be a sign of good things, as words he could actually understand soon entered his ears.

"Welcome to Pàrras, the reclaimed frontier city of Ainshard!" the darg said somewhat jovially. Eleric couldn't figure out whether the creature was actually happy or just trying to help ease his nerves.

After briefly talking with Eleric's captors, the darg motioned the grey skins to leave them alone. "Don't mind the greyborn. They don't understand Edorai, as you've probably figured out by now."

"Thanks, I was getting worried they were gonna torture me. Say, darg, can you tell me more about these greyborn? I've never seen such strange creatures."

The darg chuckled. "I haven't heard someone call me by my race in a while."

"Sorry," Eleric replied as he rubbed the back of his neck. "A bad habit from home."

"Don't worry, I just came back from Brizilum so it doesn't sting as much. Here, goblinoids are called by name, so call me Servius. I'll answer all your questions, but first, let us walk towards the grand hall."

Eleric nodded. "I'm Eleric."

He wasn't sure what visiting this grand hall would entail, but the mere fact that this darg, and probably more of his kind, were wandering through the city was fascinating to him.

It only took a few paces for Eleric to pose his first question. "Why did you decide to come here? Dargs have been getting more rights in Brizilum. Policies are changing, albeit slowly."

"Heh. I could ask you the same. Well, I'm a merchant, that's what I do. I travel to the places my wares lead me, and hopefully I make a nice profit along the way." Servius grinned.

"If I'm not wrong, this place should be far away from any of the seas, especially the White Sea. I doubt your journey here was mundane."

Servius grinned. "With great risks come great rewards, Eleric, and I've won fate's gamble. This city is still very much in its infancy, which means I can sell Brizilum clothing, equipment, and tools at a steep price and buy treasures that neither bereke nor korrigal can provide for a pittance."

"Besides that, I'm an important darg here. I can't say the same back home."

Eleric lowered his head. "It's the same for me. Well, minus the trading part."

Even though he'd only heard assuring words thus far, Elric felt his nerves return when he saw what he assumed to be the entrance of the grand hall. The last time he'd been near any "official" buildings, he'd still been a Brizilum noble.

"What'll happen once we're inside?" he asked.

Servius stopped and looked over his shoulder at Eleric. "We'll vote."

Seeing Eleric's worried expression, the darg chuckled. "Don't worry, it's not like back home. Besides, you've got my vote already. I think you'll do fine here."

"I'm a human. What makes you think I'll do fine in a city filled with goblinoids?"

"By the looks of it, you're a runaway slave. The bogeys, especially the greyborns, will sympathise with your plight. Use that to your advantage. Though, your features betray your life previous," Servius stated.

"My past? What does that have to do with anything?"

"You'll know soon enough. Now c'mon, the High Chief is waiting for us!"

The High Chief?

* * *

Eleric stood before an assembly of goblinoids of various races. They were seated in an arch around him, with the presumed head of the city, the High Chief, in the centre. He too was a greyborn.

He saw Servius whispering something into the ear of a smaller, young-looking greyborn wearing a modest but formal tunic. Eleric felt a shiver go up his spine when the youth smiled.

What are they saying? What are they even voting for?

The High Chief at the head of the assembly started speaking, though Eleric couldn't understand him.

"Human, before we decide your fate in these lands, let me welcome you to the frontier city of Pàrras. My name is Vyrga, and I'm the elected High Chief of this realm," Servius translated.

Not knowing better, Eleric gave a deep bow.

The assembled goblinoids looked on with a mix of fear, interest, and doubt. Eleric figured that apart from Servius and his kind, they'd never seen a human before.

Though considering their reactions, they've likely heard of Brizilum's reputation…

"Many thanks, High Chief. My name is Eleric, and unlike your excellence, I am but a mere Brizilum slave who found his way to this unlikely destination."

Murmurs filled the grand hall after Servius translated what Eleric had said. In the midst of all the talking, Electric noticed that there were two individuals who remained wordless—Vyrga, and the young greyborn he'd spotted earlier.

Vyrga raised his left hand, and the murmurs stopped. Servius stood up and walked towards Vyrga.

A few minutes passed as Vyrga spoke to Servius. The greyborn was calm and measured with every word he uttered, as if he didn't want to show his true feelings.

"My lordship tells me that he takes great interest in your Brizilum origin. He's never seen a human before, and as you know, Brizilum doesn't take kindly to other nations."

I knew it.

"If I may," Eleric started.

Servius nodded.

"All I want is to leave your people in peace, and find a place where I can live freely, away from slavery and war."

After Servius translated, the young greyborn stood up and said something.

Afterwards, the greyborn, seemingly bemused by his response, promptly left the assembly.

Servius pinched the bridge of his nose. "Don't mind him. Lev's a weird fella."

Eleric saw Vyrga glaring at the young lad as the latter made his way towards the door. Once he neared the exit, Lev gave one last glance towards Eleric and uttered some words before swinging the door shut.

"What did he say?" Eleric asked.

"That he wants you to stay, and his vote goes towards you staying."

"Is that what you're voting for?"

Servius nodded. "If you don't mind, could you wait in silence as we commence voting?"

Eleric remained perfectly still as a piece of parchment was passed along the remaining assembly. He tried to guess whether someone had voted for or against him, but only ended up being confused by the creatures' strange tongue and mannerisms.

After about half an hour passed, the results found their way into Vyrga's hands. He briefly glanced at them before scribbling something down and whispering into Servius' ear.

Eleric waited for Servius' translation. He could feel his heart inside his throat.

"There are three votes against your stay, and two in favour."

Eleric gulped. *Time to get out of here.*

"The High Chief, however, has decided to veto the others' decision."

How democratic of him!

"With that, you're allowed to stay in the city and its frontier lands for as long as you like. There's no slavery nor war in these lands."

"Wait, what? That's all there is to it? What's the caveat?!" Eleric blurted out loud, maybe a bit *too* loudly.

"You'll help Chief Lev with administration as his steward. Nothing I can do about that, it's the High Chief's final decision."

Great... I guess I'll see what this Lev is going to put me through. If it's too much, I guess I can always escape again.

"Oh, and one more thing!"

A rough-looking goblin walked inside of the assembly carrying a collection of leather-bound books.

Eleric shuddered with each step the goblin took.

"You'll have to study goblinoid languages. These Edorai translations, made by yours truly, will help you with the basics. Although, I must admit I hadn't expected a human to learn from them this early down the road."

Even better...

CHAPTER 10

NEW BEGINNINGS

The city quickly returned to its usual level of activity. Few knew of the troubles the council had gone through during the first election. The populace of the city didn't need to know, and most probably didn't care. As long as a strong leader emerged from this new system of governance, they were more than happy to take the extra trouble along with it.

In a seemingly modest house near the western edge of the council residence area, a greyborn rapidly paced down the hallway. His ears twitched in excitement as he concocted a plan that would both benefit him in the next election and greatly stimulate the local economy.

His train of thought halted when a knock sounded from the front door. Grinning, Lev hurriedly opened the door.

There they stood, dressed in the garb he'd grown so fond of. Lev couldn't help but admire the duo in his doorway. Rapha sported her usual bronze chestplate and shoulder piece, still painted over with the now-disbanded harem guard's striking red motif. Volker wore a refined set of his usual clothes.

The familiarity was bittersweet, as each of the three realised the sacrifices that had been made to make this meeting, here in Pàrras, possible.

Lev shook his head. *What am I doing? I need to focus on what's happening now.*

"Lev, is everything alright?" Rapha asked. Volker leaned forward as well, a look of worry on his face.

"I'm fine, really," Lev said as he motioned the two to come in.

Lev's house was nothing special, by human standards at least. He wasn't sure what size of creature the house had been built for, but its previous inhabitant certainly hadn't been a goblinoid.

The house was sparsely decorated with a few scattered pieces of wooden furniture, presumably magically enhanced to stand the test of time. A single mirror stood at the end of the halfway that led into the living room.

The house still had that same ancient scent they'd smelled when they'd first arrived—a smell that emanated not from the furniture or any of the other items Lev had deigned appropriate to fill the house with, but rather from the walls and the floor.

Lev prepared seats for them and sat down. "Trading." Lev suddenly blurted out.

"W-What?" Volker said, sweat forming on his forehead.

"It's quite simple, actually. Volker, you must have heard by now."

Volker suddenly felt overwhelmed by that weird feeling he got whenever Lev rambled off his ideas like a madman. Still, it was nice to see that Lev had recovered from his political loss. "Y-Yeah, sorry to hear that. We really thought you had it in the bag," Volker answered, before realising that perhaps he should've omitted that last part.

"I'm fine. Sit down, please. You'll want to hear this," Lev stated, his eyes glowing. "We're going to establish our first major trade route. And not just any trade route. We're going to re-establish an old one—one dating back to Ainshard's time."

Both Volker and Rapha practically leapt out of their seats.

"And," Lev continued, ignoring the sudden paleness of his companions, "we'll use those masked abominations to strengthen our intel on the old route's whereabouts."

Volker tilted his head. "The ones you said inhabited this city? Didn't they all disappear before we got here?"

Lev turned towards the wall, where a creature's mask was displayed. "The scouts have discovered remnants of their kind close to the city. I'm sure some are still alive somewhere close by."

Rapha seemed sceptical. "Even if we found and captured them, can we even communicate with them? Can they speak our language?"

"And do they really know anything about the old trade routes? Even if they do, who knows if any of the cities on the other side of those routes still exist? " Volker added.

"Rapha, Volker. I'd rather waste some time asking them, than waste an opportunity for the sake of not trying. It's not just us anymore." Lev took down the mask from the wall and gingerly inspected its features.

"We have neighbours here who know all sorts of languages—ours, Edorai, even obscure ones like ancient Ainshardian. Maybe more."

"Even stranger, a human slave from Brizilum arrived yesterday, caught by our scouts at a nearby river."

"Wait, a real human? A slave?" Volker blurted out.

"In the flesh. He'll be able to tell me all about Brizilum once he masters our language," Lev answered without a hint of emotion. "They made him my steward, after all."

Volker scratched his head. "Why did they do that? He'll have a hard time learning our language, let alone learning advanced mathematics. That's a lot of responsibility placed on a slave."

Lev walked towards the mirror and inspected his tunic. "I don't think he was a slave. By birth, at least."

"What makes you think that?" Rapha asked, curious about the new frontier dweller.

"You remember Servius, the darg merchant on the council? He told me Eleric's accent and features are a tad off for a slave. He's definitely had the privilege of a formal education—knowing Brizilum, I doubt normal citizens have access to that luxury. Which means he must've been a noble of some kind."

Volker's eyes glinted. "The human's name is Eleric? Can we meet him?"

Lev didn't seem to hear Volker's words. Instead, he clapped his hands and leaned forward. "So where were we? Right! Our beloved locals."

Rapha and Volker weren't sure how to react, but after a quick mutual glance they decided to go along with the sudden change in topic. "Why don't we use them? They should be fluent in many languages, they can surely help us," Rapha suggested somewhat hesitantly.

"Superstitions. That's why. They believe the forests in the north are cursed and fear the beasts there. They're especially wary of the northeast, which happens to be where we've spotted some of the masked creatures."

Lev continued. "There's a possibility someone'll be able to communicate with those creatures. And if need be, there's always gesturing. Even if they can't give us any information about trade routes, they must have knowledge about the terrain. We can use them to find valuable resources like mineral depots. Ideally ones without hiveling infestations."

"Okay," Rapha retorted. "Let's say we can communicate. How do we know they'll cooperate? They've treated us like a threat since our first encounter."

"Well, Rapha, I'm still certain we can... negotiate, but if we can't—"

Lev snapped the beak off the mask; Rapha and Volker flinched.

"—we still have other options."

Rapha grimaced. "I don't like where you're going with this."

"Didn't they try to kill you?" Volker interjected.

Rapha took a glance at Volker. "Yes, and I'm not against retaliating, but they're quite pitiful. For all we know, something forced them out of the city and they're lost, homeless, and wriggling around in the mud. That seems punishment enough."

Lev chuckled. "Pitiful or not, we can still get some value out of them."

Rapha rolled her eyes. "Sure, whatever you say. Now what do you need from us?"

"I want you both to gather and brief our party. Volker, I'll also need you to bring Grasha, Raban, and Orva along. We'll need their expertise for this task. Rapha, I want you to bring along your crossbowmen and some of our light ballista teams."

"Siege engines?" Rapha inquired, blinking. "Are we going out for trade or war? We need approval to bring them out, and they're incredibly unruly and heavy. They'd slow us down tremendously."

"I'll get the approval for you. We've only lived here for about a year and have barely explored the terrain north of here. It'll be good to have insurance."

Rapha shrugged. "Point taken."

"Now then, are you both ready?" Lev asked the two in a commanding tone.

Volker saluted. "Sir, yes, sir!"

Rapha responded in kind. "Let's see what we find."

"Let's."

* * *

In the depths of a forest coated by a white, serene blanket, a force of forty goblinoids marched along an overgrown path. The constant beat of their footsteps scared away the wildlife as they proceeded.

Most of the soldiers were dressed in ashen-coloured garb, complete with the red eye of Zeja sewn to the shoulder or back. While some were more armed than others, the red eye uniformly and proudly declared their allegiance to the fledgling goblinoid nation.

Amongst the marching goblinoid soldiers were two individuals dressed in differing garb. The male greyborn wore a tunic similar to the others, but with a layer of bronze scales sewn on top. His helmet had a painted red stroke, signifying his status as an officer. The female green bogey wore a thick brown robe to shield her body from the chilly fall wind.

Orva groaned. "Why did you d-d-drag me along!" She articulated through chattering teeth.

Volker smirked at her. "You're an expert in ancient languages. Why wouldn't we?"

"Then drag that damned blue clown out here instead! I heard his old ass finally learned Ainshardian after the exodus, and unlike me, he's got nothing better to do in life! Besides, who in his right mind plans an expedition to such a faraway, frigid region?"

Volker whistled in surprise. "Well, that last part's on Lev. But I do have to admire your hatred towards Gerwyn."

Orva's forehead puckered. "He's all pomp and no substance."

"I've seen some of Gerwyn's work. He's pretty capable."

Orva rolled her eyes. "Please. All he did was fix a few of the city's rune channels. Basic ones, mind you, and as soon as he finished he went and told the whole city about it. Meanwhile, I've been trying to tune and modulate an alternative magical power supply since the day we arrived. That damn orb just had to disappear! If Gerwyn weren't so busy bragging to everyone and their mother instead of d-d-doing something, *maybe* we'd have a solution by now!"

"Well, he was trying to get elected, wasn't he? Had to toot his horn."

"Tch. He didn't stand a chance against Lev or Vyrga. Even Hiltrude left him in the dust."

They continued to fight the monotony of their journey with banter. And as time passed, they finally found traces of their objective.

Volker, Orva, Grasha, Rapha, Raban, and Lev gathered over the bloody remains of what looked like a group of the masked creatures.

"What in the world happened here?" Volker muttered to himself. One of the masks had split, revealing what lay behind—a young-looking, bird-like face.

Lev knelt near the corpse and touched its arm. "It's still warm. These are fresh."

Why didn't these turn into dust? Lev examined the masks and outfits donned by the corpses. Mud and grime aside, their designs were far more elaborate than the masks and outfits worn by the creatures that had attacked them in the city. Also, these strange creatures had feathers.

Lev stood up and turned towards a few of his squad leaders. "Find any footprints. If there are any survivors, find them as soon as possible!" Then he turned to the others. "Volker, Rapha. Gather your men. You're coming with me."

"What about us?" Grasha asked as he and Raban covered a corpse missing its arms and legs with a cloth.

Lev grinned. "You two are also coming with me. The same goes for Orva."

"Great, just great," Grasha grumbled. He shuffled his feet towards the third wagon in the supply convoy to retrieve his axe.

"It'll be fine. Nothing can be worse than the horrors we faced during the exodus." Raban assured his compatriot.

"Horrors? The exodus pales in comparison to the atrocities your kind has committed against us bogeys," Orva muttered before tapping her staff on the ground. "Let's get this over with and go home already."

"Not yet. We're on a mission." Lev heard the shout of a returning scout and another grin stretched its way across his face. "Now let's go find some avian friends."

"Avi-wha?"

"Let's go find some bird folk."

Orders were promptly relayed, and the forty-strong force changed its route. Along the way, they found more and more signs of activity, from footprints and tufts of feathers, to scattered tools and other objects.

In time, the party came upon the ravaged remains of what was once a large camp. Bird-beaked corpses hung naked from nearby trees, the same symbol carved into all their abdomens—a kite-like rhombus with horn-like branches protruding from upper half.

The remains of a mother hugging a headless child caused some soldiers to vomit.

"Look for survivors!" Volker ordered. He knelt down and his voice softened. "This is horrible."

Raban could not even look. "Horrible isn't even enough to describe this."

"I'd call it barbaric." Grasha added. He covered the remains with dirt.

"Who—no. What could have done this?" Rapha asked. "Volker. You sent some scouts out earlier. Did they find anything?"

Volker shook his head. "I haven't received any intel yet" He showed Rapha some giant hooved footsteps. "Though they are a little late…"

Lev noticed a faint glow pulsing from his glaive. A warning swiftly followed. He turned to the others and tapped the glaive on the ground to grab their attention. "Grasha. Raban. Gather the soldiers and clear the perimeter. Be careful."

"Do you think we'll get attacked?" Raban asked.

"Whatever caused this is still nearby so it's possible. Maybe whatever attacked these creatures will come back for more." As the duo left, Lev turned towards Rapha. "Go tell Orva and all the shamans to gather in the centre of the camp, then gather your warriors and guard the rear. Have the ballistae ready just in case."

Rapha silently nodded and left.

"Volker, call your scouts back. We need all the information we can get to decide whether to retreat, press on, or hunker down."

Volker saluted and grabbed a large curved horn from his belt. But just as he was about to blow, another horn echoed from the woods, followed by a loud scream.

Eyes wide, Volker immediately tucked the horn. "Prepare for battle!" he roared. His squad arrayed itself into a defensive formation with Lev behind the third row.

The deep pounding of footsteps approaching forced those in the formation to steel their nerves. The bogeys' ears twitched and eyes widened as they detected three dense sources of magical energy approaching.

Three gigantic figures emerged from the forest. Their muscular figures were almost as tall as the trees, and their arms hung low enough to reach their knees. One giant carried a holster of long spikes, another carried a bloodied club, and the third appeared unarmed. The ears on their deer-like heads fluttered as their red eyes stared down long snouts at Lev and his men. Lev and his men returned the staring in kind.

Across the behemoths' chests lay hefty straps of leather that bound wicker cages to their backs. Inside the cages were Lev's quarries—masked, bird-like creatures, bloody and unresponsive.

As the first giant raised a large, green-tipped spike, the bogeys felt magical energy converging at the spike's tip.

The giant threw the spike. It flew at incredible velocity towards the goblinoids as its magical energy shielded it from the winds and kept its path true. Three bogeys were instantly impaled.

The same giant roared, and all three giants charged at the bogeys.

As Lev readied his glaive, he could hear similar roars coming from far behind him, but they were silenced by a series of fiery explosions.

He spotted four more uninvited guests attacking Rapha's side of the formation. One threw its cage on the ground, caught itself on fire, and rolled on the ground trying to extinguish the flames. The other took a ballista bolt to the chest and fell to the ground. The cages fell open upon contact with the ground and the few masked creatures who were still conscious promptly freed themselves before fleeing the situation.

Raban and Grasha went to deal with the other two.

Lev smiled. "Slaughter the beasts!" he roared.

CHAPTER 11

BEHEMOTHIAN FURY

"Crossbows!" Lev shouted. His men complied.

Bolts of bronze hailed upon the crowd of stunned deermen, who crouched and covered themselves.

Most of the arrows bounced off their thick hides and horns and tough hides. With the volley over, the deermen let out low, steady growls and slowly stood up.

Lev had predicted that the creatures would charge after the first volley let up. Instead, they held their line. Some shuffled to the rear whilst the one in the centre stood tall. Lev detected two smaller creatures behind the giant that had thrown its spear.

They're shielding the weak. Lev realised. "Quick! Shoot another volley!" he ordered.

The crossbowmen broke out of their stupor and fumbled with their crossbows. Before they could even aim, they detected magical energy building within the deermen's snouts, which now glowed green.

Lev looked at the front row of giants. The smaller ones now cowered even further away from the front row. One of the front row giants let out a deafening roar as its snout glowed even more brightly.

"Sir! We need to get out of here!" yelled one of his men.

Lev turned to make eye contact with a bald green bogey from one of the lines behind him. He turned his gaze back to the giant.

"We have nowhere to escape to, so get that thought out of your head. Crossbowmen! Aim for the— Ahhhh!" Lev's order was interrupted as the giant's roar turned into a disorienting screech.

What were once mere bestial grunts turned to a horrifying sound that wormed its way into the goblinoids' minds. Both Lev and the bald bogey covered their ears.

"I can't take this anymore! We'll never survive this!" The bald bogey cried.

He fell to the ground and screamed in agony as the other deermen started to roar. As the sound intensified, more and more goblinoids fell to their knees. Some begged the gods to save them; others fled the scene clutching their ears.

Lev felt the pressure in his ears intensify to the point where he could barely stand it, but then it suddenly disappeared. He got up and looked for the behemoths. The creatures were nowhere to be seen.

Did they flee into the woods? Lev wondered.

It didn't take long for Lev to get his answer. From the closest forest line, the sound of hooves rang through the battlefield as the behemoths charged forward.

The shamans and bogeys in the first row quickly settled into their battle stances and prepared to hold the line.

Lev raised his glaive at the approaching deermen. "Soldiers, break formation! Shamans, burn them alive!"

The shamans raised their focus amulets and staffs, aimed at the first wave of giants, and fired.

A searing beam of energy struck one of the behemoths. It let out a sickening screech as it fell to the ground, but soon stood up and crossed its arms in front of itself before advancing again.

"Look out for that one, he's getting pissed." One of the shamans gloated.

The wounded creature's eyes turned crimson red as it leapt over the wall of grey robed goblinoids, straight towards the shaman.

As the two forces collided, bone and flesh separated. The fury of the deermen was relentless.

Another beam of light penetrated an assaulting deerman and immobilised it. The red glow in its eyes quickly faded.

The nearby creatures briefly slowed down, mourning their fallen comrade before returning their attention to the battlefield.

An unarmed deerman lowered its head. Its horns blocked and entangled many of the spears thrown at it. It threw its full weight against the soldiers, readily breaching the first formation.

Four soldiers were launched into the air, their bodies horribly crumpled; one shaman lay limp, draped and skewered on the deerman's antlers.

Another deerman raised its club high. With a whistling sound, the deerman crushed an unfortunate goblinoid soldier.

Another round of soldiers charged at the creature. Their spears penetrated its hide, but to little effect.

The creature raised its club high once more, spraying the fallen soldier's blood around the battlefield. Before the soldiers could disperse, the creature brought down its club once more. When it lifted, only a pile of mangled bodies remained.

The creature advanced to the remaining row of soldiers, but before it could attack again, a spear flew into its right eye. The creature shrieked in pain and covered its injured eye with one hand. Partially blinded, it missed a passing greyborn, who stabbed at its ankles with gusto.

"I think you've killed enough of my men," Volker snarled, digging his blade into its other ankle. Squealing like a wild boar, the creature lost its balance and fell onto a wall of eager spears, which embedded themselves further when the creature tried to stand up again.

"Its guard is down. Stab it now!" Volker ordered. Aided by a few deka, he mercilessly, repeatedly stabbed the beast's neck.

The red hue beneath the creature's eyelids subsided as it choked on its own blood and drew its final breath.

Volker turned to check the situation behind him. The remaining creature was rushing towards the shaman line.

"This isn't over yet. Get back in formation!" Volker commanded.

The remaining creature grabbed a spiked wooden club from one of his fallen and lifted it high above the remaining shamans.

"Disperse!" Lev shouted as he leapt towards the creature.

The creature tried to attack with its club. As it swung, however, instead of feeling the weight of its makeshift club, it felt a stinging pain along its left arm.

Once it steadied itself, it looked about frantically and saw its club on the ground, the fingers of its left hand still wrapped tightly around the handle end.

Blood gushed out of the stub where its arm had once attached. The creature moaned and frantically reached out for the club with its right hand.

The soldiers charged in unison at the distressed creature and eviscerated its right flank with their spears. Lev jumped and swung, the cold steel of his glaive severing the creature's remaining arm.

Swinging his glaive again to clean it of blood, Lev casually approached the fallen creature, which weakly growled—or perhaps croaked, not that it mattered—and stabbed it dead.

Lev inspected the creature's corpse and equipment. *Looks like we'll need more ballistas and fire support*, he concluded.

He felt a surge of power from his glaive, and it pulsed in a purplish hue. *We shouldn't have let the young ones escape. Two more are approaching from the left flank and I fear there could be more*, the glaive told him. *Make haste, master.*

Lev quickly assessed the situation. His party had taken out a few of the giants, but had sustained several casualties in the process.

He made his way towards the left flank. There he found two behemoths, but already dead. One was covered in ballista bolts whilst the other had a female goblin pulling her sword out of its throat.

"Lev, you're finally here!" she called out.

"Rapha! What are you doing in the left flank? You're supposed to be supporting the shamans in guarding the rear!" Lev shouted, his breath still catching up with him.

"Most of the shamans fled before we could even get the siege engines set up," Rapha spat. She stared at Lev, never breaking eye contact. "There weren't many shamans left to support."

Although Lev said nothing, his eyebrow seemed to twitch.

Rapha continued. "We prioritised the crossbowmen. At least *they* stuck around."

Lev pursed his lips. "I know. How many casualties did we take?"

"We lost about four men in the flank, and I think we lost another six shamans after they broke through our defensive lines," Rapha said.

She unblinkingly watched Lev's every move—surveying the surroundings, assessing equipment condition, counting men—but when Lev bent down to examine the bloodied ground beneath them, she shivered and broke eye contact.

After a brief pause, she felt a warm hand on her tense shoulder.

"We'll manage," Lev assured.

"Sir, if I may," a goblin in bronze armour cut in. Despite the generic bronze helmet covering her face, her mannerisms and the tufts of short black hair flowing from underneath her helmet told Lev it was Rapha's second-in-command, Ruune. "I did a recount and we're at twelve dead, sixteen injured."

"Thanks," Lev told the swordswoman. "Let's regroup and see what options are left. At least we've captured some of the masked people."

Raban and Grasha approached Lev, bruises covering their bodies. Raban had a bloody cloth wrapped around his shoulder. Grasha's horn was broken.

Lev motioned for the shieldmaiden to bring healers to Raban and Grasha.

"How many did we lose?" Lev asked the deka and goblin.

"Only three," Raban replied with a heavy breath.

His knees giving in to fatigue, Grasha laid down on the ground and grabbed his waterskin. He took a hearty swig before replying. "It would have been more if we'd been any later. What the heck were those things?"

"We don't know," Rapha replied, shaking her head.

"We need to get out of here," Raban advised. "It's too dangerous to proceed."

Grasha turned to Raban. "How? We've got those things hunting us now."

Lev's left foot tapped rather insistently on the ground as he pondered, but he too was at a loss.

Until he heard thrashing about from a certain masked creature.

"Leig leam falbh thu muc damnaichte," shouted an elderly masked creature as Volker and two soldiers bound its thrashing limbs with rope. Lev wasn't sure what the creature was saying, but its aggressive demeanour suggested that the creature was cursing its new captors. Lev's eyes widened.

"I think I have an idea," he said with a grin.

"I hope it's a good one," Grasha grumbled with his arms crossed.

"Why wouldn't it be?" Lev answered.

"Well the last time you had a good idea, we built that watermill to process wood pulp and the wheel got loose. I'm pretty sure that old man didn't appreciate it when a runaway wheel came barreling down on his new ho—"

"In battle, I mean," Lev interrupted.

"Fine."

Lev's grin grew wider yet. "Then let's get Volker and Orva. And let's bring along some of our new masked friends."

CHAPTER 12

AVIAN DEALINGS

"Dè a tha thu airson a dhèanamh rinn?" the eldest of the birdfolk asked. He knelt upon the ground, his hands and legs bound together.

He had lived through the enslavers' raid of his tribe and the hunt by the forest-terrors, only to be captured by the goblinoid warriors. Having been dragged from his place of imprisonment to a newly erected tent, his greying feathers were indignantly ruffled.

"I'm sorry," Lev replied, "I can't seem to understand what you're saying." His glaive hung loosely in his grip.

"Dè tha thu ag iarraidh bhuainn?!" the old birdman yelled, thrashing against his bindings in an effort to stand. He fell again, face first, but Lev intercepted him before his mask could hit the ground. Lev tried to force him back into a sitting position, but he continued to struggle.

"An toiseach, b' e na cluasan fada mallaichte a bha gar sealg, agus a-nis, tha na gobhan agad a 'glacadh ar càirdean cuideachd!? An do reic thu thu fhèin riutha!?" the old birdman cried.

The situation was quite a conundrum. All attempts at communication thus far had been hampered by the frantic old man's bombastic tone.

"The city," Lev said suddenly. "Do you want to go back to Pàrras?"

The old man stopped thrashing at the first mention of the city. "Pàrras? Am Baile mòr?"

"Baile mòr?" Lev asked.

"Pàrras. Am Baile mòr! A bheil an criostal sàbhailte?"

Lev furrowed his brows. He locked eyes with the man and spoke slowly, enunciating as clearly as he could. "I. Cannot. Understand. You."

The old man slowly shook his elbows. "Leig às mo ghàirdeanan."

"Leig... let? Let go of your arms?" Lev summoned guards to untie him.

The old man opened his palm. "Bata. Thoir dhomh bata," he croaked.

Lev exchanged a look with the guards. No one answered—no one except a green bogey making her way into the tent.

"I'm assuming he's asking for a stick. It should've been obvious," Orva grumbled.

"Orva!" Lev exclaimed. "Looks like you've taken care of the situation outside."

Orva grinned. "Scouts confirmed it. We've zapped the last of those behemoth bastards. Don't think any more are coming."

"Excellent. Now, can you translate for me?"

"You ask too much of me, Lev. Languages evolve over time and there's only so much you can learn of a language from writing."

"And now you have a partner to help you," Lev replied with a smirk.

Orva rolled her eyes. "Oh, that's funny. Maybe you should quit being a chief and be a fool instead."

"I'll do that when you quit being a shaman and become a general."

Neither spoke. Silence filled the air and everyone, including the old birdman, curiously stared at the two. Then the two laughed, confusing the birdman even more.

"It's good that you're in the mood for jokes, Lev. You were so tense when we first set out. I thought you'd become an entirely different person!"

Lev shrugged. "Considering my luck, I honestly expected another disaster. Nothing's gone right recently."

"This might be another disaster in the making. Who knows?"

"Hah! Even if it is, we've achieved one of our main objectives for this little outing."

Orva side-eyed the avian. "Was he worth all our casualties?"

"Only time will tell." Lev tapped his glaive on the ground.

A guard entered the tent, pushing the flap open with his shoulder. In one hand he held two wax boards, in the other a pair of styluses.

Lev thanked the guard and took both boards and styluses, handing one of each to the old man. On his own wax board, Lev first sketched the outer shape of the hall where he'd found his glaive, then a large circle that he hoped looked like the orb he had found there.

The old man's eyes widened. "Am baile-mòr agus an criostal; mar sin thàinig thu bhon t-seann bhaile!"

Lev turned to his compatriot. "Orva?"

"He's realised we've been to the old city. I didn't get all of it, but I think I can manage."

"That works." Lev turned back to the old man. "Now, tell me, do you and your people want to go back home?" he asked with sparkling, almost leering eyes.

Orva slowly translated his words. The old man did not respond.

Orva frowned at Lev. "Don't look at me like that. He's hesitating."

"Are you sure?" Lev asked.

"Pfft. I'm the great Orva who spent ten months studying their proto-nonsensical language from a goddamn granite stone! Sure, I'm not natively fluent, but this much I can handle."

"Nonsensical?"

"From what I've found in what remains of the frontier's libraries, one of Ainshard's followers, a chosen one, created this language to 'teach' the natives—by force, of course. It is a bastardised version of a language from his world. Only reason I studied it in the first place was in case we captured some of their city-dwelling counterparts."

"Why would he do that? That's a lot of effort."

Orva shrugged. "Part of it seems to be nostalgia. Along with a translation from Ainshardian to their language, the granite stone told a tale about how the chosen one used to be a chieftain on some isles before his memories entered this world. The other part was, y'know, to make the natives more 'exotic' and amusing to their 'civilised' Ainshardian ears. Travelling circuses and such."

That's just wrong on so many levels! Gherm thought to Lev, full of disgust.

Every society has its deviants, master, the glaive added. *And more so its fools.*

What do you— Gherm started.

Lev cut them both off with his voice. "They really were fools. They gave future rebels a way to communicate."

Orva shrugged. "I guess? I couldn't find any records of any uprisings."

Makes sense. Documented uprisings would be bad for the empire's "strong" image, Lev thought.

The empire was always strong, the glaive replied indignantly.

Sure. That's why it collapsed, Gherm shot back.

Lev felt Gherm scurry into the recesses of his mind to avoid the glaive's wrath. He let a chuckle slip before returning to the birdman.

"Would you and your people like to return home?" He had Orva translate.

The birdman shook his head. "Cha robh an t-àite sin a-riamh na dhachaigh dhuinn. Co-dhiù, chan ann airson ùine mhòr."

"He says that place was never their home. At least, for a long time. I don't think your approach is working, Lev," Orva complained.

Hearing that, Lev couldn't help but frown. "Sadly, I don't think they have a better choice."

"You're not thinking of taking them by force, are you?" she asked with a scowl. "That'd be more trouble than it's worth."

Lev chuckled. "I'd be a fool to do so. Judging from their miserable state and the soot covering their clothes, they should have nowhere else to go. Ask him if he wants to make it their new home. If they do, no threat will touch them."

Orva grinned. "That's another big claim, Lev. You better start noting them down before you get crushed by their weight."

"Don't worry. I always make due on my debts."

"Whatever you say," Orva replied with a nonchalant shrug.

She translated Lev's words to the old birdman, then did the same for the avian's words to Lev. Orva did her best to smoothen the talks and convince the feathered elder, but it was all for naught.

Orva shook her head. "He's worried not all of his people will agree and fears for their fate."

"So? The dissenters can do as they wish. Did he think we would exterminate them?" Lev replied with a smirk.

Orva gave Lev a raised eyebrow before turning to the old man, who became visibly shocked at Lev's answer.

"Ah, excuse my manners," Lev said. "I assure you that we shall do no harm to those who wish to return home."

The old man remained sceptical.

"But," Lev continued, "handsome rewards await those who return to our capital with us."

"Chan urrainn dhomh seo a cho-dhùnadh leam fhìn. Feumaidh mi seo a dheasbad leis a' chòrr de na daoine agam."

Orva translated. "He needs to confer with his people."

Lev gestured for everyone except Orva to leave the tent. When Orva was the only one who remained, he finally let his shoulders sag. "I hate language barriers. First that human slave and his Edorai, now this bird-mess."

"That's why I'm here, isn't it? Wait... a human? When did that happen?" Orva asked expectantly.

"Nevermind!" Lev chuckled again. "You've helped me realise the research department would benefit from more experienced personnel."

"Out with it, Lev," Orva said with a faint grin.

"Well, aren't you fun? Very well. Expect an increased budget for your department's research next meeting."

"My department could benefit from more hands in general. There are so many relics and records in the city's libraries. But don't worry, I'm still going to force that sly tongue or yours to tell me about that human you mentioned once we're back."

Lev frowned. "Don't push it. Anyway, someone razed those libraries before we arrived. Barely any of them have anything salvageable."

We're fortunate enough the libraries used parchment and stone steles for their most important documents instead of paper, Lev thought.

"Suit yourself, Lev. Guess we'll never uncover what happened to the birdfolk race."

"Oh. You noticed, too?"

"Yeah. Everything about them is different from the creatures in the city. They dress differently. They don't turn to dust when they die. And if that old geezer was any indication, they're way less aggressive and more... sentient."

"I'd bet my position as Chief of Commerce that the ones in the city were the anomalies—artificial, even. Wonder how they got there."

"My department could find out. All we'd need is for you to give us more personnel."

"Or, we could find out by getting the birdfolk to cooperate with us," Lev countered. "Even if they don't know the origins of the city-masks, they still know this whole area much better than we do. They could help us map out the terrain, identify threats, and really establish ourselves here."

Just then, Lev and Orva heard yells and cries outside.

"Speak of the devil—er, the birdfolk. It seems they've decided," Lev concluded from the raucousness that insults and curses were being exchanged.

He and Orva stepped out of the tent to find the birdfolk divided into two groups. The smaller of the two seemed to have drawn the ire of Lev's soldiers, as the soldiers had surrounded and pointed their spears at the smaller group. The larger of the two groups was preoccupied with tending to a bleeding, grey-feathered figure, whom Lev recognized as the representative with whom he had negotiated.

"What in the world happened here?" an approaching Rapha asked. She had just returned from a patrol around the perimeter.

"I don't know," Lev answered, "but I'm going to get it under control. Get the injured one a healer." He waved down some dumbfounded guards to accompany him.

In the centre of the commotion, two bloodied birdfolk tussled. One had a blue mask, black feathers, and a wool cloak covering its body; the other wore only a green mask and blue pants, exposing its large, red-feathered body. As Lev arrived at the scene, the blue-mask and green-mask separated and began to circle each other.

"That's enough," Lev commanded.

The green-masked one lifted its mask just enough to spit in Lev's direction.

Lev threw his glaive aside and cracked his neck. "If you have half a brain behind that ugly mask, I recommend that you back down."

The green-mask looked down at Lev and laughed. "Dè tha thu ag iarraidh, a dhuine bhig?" It pointed at another injured bird-person and continued to talk. "Bidh mi gad làimhseachadh mar a h-uile amadan eile a sheasas air mo shlighe. Aon uair 's gu bheil mi a' dèanamh eisimpleir den amadan seo agus athair."

Lev sighed.

Before the green-mask could reply, a slightly curved bronze dagger found its way into its throat. Lev dragged the green-masked birdfolk closer before stabbing it repeatedly in its abdomen. After a few brutal thrusts he let go, and the unfortunate birdfolk dropped to its knees.

Lev thought he saw shock and horror in the green-mask's eyes, but the poor bird-person was dead before Lev could even process his actions.

Lev slowly looked up. *Damnit, I shouldn't have gone this far.*

Silence befell the scene.

Lev addressed the crowd once more. "Now, who else wants to ruin my day? I keep thinking it can't get any worse, and every time I seem to be proven wrong."

The silence continued.

"Good," Lev spat. He turned to pick his glaive back up and began walking back to the tent. Rapha, Volker, and Orva, as dumbfounded as the birdfolk were, silently followed him.

Once there was some distance between the birdfolk and the goblinoids, Lev spoke again. "I overdid it a little."

"'A little'?" Orva replied incredulously.

"You did," Rapha added, making no effort to soften her voice. "You overdid it."

"You need to calm down, sir," Volker said. "Take a break when we get back. I can handle things for a while."

How dare you throw me *on the ground like that*, admonished the glaive, but in little more than the mental equivalent of a whisper.

Gherm was silent.

Lev rubbed his forehead while pacing about. *This isn't like me*, he thought. *I've never lost control like that.*

Even so, Lev addressed his three companions yet again. "Once the injured have been tended to, leave the anti-goblinoid birdfolk alone. We'll leave without them. As for the birdfolk returning to our capital with us, prepare them for departure. We need to get out of here before it gets dark." He did not look back at them even as he issued orders. "I'll be in my tent, alone. I... need to sort some things out."

CHAPTER 13

HOMECOMING

Wet feet trampled the frozen grass beneath the melting patches of snow. Not even the cold wind blowing in Lev's face could quiet his thoughts.

Why did I lose my cool back there?

Lev shook his head and took a deep breath. He surveyed his surroundings one last time.

No sign of those giants.

On that line of thought, Lev halted and turned towards his visibly exhausted men. "Let's rest here."

His men collectively breathed sighs of relief as they moved to relay the order and set up the encampment.

Lev inspected the wagons. Their provisions were low, but their wood stock looked to be just enough to get the entire party home.

Lev fetched some wood and began piling it up near their encampment. "Get a fire started. Make sure the captives get enough food and warmth as well."

The men grumbled.

"Is there a problem?" Lev asked with a scowl on his face.

Eventually, one of them answered. "Sorry, sir, but is it right for us to bring them home?"

"What do you mean?"

"Well, didn't they attack you? Not to mention those horrifying gifts they left us." Disgust was clear on the soldier's face.

"Oh..." Lev muttered.

The soldier nodded. "Those creatures decorate with their enemies' remains. I don't know what made me shudder more, the preserved head totems or the skull throne. What says those things won't disembowel us in our sleep?"

"Our captives are not the same as those monstrous creatures."

"But the masks—"

Lev briefly went inside his tent and pulled out a mask he had swiped from the city ruins before promptly returning. The mask from the ruins was scratched, full of holes, and drab in colour.

"This is a mask, yes. But is it the same as theirs?"

"Well, no," one of the soldiers admitted. "This looks cruder—"

"Exactly. Our captives' masks have a different design. Our captives talk to us with voices instead of spears. And in case you forgot," Lev emphasised, "I just negotiated with our captives' *representative*.

"There's plenty of evidence that our captives belonged to a much more sophisticated society than the masked creatures back at the ruins did."

"Still… sir. Are you sure we need to bring them back? Our city is still being rebuilt and our campsite is safe without them."

"Not safe enough. We have no intel on the whereabouts of those antlered beasts or any other hostiles beyond the light of our campfires. Last resort, our captives can be used as cannon fodder."

The other soldiers went silent.

"And trust me. They don't want to be our cannon fodder, but having made their choice, they don't want to be abandoned, either."

Lev's men continued their impromptu vow of silence.

"Now do your damn jobs!" Lev barked.

Just like that, the wood and food was quickly divided, perhaps with some reluctance, equally among the goblinoids and the captives.

* * *

A soldier trudged towards one of the wood piles, his hands frostbitten as he kept the straps of wood on his back firmly secured. He felt the nearby warmth of a campfire welcome him as he approached a pile.

The thought of warming himself was the only thing keeping him going as he saw smoke coming from behind a nearby tent. To his dismay, however, the fire had already been taken by a group of the feathered creatures.

"Useless leeches," the soldier managed to utter before collapsing on the ground. With the promise of comfort taken by the bird people, the weight of the strapped wood on his back finally took its toll on his body.

Most bird people were startled while some tried to take some of the wood off his back to lighten the load.

Lev ran towards the soldier and helped him get back on his feet.

A few more soldiers arrived to check on the commotion. Lev turned to them and began issuing more orders. "Prepare more tents and bonfires. We can't lose more men to this expedition. Not to the beasts, not to the cold."

"Oh, we'll lose some for sure," the injured man said under his staggered breath, "and it won't be to those vile beasts this time."

Aside from the growing strife within the expedition force, Lev was dealing with plenty of conflict within himself. Something felt different.

I don't know what came over me. When I killed that green-masked avian, it felt as if something was whispering into my mind. Turning everything into a dark sea of red. Am I being manipulated?

Neither Gherm nor the glaive would do this, he told himself. *Actually, Gherm wouldn't, but the glaive...*

Taking a seat near a bonfire, Lev reached forward to warm his freezing hands and looked up at the sky. The crackling of the fire and the gentle descent of snowflakes provided him a sense of relief.

Yawning, he tiredly rubbed his eyes. *A little nap shouldn't hurt. The scouts have us covered*, he thought, and lay down to rest.

Master, I sense you are troubled.

Before Lev could even close his eyes, the unmistakable voice of his glaive jolted him back awake.

Lev stood up, took one last glance at his men and the bird people, then snuck out of sight. Once he was sure he hadn't been followed, he communed with the glaive. *I'm not sure if I was fully in control back then. Did you sense something?*

A few moments of silence passed, and just as Lev was about to repeat himself, he felt another consciousness join the conversation.

Leave, Lev told the glaive. *I want to discuss something with Gherm.*

The glaive quickly responded. *If it benefits you, I shall gladly obey.*

As soon as the glaive departed Lev's consciousness, Gherm spewed question after question with full force. *Why did you do that, Lev? What happened to you? Wh—*

Stop, Lev commanded.

Gherm paused, apprehensive.

I... no. We. We have found ourselves influenced by outside forces since we began sharing this body.

Gherm felt confused. *I don't feel any different. And 'external powers'? It's just you and me here.*

Then let me correct myself. Only I have found myself influenced by outside forces, and I'm certain you're not the culprit.

Of course. But then, who? Gherm pondered. *Wait. Don't tell me—*

Looks like that contract I signed with that being was binding after all. For me, at least.

Lev had taken great pains to conceal Gherm's consciousness when he had entered into the contract with the ghostly white being. Still, Lev was somewhat surprised to hear that Gherm had escaped the contract's bindings. It was a clear indication of the white being's limitations.

Ainshard's key, huh, Gherm replied.

Despite the clear distress Lev could feel from Gherm's consciousness, the latter's delivery was quite calm and collected. *Heh. Guess I'm starting to rub off onto you, too*, he observed.

Lev heard the sound of boots crunching in the snow near him. In front of him stood Rapha, followed by a few guards.

Unfortunate. I wanted to discuss this further, but it seems it'll have to wait, Gherm.

Watch out, Lev. This is proof that you need to keep an eye on the guides. Don't let them dupe you.

I won't, Lev replied.

Rapha furtively eyed the surroundings before speaking in a low voice. "Lev, there's something you should know. The bird people are up to something."

When Rapha and Lev returned, the creatures were gathered around a fading fire pit, repeating a guttural sound that resembled their language. Orva stood nearby, quietly but not covertly observing.

Lev's eyes met Orva's. "What are they saying?"

"It's hard to describe. They're speaking some kind of dialect—might be a mix of their original tongue and the one taught to them. Not that I'd know, since I couldn't find any written records of their original language."

"Can you guess?"

"I think it's some kind of chant."

Lev raised an eyebrow. "I don't feel any magical energy being released."

"I don't think they're casting magic. I think it's a... song? Might as well ask." Orva approached the chanting captives, knelt down in front of one of the smaller bird creatures, a child perhaps, and spoke in its strange language. The creature in turn pointed at the fading fire pit Lev's men had lit moments ago.

Lev watched the ash float through the air as Orva returned. "Are they talking about the creatures from the ruins?" he asked. Back at the ruins, the masked creatures' corpses had turned to ash within seconds of death.

"They are. Our captives seem to be both fearful of and intrigued by them. They call them the ashborn."

Lev placed his hand on Orva's shoulder. "Maybe we can confirm that they're different after all. Press them for more information."

With memories of the bloodthirsty, screaming creatures still fresh in her mind, Orva clicked her tongue and approached one of the older birdfolk.

After a few brief exchanges, she returned to Lev. "Seems like there's a legend about the ashborn. These birdfolk are unsure of when these events transpired, but they're certain of one thing."

Lev stared at Orva expectantly, unblinking even as he rubbed his hands together to shield from the cold wind.

Orva cleared her throat. "Legend has it that the god-king once had a cursed citadel, and there were bird people who stayed behind after his departure. Assuming this citadel is Pàrras, those same bird people who stayed in the city all those years ago were the creatures we barely managed to escape from when we'd first arrived."

Although Orva's words were incomprehensible to the feathered creatures who had gathered around her, they listened intently nonetheless.

She continued, "According to their legend, those who stayed paid with their souls to do so."

Lev frowned. He had hypothesised that the beak-masked creatures were leftovers from one of Kram's experiments, brought into existence and abandoned on their creator's whims. Until their creator was forcibly sealed away, at least.

"My guess is that the one they paid their souls to was Kram."

One of the younger-looking birdfolk screeched immediately after Orva's last word.

Lev quickly noticed that many of the other masked creatures were shivering. *Kram*, he thought. *Is he a bogeyman to them or something?* Lev motioned to Orva to continue.

"I'm sorry, I didn't understand the rest of what they said. It seems that recalling their legend brings them great distress. I heard a mention of Kram several times, but the rest was incoherent."

Lev stood up with a relaxed expression on his half-frozen face. "It's fine, I have a good hunch of where this tale ends."

Orva nodded, but Rapha was clearly still confused. "What are you implying?"

"It's quite simple. Our feathered captives here are probably one of the few pure tribes left."

"'Pure'?"

"Yes, pure. I believe they are closely related to the frontier's original inhabitants, from Ainshard's golden age."

An agonising scream interrupted their conversation.

"Waaagh!" One of the bird people broke away from the others and ran towards the nearby forest.

One of the soldiers stepped out of line to chase after it. "Stop, get back here!"

Lev's frame suddenly blocked his way. The soldier looked past Lev at the fleeing birdfolk, then at his superior. "Sir, are you sure about this?"

"They may be our captives, but they're still here by choice."

The soldier briefly cast his eyes over the remaining bird people before returning to his position. All the while, the creatures continued their chant about Kram, then Ainshard. Those were the only two words Lev recognized from their strange tongue.

Orva shook her head. "It's better to leave them be."

"You're probably right," Lev conceded. "What was up with that one, the one that ran away?"

Just as Orva was about to respond, Rapha cut in. Well, the city used to be mostly inhabited by goblins, and all of us are goblinoids. My guess is that there are some goblin tribes further to the north who worship Ain—erm, *him*. If I'm right and they're like the Jiira, they likely made sure to reinforce the birdfolk's fear of him."

"Hmm. That *would* make sense," Lev mused. He turned to Orva. "Are they still singing about the ashborn and you-know-who?"

Orva lifted her hand up towards her chin and leaned in closer towards the creatures.

"Yes, but their tone has changed. It sounds like they're asking their gods for protection."

Lev looked in the direction the beaked creature had fled. He could barely see the outline of the creature running over the hills towards the dense forest behind it. "Why would that one run back to enemy grounds instead of returning with us to their ancestral home?"

Rapha shook her head. "Ancestral home? From what you two said, it sounded like the city was their prison."

"Yet we still have bird people wanting to come back with us," Lev rebutted. "From what we understood when negotiating with their representative, they need our protection.

"Besides, surely the city must hold some value to them. The only thing I can think of is the crystal, but tough luck if that's what they're after."

"Who knows?" Orva shrugged. "If there's something else they want in the city, good for us. Unfortunately, they seem to think the ashborn may still be hiding within the city. Which is very possible. We've barely explored its depths." Orva hesitated. "Like the underground sewers."

The sewers. They should have been flooded out long ago... right? Lev thought. When the caravan arrived at the abandoned city a year ago, they had carefully scoured most of the above-ground sections of the city, including the high-rise buildings, for enemies. To their surprise, they'd found no sign of the creatures they'd escaped from during the expedition.

Orva saw the blood drain from Lev's cheeks. "Hey, don't worry about it. If they were hiding in the sewers, we'd have seen them already. I'm sure even creatures made of ash need to eat."

Instead of calming Lev, these words instead worried him further. "Who's to say they need to come above ground to get food? Maybe they can rely on vermin and insects, or are cannibalistic in nature. Think about it. To have survived in the city for as long as they did, they must have found other sources of sustenance."

It was Orva's turn to turn pale at this conjecture.

Lev quickly changed his tone. "Or, yeah, you might be right. There's a nonzero chance they all died of starvation long ago. Let's get back to the city before we think any more about this."

Rapha nodded frantically, and Orva's expression returned to its usual nonchalance before she excused herself to get some rest.

Lev and Rapha stared at the chanting bird people for a few long, heavy moments.

Rapha let out a sigh. "It's one problem after another. We just can't catch a break."

"We'll do what we can with our heads held high. Just like we've always done."

Rapha smiled. Lev received her smile with a blank stare. She shook her head. "Yeah, you're right. Now get some rest. We'll be back on the move soon, and we need you in top form. I'll make sure no one bothers you."

Lev chuckled. "You're starting to remind me of Volker. Thanks, Rapha."

CHAPTER 14

FINAL SPRINT

"Looks like we're on the right track," Volker told Lev as he packed their cookware.

Two days had passed since they'd left the woods, one since they'd last encountered the behemoths.

"It doesn't feel right to call them behemoths," Lev grumbled. "They're big, but we've seen bigger."

Volker smiled apologetically. "The men like the name. Not much we can do about it for now."

"Seems you've stopped with the formalities," Lev mused as he checked his gear.

"Only when others aren't around. After all this time working under you, I've found you're not a fan of stiff behaviour." Volker moved to strap on Lev's spiked leather gauntlets.

Lev nodded, then motioned towards a few approaching figures. "Even so," he whispered to Volker, "formalities have their place. Especially around subordinates."

Volker moved behind Lev. "Yes, sir."

The approaching soldiers slowed, then halted their steps. It took a few seconds before one overcame his hesitation and stepped forward. He saluted.

"What's on your mind?" Lev asked the soldier with sharp eyes.

"Sir, is this the path you mentioned when we prepared this route?"

Lev gestured for Volker to pass him the map. Once he received it, Lev unfurled the papyrus sheet and brought it closer to his face.

His index finger traced the path they'd taken previously until it stopped at two identical hills. "We're currently here. According to our feathered guests, the area left of these hills are outside the behemoths' usual hunting grounds. We should be able to avoid them if we take this route."

A chorus of sighs escaped from the gathered soldiers, and while some were clearly still sceptical about Lev's plan, his words had seemingly brought them some well-needed peace of mind.

Lev grimaced. Some of his men had sat down a distance away, bantering away their worries.

He turned and pointed towards a distant clearing surrounded by several hills, raising his voice so that all could hear. "This is no time to relax. A single misstep could provoke them to cross the hills."

One of Rapha's shieldmaidens stood up. "If the hills aren't safe, then why are we walking through them like a bunch of idiots?"

"Our stocks won't last us if we take a longer route, Ruune," Volker attested.

"Exactly," Lev said. "Using the hills as cover gives us the best odds of making it home safely, with full bellies." Lev's index finger gently tapped on a blue line on his map. Behind the river was drawn a dotted red line, with the words "frontier outer lands" crudely written next to it. "As long as we can safely reach this river, the rest of the trip should be simple."

His soldiers remained visibly confused, the newer recruits the most so. Lev clicked his tongue. *Once I get back, I should push for improving the literacy rate of our military.*

After Lev explained what was written on the map, one of the soldiers raised a hand. "So we're supposed to just hope that they don't see us? Sir, with no disrespect, are you sure we couldn't just ration our supplies?"

"Can we even trust the bird people?" Ruune added.

Tch, Lev thought with a stern expression. *They're so afraid of further losses that they just want to hurry home, without even a plan to do so properly.* "Well, then. Does anyone have any better plans?"

No one responded.

"Then prepare to depart. On the double!"

The soldiers reluctantly packed their bags and the march continued. It took them several hours to reach the hills, as they needed to stop several times to avoid being discovered by the behemoths. Still, the plan seemed to be working.

When they were about to reach the last hill, however, they heard the sound of something massive pushing its way through the trees.

Lev's glaive glowed brightly, something Lev had warned it to not do unless absolutely necessary.

Seems our luck's run out, Lev thought.

A soft yelp escaped from one of the soldiers at the front, still audible enough for the rest to hear.

"B-Behemoths! I can hear one on the other side of the hills!"

The soldier readied his spear and took a few steps backwards, bumping into the shaman following close behind.

Lev ran to the front and spoke in a low, but firm voice. "Stay in formation. Stay calm. They haven't noticed us yet."

The soldier's spear still shook. "But sir, what if—"

"We'll take them out if we can."

"And if we can't?"

"We advance as close to the river as we can. Then the rear guard will hold the line while the captives and supply train make a run for it, with us right behind them," Lev replied solemnly.

The man gulped, tracing the tree line with his eyes.

Lev turned towards Volker and Rapha. "You two will lead the rearguard. Those beasts must never get the chance to close our path."

"Sir, yes, sir!" Volker said.

"Got it," Rapha affirmed.

"What about us?" Grasha interrupted. He pointed at himself and Raban, who had just finished organising his men.

"You and Raban will guard the ballista crew and crossbowmen," Volker said.

Grasha groaned. "Do you really think you can handle things by yourself?"

"Both of you are still injured. Do you really want to throw away your lives?" Lev retorted.

Grasha shrugged. "Not at all. I've still got much to live for."

"Lev," Raban cut in, "are you sure you can fend off those giants alone?"

"I'm not alone," Lev remarked. "I have my men, and Orva, with me."

Orva, flabbergasted, threw her hands up in the air. "Oh, come on! Don't I have a say in this?"

"You'll lead the shamans, unless you'd like me to cut your funding."

Orva snarled. "You wouldn't dare."

"This goes both ways. Do well and I'll see to it that you get more."

"You better."

Raban nodded. "Very well. But if you're ever in danger, we'll step in."

"I'll be fine. As long as our ranged support stands, we can avoid the worst outcome," Lev reassured the two.

Lev turned towards his soldiers. "Relay my orders. Prepare the ballista on high ground, and have the shamans prepare their focus amulets. We'll kill the beasts before they get the chance to disorient us. Get some scouts out in advance so we know the enemy's position."

"Sir, yes, sir!"

Lev kept his attention on the tree line. His ears twitched at the rustling of the trees and the clopping of hooves, but he did not move. A soldier close to his right shifted, clearly distressed.

"W-What's that sound—"

To the east, the glaive warned.

The men soon heard the distant sound of a horn. "They're coming from the east," Lev declared. "Soldiers. Face east!"

The formation quickly reassembled to face the eastern hills. The soldiers waited, breath bated and eyes wide, searching for signs of the gigantic beasts. Lev calmly stood his ground, right hand raised high.

A loud roar echoed through the woods, followed by more responding in kind. The soldiers saw a giant hooved foot emerge from the tree line, and the proud form of a white behemoth emerged from the woods on top of a small hill.

It stared down at Lev and his men with its red eyes, huffing in distaste. Lev sneered.

It raised its crude stone axe into the air, but just as it was about to unleash a war cry, Lev lowered his hand. A ballista bolt followed by streaks of lightning slammed into the startled deer man's bulky frame.

As the white behemoth fell, the enraged cries of its brethren sounded throughout the woods.

"I hate showoffs," Lev grumbled, slamming his spear's butt into into the ground. "Soldiers, prepare for battle!"

Several behemoths charged towards them.

The first three rows of spearmen dug their feet into the ground and pointed the tips of their weapons at the attackers. Once the behemoths were roughly ninety killigs away, Lev's counterattack began.

Crossbow bolts, fireballs, and beams of light showered the behemoths. Four fell to the first volley. The remaining behemoths howled in anger and sped up their charge.

"Fire again!" Lev yelled. Another volley of projectiles flew through the air down upon their beastly foes.

In an attempt to dodge the spells and projectiles, the behemoths quickly dispersed amongst the trees, using them as cover.

"They sure learn fast," Lev cursed under his breath.

One of the behemoths stepped out from behind a tree, bellowed a war cry, and threw its wooden spear.

The spearmen could only helplessly watch as the spear flew over their heads and impaled the chest of a young shaman.

"Markolf!" a blue bogey next to the shaman screamed in anguish. The blue bogey turned to the approaching behemoth and summoned a torrent of flames so great that his focus amulet cracked.

The burning beast rolled on the ground to no avail. Ignored by its companions, it burned to a crisp.

"Another roar incoming!" yelped a bogey soldier. Many of the greyborn could feel magical energy building up behind one of the trees.

"Not on my watch!" Orva shouted. She raised her staff, and a trio of swirling balls of fire hurled themselves at the behemoth's location.

The behemoth leapt from its hiding spot to avoid it, only to receive a ballista bolt to its head. The force of the ballista bolt carried it a few killigs before impaling it to the tree behind it.

Two of the behemoths were approaching the formation at a rapid pace.

"Brace yourselves!" Lev yelled above the din.

The men held tightly to their spears and shields, their hearts hammering in their chests, as the two giants closed in on them. They did not break formation.

The younger-looking of the two behemoths slowed down.

The older-looking behemoth shielded his face with his hands. Most bolts bounced off its horns.

The goblinoids hid behind their shields and gritted their teeth as they braced themselves for impact.

With a loud bang, the older behemoth sent the spearmen in its vicinity flying, leaving a small hole in between the first two rows of defenders.

Just as the behemoth raised its club, a fireball approached. The beast instinctively jumped backwards to narrowly dodge the fireball, which smashed into a rock.

Seeing how easily the behemoth evaded the shaman's attack, Lev rubbed his forehead. "I hate magic," he cursed before running straight at the behemoth.

The behemoth roared in indignation and swung its club. Lev ducked, leapt towards the beast, and thrust his glaive into its left ankle.

It let out a loud cry before trying to stomp Lev.

Using the glaive's ability to slow his perception of time, Lev barely avoided the gigantic hoof. He pivoted behind the behemoth's feet and swung his glaive.

"Too slow!" he taunted. His blade pierced deep into the beast's ankle, severing its Achilles tendon.

The beast fell to one knee and let out an agonising cry until its cries were cut silent.

The behemoth stared at Lev, his glaive thrust forth, with a bitter look in its eyes.

It reached toward its neck with a claw, probing its pierced jugular. Muttering incoherently, it collapsed to the ground, never to move again.

A thunderous boom sounded out, followed by bestial cries.

Lev turned to face the younger behemoth. It hastily crawled away from the battlefield, smoke emanating from its singed fur. Lev could hear the wheezing from its burnt lungs mixed with a few sobs.

It's... crying?

"Just die already," Orva grumbled as she zapped the young behemoth again.

It twitched and seized, strongly at first, but it quickly lost strength and fell limp to the ground. On his way to rendezvous with his men, Lev encountered two more dead behemoths and a practical stampede of behemoths retreating to the hill.

Lev took a few glances at the charred cadaver still in front of Orva. "Wouldn't it have been better to kill it instantly? I know you're capable of that."

Orva merely shrugged. "I thought the first lightning bolt would've been enough."

"Right. If you say so," Lev replied. He sized up the casualties. Three soldiers had died; seven more were injured. Thankfully, their shields had done their job and taken most of the damage.

"So, did we win?" Orva asked, her eyes scanning their surroundings for any magical anomalies.

Lev turned his eyes back to the hill. The remaining behemoths had not retreated after all—he could see large, antlered shadows accumulating behind the trees.

"They were just testing us. Orva. We need to get out. Now."

"Shit. Won't they chase us?"

Lev thought for a moment. "Can your shamans raise a wall to give us cover?"

"Impossible. We can raise a few stones, but a wall tall enough to cover us would—"

"It doesn't have to be a strong one. We just need to stall them."

"Even that would take time I don't think we have."

Lev paced about. His eyes fell upon the river.

"Are you thinking what I'm thinking?" Orva asked, grinning.

Lev responded in kind and immediately blew the retreat horn. "Fall back, in formation!"

With the order relayed, the men began their tactical retreat.

For a while, the behemoths had stayed atop the hill, cautiously observing rather than making a move. Once Lev's troops had almost reached the river, the gathered behemoths' numbers had reached fifty. The beasts charged towards their enemies with a unified roar.

A shower of projectiles, lightning, fireballs and fiery beams slowed the behemoths' advance.

Lev took out a focus amulet and threw several fireballs at the beasts, to little effect. Compared to Orva's, or even to the average shaman, his fireballs were laughably small.

Orva eyed Lev. "You're really bad at magic, you know?" She released a torrent of flames large enough to cause the behemoths to stop.

"I only had a year to learn," Lev responded indignantly.

"Somehow I expected more from you."

"Yeah, I get it. I'm a genius, just not at magic." Lev returned his attention to the behemoths. "Let's just cross this damn river."

Once every goblinoid had crossed, Orva directed the best of her shamans to collect their energy into one huge ball of concentrated light. "Time to show you *real* magic, genius," she boasted, her staff glowing ominously in her hand.

Though some of the behemoths stopped in their tracks, most of the furious beasts mindlessly continued their charge. Soon their hooves were in the river.

"Now!" Orva yelled.

A blinding flash covered the river, which gave way to a cacophony of wails and screams. The behemoths' bodies spasmed, almost dancing. The smell of cooked venison filled the air.

The remaining behemoths covered their eyes, and Lev's counterattack began.

The remaining shamans and crossbowmen unleashed everything they had at the behemoths—an unrelenting spray of fireballs and crossbow bolts, followed by the occasional ballista bolt, repeatedly struck the behemoths on the other side of the river.

At long last Lev's men saw the remaining tens of behemoths turn tail and run towards the hills, with nary a glance at their barbecued brethren before they disappeared into the woods.

Lev awaited a possible counterattack. It never came.

After a few moments, a few of the shamans stopped firing. Slowly, the others including Orva joined them. Orva fell, first to her knees, and then softly onto her back, with no energy left in her body.

Once Lev and the others approached, she lifted her head. "If you're going to ask me to do anything else, you can throw yourself in a ditch. I'm done."

"Don't worry. We've won."

Everyone erupted in cheers and cries of victory.

Orva yawned and crawled towards a wagon. "Finally. Now if you'll excuse me."

CHAPTER 15

A RIVAL'S GAME

They had finally made it. If all went well, they would see their home in just a few days. *If.*

Exhausted as the soldiers were, some were barely managing to place one foot in front of the other. The numerous wounded were putting a strain on their herb supply, and it wouldn't be long before they ran out. With dwindling supplies and only a handful of shamans with enough energy to heal others, Lev knew he couldn't slack.

He repeatedly scanned his map, ensuring that they'd taken the right path after the clash at the river. He'd done his best to not deviate from their intended path, but with all the chaos and their limited margin for error, he wanted to be sure.

"Are we still going the right way?" one of the wounded asked, hoping for a break as Lev reassessed their location.

Lev merely glanced at the map before responding. "Yes, I'm certain of it."

They continued their pace until reaching the remains of a broken monument. Lev's face lit up once he saw they'd finally passed the familiar dotted line. Near the line was a representation of the monument with something written above it.

Frontier Outer Lands. His eyes drifted to those familiar words, but soon focused on something entirely different.

A group of goblinoids wearing a familiar colour scheme were now visible in the distance and rapidly approaching.

Lev breathed a sigh of relief as he recognised the approaching goblinoids' grey garb. It was a welcome sight, one that nearly brought tears to his eyes.

At the front of the approaching group walked a familiar figure. He wore regalia typical of scout squad leaders: a grey tunic with a small bronze chest piece, accompanied by a horn swinging around the neck.

As the lead figure came close enough for Lev's squad to discern his facial features, even Volker's wariness faded away. "Is that Hemgall?"

Lev took a closer look. It really was Hemgall, and he had brought both a decently sized scouting party and a wagon filled with provisions. The wagon in particular almost made Lev believe in miracles.

But alas, a lifetime of hardship had taught Lev to not believe in miracles, especially not in one this close to home. After all, how could Hemgall have predicted the path they'd take back to the city?

In a landscape as vast as the forests and hills now beyond the river, mere cardinal directions would not have been enough for a small scouting party to pinpoint Lev's location with such accuracy.

Who sent him? Lev wondered. He visualised the faces of Vyrga's appointees to various other chief positions. The only chiefs Lev imagined capable of predicting his path were Rak and Vyrga. *Was it Rak? No, he's not the type to organise a scouting party. He'd rush over himself.*

Volker hurried to Hemgall. He could barely believe his eyes. "Hemgall!"

Hemgall's face lit up. "Volk! Glad to see you in one piece, kid!"

"Who sent you? Was it Rak?" Volker asked.

Hemgall groaned. "I wish. It was our least favourite pain in the ass."

Lev stepped in. "Vyrga."

The mood dampened.

Rapha walked in between the three. "What's most important now is that we've got more men—" She eyeballed the wagon. "—and supplies."

Orva was suspicious. "That's weird. Aren't scouts supposed to carry their own supplies? How far did you plan to scout, Hem?"

Hemgall laughed. "We were prepared to go beyond the outer frontier."

"Vyrga appointed you to lead this group?" Lev asked, circling around Hem. He found no other familiar faces in Hem's party.

The scouts nervously observed as Lev circled them like a vulture. It was as if he was looking for their weak points, threatening to strike if they moved.

"Lev," Hemgall suddenly said, placing his left hand on Lev's shoulder, bringing Lev to a sudden halt. "Everything alright?"

"Yeah, it's... nothing. I was just conducting a headcount." Lev ambled to a nearby boulder and climbed on top of it.

Both his and Hemgall's men instinctively turned to listen.

"We're almost there," Lev announced. "It's only a matter of time until we reach one of the farming settlements."

The sun was already setting.

"See if there's medicine for the wounded, and set up camp for the night."

That was all the soldiers wanted to hear. They quickly started moving in pairs, setting up tents whilst the shamans tended to the wounded with the scouts' provisions.

By nightfall, the entire camp was in boisterous spirits. Left and right, goblinoids were cheering, singing folk songs, and sharing boastful tales about the expedition.

Hemgall took a sip from his mug, which by that point had been refilled ten times. "Say, Orva, I heard from one of your lads you killed most of those giants by yourself?"

Rapha giggled. "She sure did! She decimated them left and right!" she boasted. Rapha wasn't usually this chatty, but it was their friend who was asking—that, and a couple of drinks had done their job.

"You're exaggerating," Orva declared between hiccups. "It was a combined effort. Lev and the others dealt with the grunts. I only took out the stronger ones. Gahahaha!"

"Very funny," Volker replied, rolling his eyes.

Orva looked to her side, expecting Rapha to laugh with her, but she was silent.

"What's the matter? Did I say something wrong? We survived, Rapha. Remember that."

Rapha looked at Orva, life returning to her eyes. "You're right, we're alive. We should enjoy this evening for as long as we can."

"That's the spirit!" Hem bellowed. "Speaking of which, where's my mug?"

"You mean that empty one over there?" Rapha snickered. Hem's inebriated, disoriented face was a sight to behold, and very soon she, Orva, and Volker had all burst out in laughter.

If it weren't for his political worries, Lev, too, would have relaxed with the others. He definitely needed some rest and relaxation. He just couldn't find the will to. Instead, he sat in a clearing a few killigs away from the camp to contemplate his thoughts.

So he wants to keep tabs on me through Hem, Lev thought. *Too bad. I know how dirty you play, Vyrga.*

Lev was cautious about sharing information with Hem's group. Anything he knew could be leaked to Vyrga, and with the pendulum of public approval in favour of Vyrga for the time being, Lev was worried that Vyrga's propaganda could make any of their costs—from the casualties in the behemoth encounters, to the very beginning of the expedition itself—look like an utter tragedy.

Even sheltering the birdfolk refugees could be something Vyrga could hold against Lev. As far as the goblinoids were concerned, the birdfolk were additional mouths to feed and additional bodies to house, with limited capacity to communicate, and almost nothing to contribute to goblinoid society.

At least, not immediately, Lev reminded himself. *Integration could take years.*

But that wasn't all that bothered Lev. Hem was a good friend from even before the revolution against the Jiira, and if Hemgall hadn't taken such a liking to Lev when they'd first met, Rak would have never come around and become the reliable friend and ally he now was.

A smirk appeared on Lev's face. *Heh... Maybe even Vyrga's just a friend in the making.*

He quickly shook the thought away. Perhaps Vyrga seemed to be full of selfish desires to the others, but Lev could tell they were cut from the same cloth, only weaved differently. The sly greyborn, like Lev, simply wanted what was best for the frontier. It was just that his means and guiding principles were diametrically opposed to Lev's.

The current problem didn't lie in Lev and Hem's friendship, but in Hem's scouts. Hem wasn't the type to keep secrets from his men, especially when drinks were involved. He also rarely questioned their loyalty. With Vyrga easing tensions with Rak and mending his relationship with Hem, it wouldn't have been hard for him to worm some of his spies into their ranks.

Lev stared at the night sky. Whether it was the smog above Neue Berlin or the cave ceiling in Gherm's previous home, it had been a long time since he had seen the moon clearly, and he wondered if the stars had always been this bright.

He stood up and resolved to spare Hem—or whoever was eavesdropping on Hem—the details, or at least the important ones.

He walked back to his companions, advancing past a tent full of drunken soldiers boasting about the previous battle, and only stopped when he reached a campfire whose lively crackle intermingled with familiar voices.

"No way! They danced? Those creatures really danced in the river?" a deep male voice said between incredulous laughs.

A few giggles followed before another voice answered on cue. "With weapons to boot! The way they caught fish without breaking their rhythm was a sight to see!"

Lev's expression relaxed. He took a seat next to Volker on a nearby log.

"Oh, and who have we here!" Hem said whilst trying to keep a straight face.

Lev let a smirk slip.

Volker jumped from his seat. "Lev—I mean, sir! Is everything alright?"

Lev looked at Volker. "Yeah, everything's fine, Volker."

Hemgall took another gulp from his mug. "What's the deal with those bird things?"

Orva did not respond. Rapha side-eyed Lev.

"They're casualties from the battle," Lev blurted out. "We rescued them from the behemoths and decided to take them back with us."

Hemgall placed his mug on the ground. "I see. Why though?"

"They'll prove useful to us. We'll discuss why later. Once we get back to the city."

"But how? Come on, Lev."

Orva looked at Lev expectantly, whose continued silence unsettled Rapha and Volker. "Well, it's pretty late," Orva said. "We should go to bed. The gods know we haven't been sleeping well all this while, and even Zeja must've needed her beauty sleep."

Hem stood up, turned away, and stretched with an enthusiastic grunt. "It is. You all should do the same." He left the campfire for his tent, trailed by Rapha and Volker, who also headed back to their tents, leaving Orva and Lev alone at the fireplace.

"Lev," Orva started, "why didn't you tell him? He's been through so much with us, and I assure you, he noticed how strange you were acting."

"I know."

"Then why?"

Lev picked up Hem's empty mug, scanned the campfire one last time, and turned to walk to his own tent.

"Don't ignore me!"

Lev looked over his shoulders at Orva. "It's precisely *because* he's been through so much with us that I don't want to involve him in my political games with Vyrga."

Orva didn't respond with another question. Instead, she simply followed Lev until he reached his tent.

"He's already involved. We all are. Did you forget we all made deals even before the exodus? Even Rak made a truce with the guy!"

"There's a lot at stake, Orva," Lev responded in a low voice. "I don't want him, or Rak for that matter, to be tricked into acting as Vyrga's pawns." It was then that Lev stepped into his own tent, leaving Orva to return to hers.

The following morning, the two goblinoid parties prepared for their final trek.

Volker ran towards Hem and saluted. "Hem, are you sure it's alright if you abandon your scouting duty and join us? We've got enough supplies now, thanks to you, and the trip home is safe from here."

"Yeah. You all in Lev's group already mapped the terrain around the behemoths' territory. There's no point in us going any farther."

Volker nodded in agreement, but something in his mind began to whisper words of doubt.

Hemgall walked past Volker. "Anyway, I've heard so much about these captives. I'm going to go see them for myself."

It slowly dawned upon Volker that their trip back home might not be as fun as he'd hoped. Still, with a fanciful flourish, he raised the expedition horn and signalled their departure.

CHAPTER 16

STRANGE RAIDS

After another day of trekking through the woods, everyone was finally able to relax. There hadn't been any signs of behemoths in recent days, and the scouts were sure they weren't being followed.

In addition, they were still several days' travel from Pàrras, so they had made their way to one of the few farming settlements in the north to rest. It was the very same settlement Rapha and Volker helped build before the elections..

Lev and Hem's forces strolled towards the settlement at a leisurely pace. Rapha, with Ruune by her side, was diligently guarding the front, with the now recovered Raban and Grasha guarding the tail of the expedition. Orva, as exhausted as she was, was sleeping off a nagging hangover in one of the wagons. In the centre of the army walked the leaders of the two forces accompanied by Volker.

"Are those deer people really that big?" Hem asked, slightly relaxing his stiff posture. "Good thing we ran into you first."

Volker slowly smiled. "Yeah. It would have been rough for your men without magic or artillery."

"Don't worry!" Hemgall laughed. "I've got all the magic I need right here." He dramatically drew his double-headed axe.

Volker couldn't help but shake his head. "Sure, sure you do. I'm just glad those damn things decided against following us again."

"Yes," Lev added, "but we'll have to deal with them at some point. We still don't know much about their behaviour, much less their physiology. I think we got lucky with Orva's lightning and the river back there."

Hem scratched his head. "Fizzy-what?"

Lev glanced at Hem. "Sorry. Their insides, and how their muscles and organs and whatnot work and fit together."

"I see. Knowing how their bodies work would make killing them easier."

Once I get the approvals, I need to add biology to the army curriculum, Lev thought. *It shouldn't be too hard since—*

Lev halted in his tracks to look at the sky in the distance, causing Hem to bump into him.

"Watch where you're going!" Hem scolded as soldiers bumped into him from behind. He heard similar complaints from other soldiers, but without warning, the complaining went silent.

Hem looked where Lev was looking. "Is that smoke?"

"It's coming from the settlement!" Volker cried.

"Lev, we know these people!" Rapha shouted, her lip quivering.

Lev urgently blew his horn. "Combat formations! We need to move! Quickly!"

The army quickly organised itself and sped towards the settlement, encountering no enemies en route. They soon reached the settlement's periphery, where the smoke was considerably denser.

With a wet cloth held against his nose and mouth, Lev hurriedly surveyed for any signs of life, friendly or otherwise, but found no evidence of survivors among the burnt fields and blackened husks of sheds and watchtowers.

"Sir!" yelled one of Volker's soldiers. "There's something in the ash!" He tentatively dug it out, revealing a curved blade.

"A sickle?" Volker said. "What in Ainshard's name happened here? Where are all the farmers!"

Lev flagged down a messenger. "Get the scouts to search the area for any more clues." He then turned to the now approaching Orva. "Might any of our beaked friends know who or what could have done this?"

"I already asked them," Orva replied to Lev's dismay. "They said it could be the same beings who forced them to take their chances with the behemoths, but we need more information."

"Already on it," Lev said. *All that work for nothing!* he silently lamented. *We need to find whatever civilians we can and relocate them—*

Lev's sudden wide-eyed expression startled Orva. "Wha—Lev? What is it?"

"If this…" Lev's voice trailed off. His hesitation was palpable. "If this settlement is like this… what about the others? How far does the damage spread?"

Orva was speechless.

Many of Lev's men were inspecting the charred townscape, but some were too stunned to move.

After mentally scolding himself, Lev quickly found his resolve. again. "Morale. We need to preserve whatever morale we have left. If the soldiers panic, we'll be in a much worse state."

"I-I couldn't agree more," Orva said.

"We'll hear what the scouts have to say. We move immediately after."

"S-Sir!" one of the scouts yelled, sprinting from the direction of the village centre.

Lev's body tensed. "What did you find?"

"The settlers," the scout replied in a grave tone, "or at least what's left of them."

Lev's pallor blanched. "How bad is it?"

The scout shook his head. "It would be best to see for yourself."

Lev and Orva could hear nearby soldiers muttering. The two quickly exchanged glances and proceeded to the village centre. They were joined by Rapha and Volker as they passed the wooden wall separating the village from the fields.

"Wh-What is this?" Rapha barely choked out as her body shook.

In the centre of the village stood a hundred stakes. On each stake a goblinoid's corpse had been impaled through the abdomen. Their entrails wrapped around notches carved below and their ashen faces bathed in the sun. Men, women, elders, and children—none had been spared.

Lev grimaced. He could hear some of his men emptying their stomachs. Eventually, he turned around, and to his surprise, found Volker with his back turned, dry heaving.

Orva averted her gaze. "This is despicable."

Hem rushed past Lev, accompanied by a few soldiers. They began removing the corpses from the stakes and laying them on the ground.

Lev turned to the rest of his men. "What are you waiting for? Take our people off those spikes!"

The gathered men split into two groups, one to collect the corpses and the other to light a pyre outside of the village.

Weeps could be heard among some of his men. Some of them had recognized familiar faces among the corpses. Volker and Rapha too had seen better days.

Raban approached Lev. "I'm sorry, sir, but I can't do this. You know how we goblins feel about burning our dead."

Lev frowned. "We don't have time to dig graves. The sooner we're done here, the sooner we can rescue whatever's left of the rest of the villages."

"I understand that, but my men demand that we at least bury the goblins.

"Let me rephrase. We don't have time for your men's superstition."

Raban grimaced. "And freeing souls by burning bodies isn't superstition? If that's the case, it's better to leave the bodies and go deal with the threat that caused them in the first place!"

Hem suddenly approached Raban, detaching his great axe into two axes.

"Say that again. I dare you," Hem snarled like a beast.

Raban warily looked up. "I didn't take you for the religious sort, but one must respect Jiira culture!"

Hem sneered. "Jiira 'culture'? I know how it works. We all do. Don't know how you got lucky but your men would be much brighter if you Jiira didn't try so hard to keep your precious Ainshardian blood pure."

"Why you—"

Before Raban could lunge at Hem, Lev swung the blunt side of his glaive between the two, causing both to step back.

"That's enough," Lev admonished. "We have bigger priorities."

The three were silent until Lev turned to Orva, who was having an impassioned discussion with a birdman sporting black feathers and a blue mask.

"Is something wrong?" Lev asked the shaman.

"Some of the birdfolk seem to be having second thoughts."

Lev mulled over Orva's words for a while before turning back to Raban. "Seems we can compromise. We'll split our forces. Raban, you and Grasha will stay here along with the birdfolk and those too injured to march. Take care of both the burials and cremations."

Lev eyed the horizon. The sun still stood high in the sky. "I'll survey nearby settlements for damage or casualties."

"Deal," Raban replied. "But what should we do if we get attacked? I worry my men lack the morale, armaments, and manpower to defend these... remains. And who knows if those birdfolk will stab us in the back."

"I don't expect your men to defend the settlement. Order your scouts to lay some traps in the vicinity. If something comes up, send a messenger if possible, but your top priority is to evacuate. As for the birdfolk, if you don't trust them, trust me."

After a brief moment of contemplation, Raban firmly nodded. "We'll do what we can."

Lev nodded. "That's all I ask." He blew his horn to signal for departure, and a moment later his considerably smaller force left the desecrated village.

As much as Lev hurried, the next few villages his forces rushed to were all the same as the first. Everywhere they looked, buildings and fields had been razed to the ground.

Interestingly enough, though, they found large piles of cremated remains next to large chest pieces, which themselves were large enough to fit large bodies—significantly taller than the average goblinoid, though not as bulky. Their attackers were far taller than them.

Lev felt Gherm stirring.

At least the settlements closer to the city don't seem as bloodied, Gherm offered.

Our countrymen probably got the evacuation orders right away because they were so close to the capital, Lev replied. *The soldiers who defended the retreat, though...*

Lev watched as his men covered their fellow goblinoids' bodies with cloth and cremated the rest.

Ugh, he lamented, *we would have caught up to the enemy by now if we weren't so preoccupied with pointless traditions like this.*

Pointless? Gherm asked.

The corpses in the funeral pyres we found here are way too tall to belong to goblinoids. I'm pretty sure those pyres are theirs. Lev sighed.

Lev's group repeated their surveys and funeral rites at another few settlements. The closer they travelled to the city, the more palpably Lev felt Gherm's unease.

Do you think the city will be safe? Gherm asked.

Don't worry. I'm no fan of Vyrga, but he and Rak are more than capable of defending the city.

Gherm's unease did not abate.

Ghorza will be fine, Lev intimated.

Gherm eased slightly. *She does live close to the city centre.*

Just as Lev felt Gherm begin to disengage, the glaive interfered. *Master*, it said, *I humbly request your hypothesis as to the nature of our enemy.*

Gherm spoke up. *Some sort of bandits?*

Lev contemplated for a moment. *No. This attack was too coordinated. Too… efficient.*

Gherm promptly re-engaged. *What do you mean?*

They razed the fields. Attacked multiple settlements seemingly concurrently, even fortified ones. Left no witnesses. Lev clenched his teeth. *Most tellingly, our soldiers still had all their equipment. Whatever the enemy is, they haven't done any looting.*

If not bandits, Gherm replied, *then what?*

Isn't it obvious? It's an army. Some sort of sophisticated alliance of sentient creatures like us. I don't know why they're attacking us or how strong they are, but I do know one thing.

Which is? the glaive cut in.

Lev's grip tightened around his glaive. *We'll meet them when we reach the city.*

CHAPTER 17

BLOOD OMEN

"How did it come to this?" Kathaga muttered. Blood dripped down her chin onto her tattered ceremonial robes as Pàrras, the city promised to her people, was set aflame in front of her eyes.

She wanted to cover her ears to keep out the wails of her people as they cried to their goddess for help, pled for her to not forsake them... but she could not. Her entire body was chained to a pole in the ground.

She tried her best to move, grinding against the shackles to raise her head. Once raised, she found the severed heads of what should've been the bogeys' saviours. Zeja's champions, all of them now dead.

Lev, Vyrga, and Rak had been part of Zeja's plan for the liberation of her children and their eventual rise, but now their lifeless heads decorated the gory scenery.

"Oh, Zeja. What are you trying to tell me? Is this one of your tests?"

As if to answer her prayer, she heard a squawk to her right. When she turned to look, she gasped.

"No... This can't be..."

In front of her was a crumbled statue of Zeja. On its head was a golden eagle with crimson eyes, digging its beak through the statue's eye socket. From there, it picked off the red jewel inside. Satisfied with its loot, the eagle fluttered away as black ichor spurted forth from the gaping hole it had left behind.

Shortly after, the statue crumbled to dust.

Some distance away, the eagle swallowed the jewel; its body underwent metamorphosis.

Feathers were replaced by armour as the eagle changed into an armoured giant.

No longer able to maintain flight, the giant fell to the ground, leaving a sizable crater beneath its feet. "At last, I am complete," the giant declared, standing two killigs tall.

"Or I will be... for this fate is inevitable."

Kathaga thrashed in her chains. "No! This will never happen!"

She struggled to break free. "The past won't repeat itself. We will surpass your misbegotten empire, Ainshard!"

Kathaga felt a hand on her shoulder. Under that firm but motherly touch, the chains binding her body rapidly decayed. *You're right about that, Kathaga. We won't repeat the sins of our past.*

With the remainder of her strength, Kathaga raised her head once more. "Zeja!"

The scene in front of her changed. Gone were the flaming ruins, and in their place were the insides of the new temple they had erected in Pàrras. It was there she was, kneeling in front of a statue of Zeja.

If the dogs of Ainshard weren't so lacking in wit, they wouldn't have created their own downfall. We might play along for now, but they won't rule again.

"We won't fail you. Even if it cost me my life, all enemies of our people shall be crushed," Kathaga vowed.

Remember. Every creature has its uses, even the vile ones. For now, listen to what I say. Enemies are approaching from the east. Evacuate the settlements and prepare for war.

Kathaga stood up and turned towards the exit. "As you command."

* * *

"This mission is a fucking joke," Lachas cursed as he and his men looked on towards the ancient city they sought after. What was supposed to be home to a threat to their kind had its gates open and its nobility standing outside its walls.

"A new threat appeared in the west, they said. Abandon your cover once you hand over Briecka, that damn fortress city, and deal with it, they said. You'll be highly rewarded, they said," he grumbled as he dismounted his tall, armoured frame from his horse.

"The only good thing about this assignment is that I won't be stuck in that hellhole of a city," he grumbled.

"You're going to meet them?" one of his men asked.

"Better to get this over with before her accursed birds find us."

"But boss, don't you think this is too easy? They put up quite the resistance in their hamlets. Why would they give up now?"

"They've been evacuating their people since they caught wind of our first attack. However, many of their men died protecting the farmers. They've got nowhere to go now but the city."

"But the city walls have been partly rebuilt, enough to withstand a siege. From what we've seen, their magic isn't too inferior either."

Lachas laughed. "In terms of power, perhaps. But technique? They're hardly worth a notice without their little amulets. Surviving sieges require food, and those farms won't be able to cultivate the land. So stop wasting my time and let's get this over with!"

Heeding his superior's command, his aide swallowed his complaints and followed Lachas to meet with the city's nobles.

It was a group of four people, three goblinoids who looked to be from the same species and a darg. At their helm was an old blue-skinned goblinoid holding a sceptre.

Lachas had his men surround the four and studied the old man's reaction. Despite the odds, he stood firm, still facing his much taller adversaries.

Lachas whistled. "You've got guts for a goblinoid. I thought your kind would just take your treasures and crawl back into a cavern."

"The name's Meinrad," the old blue-skin said.

Lachas hummed as he scrutinised the other goblinoids. "Meinrad, eh? Never met a blue goblinoid before. The only critter I know amongst your so-called nobles is the republic's dog. I can tell a Brizilum merchant when I see one, but why is he with you?"

"Servius is a part of our council. He is also here to act as a mediator in case you did not speak our tongue."

Lachas grinned. "Smart. He would've been useful in most cases, but in my previous line of work, speaking goblin was considered useful. They make the best customers for… special wares. You see, goblins and my kind normally don't get along too well."

Meinrad frowned. "So we have figured. You have caused quite some carnage."

Lachas shrugged. "Orders are orders. We thought goblinoids knew better than to move to the old cities, but my superiors informed me otherwise. Rhey didn't like it, so here we are. No hard feelings!"

One look at the fuming goblinoids' faces was all that Lachas needed to grin from ear to ear. "It seems I overestimated you. It's a shame, really. If you're as unreasonable as the rest of goblinkind then, well, it will be quite hard to settle things in a civil manner. The loss of so many lives over a minor grudge would be such a shame."

Meinrad sighed. "There won't be any need for that. We'd like to welcome you inside so that we may discuss things peacefully. While your superiors might want us to leave the city, surely we can come to a deal that benefits us both?"

"I'd love that. We'll gladly accept such an offer. We're all rational men, after all."

Meinrad nodded. "Then allow me to welcome you to Pàr—"

"A moment," Lachas interrupted Meinrad. "I'd love to strut into your *remarkable* city, but there are measures that need to be taken. My men need to investigate the city for my safety. I want to trust you but knowing how goblins operate, I can't be too careful."

Meinrad grit his teeth. He took a deep breath and answered with a simple, "Of course." before guiding half of Lachas' retinue into the city.

"Damn it, Lachas! What are you doing!?" His aide whispered into his ear.

"Pipe down," Lachas said as he mounted his horse. "Once our men are done, we'll relax for a few days while our engineers sabotage the gates. We'll capture the city and gain a city's worth of ancient treasures and exotic slaves never before seen in the north.

"I'm sure the brothels would appreciate some exotic wares. After all, these goblinoids do look like miniature versions of us."

The aide frowned. "These aren't normal goblins, and they have dargs amongst them. They definitely have some tricks up their sleeves."

Lachas turned to his aide with a grin on his face. "They might, but they're desperate. They understand that even if they kill us, our people would come to slaughter them all. Once our men have secured the city, we're going in. And that's final."

The aide sighed. "You're the boss."

Once they received a signal from their men, Lachas, and the rest of his retinue entered the city.

He frowned once inside. "It looks shabbier than I expected. I'm not surprised you goblinoids haven't been doing a good job maintaining it. It would need the refined touch of a master bereke artisan to restore even some of this city's former glory. But I doubt you could afford it. In the end, it's just a miserable wreck that belonged to a miserable myth, after all."

"Miserable?"

"Ainshard. A name that is used to scare children of my kind. He's been inflated into a legendary devil over the centuries, but one look at the city is all I need to know why his empire fell. Even the runes he used in his city were stolen from us."

Lachas laughed. "The mighty and feared goblin emperor is nothing but a jok—"

His laughter was cut off when he heard a loud *clank* from behind. He turned around to find that the gate had been closed, trapping most of his troops outside the city walls.

He turned to Meinrad and sneered.

"What is the meaning of this!?" He yelled at the old bogey, who was now grinning. With a tap of Meinrad's sceptre, various bogey shamans emerged from the nearby buildings with magical energy coursing through their staffs and amulets.

Lightning followed, killing off most of Lachas' men.

"You dare attack the mad one's envoy? Very well!" Lachas yelled as the runes on his armour activated, forming a protective barrier around him and the remainder of his men.

A bogey accompanying Meinrad bludgeoned Lachas' aide with a mace he'd hidden beneath his robes.

Lachas hesitantly tried to back off and turned his attention to Meinrad. "You're making a mistake! We can—"

"I think our little parley is over," Meinrad declared before unleashing powerful flames from his sceptre. Lachas' armour withstood the attack for a short moment, but the runes' innate power diminished quickly, shrinking the barrier.

That day, the loudest noises in Pàrras were the wails of bereke soldiers and their commander as they crawled towards the closed city gates.

"It's time for war!" Meinrad announced.

A shaman perched atop the walls launched an explosive fireball into the sky, signalling to Vyrga and the others that it was time to attack.

CHAPTER 18

VILE DEATH

The remaining bereke soldiers outside the city gates patiently waited for their commander, unknowing of what was hiding nearby.

Perhaps it would have dawned on them to check under their feet if they'd noticed the lack of wildlife.

Vyrga and the others sat inside one of many hidden tunnels that stretched outside of the city walls, expertly covered by snow.

"I can't wait to make them pay…" Rak hissed.

"Patience, Rak. A good hunter knows when to strike," Vyrga advised. "It won't be long now."

"I hope so, my clothes are getting wet," Ludger complained. He kept fiddling with his spear, accidentally bumping it against the dirt walls every now and then.

"I hope Bolo's fine. All our best fighters are here, and all he's got is a former overseer turned city guard and a grumpy blue-skin."

"You shouldn't underestimate Thorst and Gerwyn. And you clearly don't know your brother well enough if you think he needs our help. His only purpose is to flank the invader's left, an easy task since our reports tell that's the weakest part of their formation."

"I hope you're right, Vyrga."

Rak's ears twitched. "Quiet. I can sense someone casting spells."

Rak and Vyrga took a peek through one of the snow-covered trapdoors and grinned. The city's gates were closed, leaving the berekes utterly confused.

Rak took out his axe. "Get ready, men. Any second now and we'll make sure the bastards are Dorn's problem. I hope they have coins to pay the ferryman!"

Rak's men let out a silent cheer and leaned forward. They were barely able to keep their animosity in check. Many had families that had only recently transferred to the settlements. Rak could sense his men's bloodlust.

Vyrga's own were the same, and it wasn't just his elites. The expedition, war with the Jiira, and exodus had honed the former rabble of the bogey caverns into a formidable fighting force. One that was ready to face any threat, at any price.

The commotion above increased. From under the trapdoor, they sensed spells being launched, followed by a fireball shooting straight into the sky.

It exploded in brilliant flames, heralding the start of the ambush.

The bereke soldiers panicked as roars sounded from beneath them. Rak was the first to charge out of the tunnels like a rabid dog, closely followed by his men. With the underground ambush now serving as their vanguard force, the goblinoids smashed against the stunned bereke forces, disrupting their loose formation even further. With the area surrounding the exits secured, Vyrga's men also joined the fray.

Rak's axe cleaved through the enemies' armour while Vyrga's bow sniped the bereke squad leaders from the back.

With his spear in hand, a bereke cavalryman sped towards Rak.

Rak sidestepped the attack. With a grin on his face, he grabbed the man's spear and flung him off his horse.

Before the cavalryman could come to his senses, Rak dug his axe into his face.

Seeing Rak's rampage, the Bereke elites hesitated and turned to deal with Vyrga instead.

With every twang of his bow, the approaching attackers fell one by one. Those who escaped past Vyrga's eagle eyes were easily offed by Ludger's spear.

"Why did you force me to stay behind? Can't you protect yourself?!" Ludger complained.

"It's to protect you. From what I heard from the dargs, the enemy can gather energy from their surroundings and use it. The moment they catch you off guard, you're dead."

"Vyrga's right, boss. Even I'd have a hard time watching your backs around these tall guys," Willibald advised.

"You're making too big a deal out of them. From what I see, they absorb magical energy directly into their bodies instead of a medium like our amulets and staffs. It's even easier to tell when they're casting spells," Ludger argued.

Vyrga shook his head before shooting another bereke in the head. "There's still a risk."

"Duck!" Willibald yelled as a fireball flew over his head. He lunged forward and smashed the offending bereke in the face with his mace.

Once he'd crushed the magic user's face to a pulp, he turned to Ludger. "See what I mean—"

"No!" Ludger yelled as a boulder smashed into the back of Willibald's head.

With one of his oldest comrades dead, Ludger charged towards enemy lines through teary eyes.

"Have you gone mad, boy!? Stop!" Vyrga yelled. He wanted to aim at those who opposed his son, but couldn't.

I can't jeopardise the plan. Don't die on me, Ludger!

Refusing to heed his adopted father's commands, Ludger strode forth with a vengeance. Using the spear's range, he fended off every bereke on his path. His comparatively smaller body danced through their lines..

With Ludger distracting the berekes, his men were able to catch up to him. Once Ludger, after much bloodshed, managed to calm down, he commanded his men to assume an offensive spear formation.

The berekes couldn't approach the marching wall of spears and every attempt at magic was met with an arrow to the head.

Under the onslaught of the goblinoids, joined by the ballistae on the city walls, Lachas' forces began to dwindle rapidly.

Whether it was through magic, artillery, or tactics; they were outclassed by the same foes they had looked down upon. The only advantages they had over the forces of Pàrras were their gear and their height.

"Sir, Bolo's arriving from the left!" one of Ludger's men yelled.

Ludger laughed. "He doesn't want me taking all the glory! Men, leave some scraps for my dear brother!"

The sight of Bolo's forces approaching gave the berekes pause, if only briefly. As more berekes fled the battlefield, one of the remaining bereke squad leaders desperately tried to counterattack Bolo, preferring to die with honour instead of being pushed into Ludger's spear wall. All it took to break the squad leader's resolve was a strike from Bolo's shield to the guts, followed by a swing of his mace, ending the bereke's life.

"How are you making them flee so fast? Is it the mace?" Ludger yelled with a cheer.

"Business as usual," Bolo answered before caving another bereke's skull.

Ludger chuckled. "It's the mace…"

Bolo's reunion with the other goblinoid forces outside of the wall was a sign that the left bereke flank had been crushed.

In the beginning, only a small portion of the berekes had fled the battlefield, with most deigning to hold on despite the terrible situation.

A testament to their training.

But slowly, surely, their resolve crumbled. A bereke soldier slowed down, letting his compatriots march in his stead. The next moment, his fellow bereke found him running towards the nearest tree line.

A few rats was all it took to break the army's resolve. Individual soldiers became squads, squads became entire battalions. Soon, all that remained of the bereke forces were their elites and most loyal combatants.

As the fleeing berekes scurried towards the woods in hopes of salvation, the sound of bronze meeting flesh made them stop in their tracks. The decapitations had begun. On the orders of the same giant grey goblinoid that terrorised the battlefield, the cowards were beheaded one by one.

They were surrounded by Rak and his men; the woods had clearly been a false beacon of hope.

Another head left its shoulder when a bereke tried to force his way through the encirclement.

Rak laughed when his enemies began to cower in fear. He didn't need to know their tongue to understand their feelings. The hatred and vitriol behind every cry they yelped was enough to carry their message across.

You didn't show mercy to my people, so why should I? Rak wanted to yell back. But he didn't. Why should he waste his breath on dead men?

Vyrga had expected the bereke to break and flee; he was shocked at their ability to retain control of their forces. When he saw the encirclement, he was livid.

Rak, you dolt! This isn't part of the plan! He cursed. *You're spreading our men too thin, and without the means to escape, the enemy's desperation will turn to anger! You're killing our men!*

Just as he predicted, without the possibility of escape, the fleeing berekes steeled themselves and rejoined the battle.

"Things aren't looking good," Bolo commented

The berekes shouted and cursed till the moment they dropped dead.

Bolo's ears twitched. He turned to find an unarmed bereke running towards his brother, his glowing body overflowing with unstable magical energy.

"Ludger, watch out!" He screamed before bashing the bereke with his shield, flinging him away from his brother. Mere seconds later, the bereke exploded with blood and guts spraying the surrounding area.

"What the hell was that!?" Ludger yelped.

"Some of the bastards have gone crazy! They're intentionally turning their bodies into bombs!".

The few remaining berekes intensified their fighting, refusing to submit to their eventual demise. Some even tried to break through the encirclement, but most failed miserably.

As the sun began to set, the goblinoids looked upon the last vestiges of the battle. The carnage was almost over.

"Do you think the fighting will ever end?" Bolo listlessly asked.

"It looks like it's ending to me," Ludger responded casually.

"Don't mess around, brother. You know what I mean!"

Ludger shrugged. "Heh. I do, and I hope not. We'll be out of a job if that happens."

Bolo shook his head.

He silently observed the berekes' last struggles as they met the same fate as their brethren.

A bereke soldier jumped out of a mound of corpses a few killigs away. Despite the hole in his abdomen and his flailing guts, he sped towards Bolo.

Judging by his iron armour, it was one of Lachas' elites. One of the *lucky* few who'd managed to sneak past the encirclement.

"Die, you ungodly abominations!" he screamed before getting skewered by an annoyed Ludger.

"Shut up!" Ludger complained.

To his and everyone else's surprise, the elite grabbed Ludger's spear and plunged it further inside his abdomen, locking it into place.

All the greyborns and shamans in the vicinity could feel the magical energy being abruptly sucked out of the air and into the elite's body.

With Ludger still struggling to free his spear, the bereke grabbed his head with both hands and let out a surge of lightning.

"No! Ludger!" Bolo yelled before throwing his mace at the elite's head, shattering his skull into a million pieces.

Feeling the unstable magic and hearing Bolo's scream caught Vyrga's attention. When he turned to see what was going on, his bow fell to the ground.

"No…" he whispered, before abandoning his post and making his way towards his sons. He wasn't needed anymore. The battle was over.

Despite all of the deafening cheers and the men's triumphant roars, none of it made it into Bolo and Vyrga's ears. On this day, one of their kin had died.

CHAPTER 19

THE FRONTIER'S NEMESIS

"Shit," Lev muttered. "Are we too late?"

His forces had rushed back as soon as they'd seen the smoke in the distance. Despite preparing themselves for the worst, they now stood, shocked, on the periphery of the city.

Hundreds of pikes had been erected outside the city walls. Each wooden spike was topped with a head—but not that of a goblinoid.

Hem gawked at the heads. "What are these creatures? They look so much like... us."

Lev gave a brief nod as he approached a blond-haired head. He peered into the blue eyes—or rather, eye, as the other one was flailing about outside its socket.

If not for their long ears, Lev worried, *I'd have thought they were human. They look like elves... At least it seems they might not be from Brizilum. Fighting them head-on would be suicide.*

Some of his men cheered, while others breathed sighs of relief. Despite the gruesome sight, the city was still safe.

"Volker," Lev called, "have the scouts search for any remnant enemy forces."

"Way ahead of you, sir," Volker cheekily replied. He gazed back at the city. "I'm just relieved the walls held them back."

"It wasn't just the walls," Lev wryly responded as he studied the remains of the battle, particularly noting the underground tunnels. He turned towards a nearby wagon and grabbed a large, curved horn. Unlike his military horns, this horn's purpose was to signal the city.

Lev licked his lips and blew the horn. Its deep sound echoed throughout the desolate battlefield, scaring away a group of nearby vultures.

Tension filled the air for an uncomfortable length of time, but at last the city's horn replied.

That's a relief. Lev immediately blew his military horn to signal an order to march, and his men carefully made their way through the garden of heads all the way to the southern gates.

The gate's heavy doors slowly opened and a familiar grin greeted them from the other side.

"Good thing you're all back," Rak said. "Many of us thought you'd died."

Hemgall laughed. "You'd need a god to kill us. Several."

Lev's lips curved upwards. "Did you?"

Rak shook his head. "It would take more than the berekes to take you down."

"Berekes?"

"Berekes. That's what the dargs call them. I have a few less pleasant names I'd like to call them instead though."

Lev ordered his men to continue into the city before subtly motioning at Rak to meet him inside the garrison barracks near the southern gate. Hemgall followed the two. On the way, they found Thorst on patrol and brought him along as well.

Lev closed the door behind him as they entered an unoccupied room. "What are our losses?"

"First things first, welcome back. Ghorza's worried sick about you," Thorst answered.

Lev's brows wrinkled. "Is she alright?"

"Don't worry, she's fine. She made it to shelter before the battle."

"Where is she now?"

Thorst let out a tired groan. "She's currently helping the wounded in the plaza. Despite my best efforts, she refused to stay in the shelters."

"Alright. I'll head there after this. Now, how big was the enemy force and what are our losses?"

Thorst lowered his head. "We lost many good men."

Rak nodded. "According to the reports, the enemy was several hundred strong. We wiped most of them. Only a few managed to escape before I blocked their rear. Of those, we managed to capture about fifty. Unfortunately, we lost two hundred of our own."

Lev's sorrowful expression betrayed his thoughts. "Their sacrifices saved the city."

Sadness clouded Rak's features in kind. "I can't speak for all the dead, but the ones I knew were good men. They'd followed me for years, from when I was a gang leader in the cavern until…now." A warm sadness filled his heart.

"These, buh-ree-ks, as you call them," Lev said, "do we have any intel on why they attacked us?"

Thorst's forehead creased. "They're being interrogated as we speak. They were ordered to attack us and told us who gave the orders, but I think they're only giving half the truth. There were conflicting answers. We're throwing everything we have at them, but still haven't gotten anything worthwhile."

"Seems we need to be more creative."

Rak leaned into Lev's ear. "Whatever you come up with, show no mercy. You'd understand if you saw what they did."

"I do. We passed by the settlements before we rushed here. Speaking of the elv—berekes," Lev corrected himself, "how did you beat them with so few casualties?"

Thorst's eye twitched. "Two hundred dead isn't enough?"

"From what I saw of the battlefield, there were more than a *few* hundred. With so many of them and so little intel, it easily could've been much worse."

Rak snarled. Lev tried to ignore the disgust emanating from Rak as he continued. "As for who could both conceive of and execute the strategy that led us to victory, let me guess. Vyrga?"

"With some help from Kathaga. She warned us of the attack in advance." Rak answered. "We're falling behind, Lev. His plan annihilated the attackers. He's won the favour of both the regular folks and the council. His chubby blue pet even dared to slander us in public after turning Vyrga's spear-wielding runt into a martyr."

Hemgall gasped. "Spear-wielding... No! That can't be true!" he yelled.

Rak sighed. "It is, Hem. He fought hard but one of the bastards did him dirty in the end. Ludger's dead."

A dreadful silence filled the room. In the end, Hemgall took a deep breath and faced Rak.

"Rak, I'm sorry. I need to check on Vyrga and Bolo. I also need to give the shortstack my goodbyes."

Rak nodded. "Do so. Vyrga wouldn't let his new pet even think about slandering us in public if he was right of mind."

"Thank you." Hemgall quickly left the room.

Once Hemgall was gone, Lev turned his attention back to Rak. "New pet? Did you mean Bodobert?"

Rak grit his teeth. "The one and only. Council member. Fat. Blue bogey. Wears stupid, bizarre outfits. Loves spouting shit about Vyrga's *glorious* victory."

"That's Bodobert, alright. It's good you didn't cut him down right then," Thorst said. "Killing each other over some clown's words should be the last thing we do."

Rak rolled his eyes. "Tell me things are going well on your end, Lev."

Lev lifted his shoulders in a half-shrug. "Not as much as we'd hoped for. We couldn't achieve our main objective, but did cover all the secondary ones."

"Secondary?" Thorst asked.

"Have you heard about how we discovered this city?"

"Who hasn't? There were some masked inhabitants here, you ran into them and were chased out of the city. Do they have something to do with your secondary objectives?"

"That—yes, but it's a bit difficult to explain. It seems that most of those creatures left the city shortly before we arrived. The ones that remained had little life force left, and swiftly withered away. At first we suspected they'd fled into the city's sewage system, but our searches proved fruitless."

"So Vyrga was right. The city was safe to enter," Thorst stated with a raised eyebrow.

"Vyrga was focused on the situation at hand, not the future. There's always a chance they could return, looking to reclaim their city." Lev warned.

Thorst sharply inhaled. "So we could be attacked at any moment. Why hasn't anyone told us about this?"

"Calm down," Rak retorted.

Lev clenched his teeth. "Why scare the populace? It's not like we should evacuate the city just on the off chance of an attack. We have nowhere else to go, and the city is as defensible a location as any in the area.

"Still," he continued, "I agree it's a fool's errand to simply wait to be attacked. My secondary objectives revolved around finding traces of the creatures that fled the city and learning more about them by whatever means necessary. I must admit, though, I didn't expect to find what we did."

"Don't tell me. You found some of those angry masked things?" Thorst guessed.

"You could say that."

"Eh? I don't believe it."

"You'll believe it when Raban and Grasha enter the city with them. More importantly, what was Vyrga's plan to deal with the berekes?"

"We faked a surrender, baited their leaders inside, and killed their leaders. Meanwhile, Rak, Vyrga, and his sons led an ambush to catch the tall pieces of shit by surprise. Then we slaughtered them to the last man. I was placed under Bolo's command to attack the berekes' left flank."

Rak flashed a bloodthirsty grin. "As soon as the fighting started, we rushed out of our hiding holes like hivelings and swarmed the bastards! Those murderous shits didn't know what hit 'em."

His smile slowly gave way. "As much as I hate Vyrga, his plan got those damn berekes off our turf."

"You should've seen it," Thorst added. "The moment things turned sour for them, the bastards lost their heads and tried to force their way through Rak to escape. I've seen corpse-eaters smarter than that."

"Good for him," Lev said. "Sounds like Vyrga's choices secured a favourable result for our people."

"That's one thing we can all agree on," Rak remarked. Thorst nodded in agreement.

"Any other happenings I should know about?" Lev asked.

Thorst rubbed his chin. "The refugees from the settlements were relocated to the western district. Those houses we rebuilt came in handy."

Lev's brows creased. "I was planning on settling the birdfolk there. This is quite troubling."

Thorst dismissed the idea with vigorous hand-waves. "Our people need the place more. Why not settle the bird creatures in the north?"

Lev shook his head. "All we've done there is repair the wall. And the buildings in the north are barely inhabitable."

"It's better than nothing. What if we make them share the western district?"

Lev frowned. "The birdfolk don't speak our language and the refugees have just seen their homes and families destroyed. I worry even a single misunderstanding could spark a fight between them."

"Then why bring them here in the first place?" Rak probed.

"They have so much knowledge we don't. They know the northern region and its people. Even better, they're vulnerable. It won't be hard for us to win them over. Besides, they may know a few magical tricks that we don't—"

Lev stopped upon hearing a commotion outside.

Rak and Thorst looked out of the barracks' windows and saw masked, bird-beaked creatures pouring into the city. The bird people gawked at their surroundings in awe and appreciation as they entered. Flanking them were those who'd sustained injuries during the expedition.

"Looks like they've arrived," Lev commented.

Rak scratched his head. "Our men can handle mapping the place and improving relations within our domain. And with shamans like Orva and Gerwyn handling our magic research, do we really need help? I'm sure we'd be fine without them." He motioned toward the window.

Lev shrugged. "There are many inconsistencies and gaps in our theories and knowledge of magic. The birdfolk may have information that can help us further our understanding of the subject. Besides, they may know more about these berekes."

Thorst cocked his head to the side with a peeved expression. "Not to be rude, but aren't you pretty bad at magic? I've seen you try. Even with a quality haze crystal in hand, your fireballs are the size of my boogers. You should stick to physical combat and leave magic to the experts."

"My proficiency in magic aside," Lev replied through clenched teeth, "the fact remains that our people have reached a standstill with their research. A new perspective, especially a non-goblinoid one, could help."

"But... um..." Thorst's mouth opened and closed a few times. "Whatever."

"I still think the timing is terrible," Rak commented. "We're still recovering from the attack. Tensions are high."

Lev lifted his palms and shrugged. "Sorry, but as you can see, they're already here."

Rak groaned.

"It sounds like our only option is to put them in the north." Thorst repeated.

"Thorst is right. You said it yourself. It's too risky to place them with our people. The north is their only option."

"I suppose it is, isn't it?" Lev conceded with a sigh. "Alright. For now, we escort the birdfolk to the northern district. After that, we reconvene at my place to plan our case for the council."

"This won't be easy," Rak mumbled.

"When has anything been easy?"

CHAPTER 20

A LORD'S DISPUTE

Long after the battle and before Lev's arrival, Vyrga held a funeral for the lost. Every fallen soul was accounted for. With the exception of the goblins, whose kin decided to perform their own ceremony, the remaining goblinoids had been placed on a grand pyre. At the top of the pyre lay Ludger.

The crowd seemed unsure what to think about the ceremony. Most had come to see the bodies of their beloved ones one last time before they were engulfed by flames, becoming one with the cycle again.

"He placed one of his own men at the top? First it was Lev, and now Vyrga out of all people. What is Kathaga thinking?"

"That man was his son, but there are better bogeys deserving of that honour. May Zeja forgive our head priestess."

"There goes another of his sons. Our dear High Chief must be having it hard."

"Ludger shouldn't have died. That cocky bastard owes me money!"

"What were you doing gambling with a greyborn thug? People of our stature shouldn't deal with the scum of society!"

Despite all of the murmurs, Vyrga kept quiet.

Even Bolo, who was known for his calm and gentle demeanour, had a hard time keeping his emotions in check. Especially when it was the priests who had arranged the funeral rights, not Vyrga.

"Don't waste your time on them. These corpse-eaters only know how to yap their mouths," Vyrga whispered in Bolo's ear.

"But father—"

"There are other ways to deal with them," Vyrga interjected.

Bolo softly growled in response.

Kathaga approached the platform, torch in hand. To everyone's shock, Vyrga stepped forward and stopped in her way.

He opened his palm. "Priestess?"

The priests were the first to complain.

"What are you doing!?"

"This is Outrageous!"

"High Chief or not, how dare you stand in the high priestess's way!?"

Vyrga barely gave them a glance before returning his attention back to Kathaga.

Kathaga smiled. "Can you elaborate on your decision, High Chief?"

"It is out of respect for our faith. Funerary procedures of such scale are meant to be held by the high priest of Dorn, isn't that correct?"

"Indeed, but he died during the exodus!" One of Zeja's priests yelled.

"He did, didn't he? And have the priests of Dorn elected a new high priest?"

"Don't mess around with us, Vyrga! Dorn no longer has any official priests. Who wants to be known as the servant of that stubborn god of death anyways!? With their diminished status, only we can represent Dorn! Times have changed!"

Vyrga turned to the people and grinned. "Do you hear that? Even the priests admit that times have changed! But is it right to leave such a burden to these wise men and women? They bear our hopes and dreams before battle, but should we let them bear the weight of our dead too?"

Kathaga laughed. "What do you have in mind, High Chief?"

"My dear priestess of Zeja. The High Chief is both leader and servant of the people. We, who were chosen by the people, sent our kin to die for the nation and fought by their side. Only we should be tasked with handling the weight of our actions, so we should be the ones sending them to the cycle."

The priests of Zeja wanted to laugh at Vyrga's arrogance, but were rendered mute when they came to a realisation. The crowd was actually discussing such a scenario, and even Kathaga was contemplating it.

That damned traitor! She isn't fit to serve our goddess!

Shit! If it weren't for her, we could've repurposed the new temples as communal grounds!

She's contemplating such blasphemy!? That old crone must have finally lost her mind!!

With bated breath, the priests awaited their high priestess's decision.

Their hearts sank when Kathaga handed the torch to Vyrga.

"War leads to death, but that does not mean people should mistake them for one and the same. It is now your duty, high chief. May you be up to the task."

The people cheered as Vyrga gave Kathaga a curtsy bow.

He went up to the pyre and looked at Ludger one last time.

Vyrga dropped the torch on his son's pitch-covered body. *I'm sorry it led to this. May there be a better place for you in the next cycle. Goodbye, Ludger.*

"This is how you deal with foul priests," Vyrga whispered to Bolo once he had returned to his position.

"But why did Kathaga agree?"

"We planned it beforehand. She hates her fellow priests more than I do."

* * *

With the funeral over, Vyrga relieved himself of his duties and returned to his office. Once inside, he swiftly strode to his desk and slumped down in his seat. After a few moments of contemplation, he leaned on his right arm and wearily stared at a set of wooden carvings he'd made a few months prior.

He reached forward. The tips of his fingers carefully stroked the faces he'd lovingly reproduced from his most tender memories. His eyelids drooped and he let out a deep, exhausted breath. "Os. Heimo. Gelmar, Ludger... Could I have done better? Could I have saved any of you?"

Vyrga stared longingly at the carvings, almost as if he could speak to the people they represented through them.

A knock sounded from his door; his ears perked. He straightened his back and tightened his expression.

"Enter."

A familiar fat, blue bogey entered the office. His overly pink, puffy shirt, styled after legendary figures in surviving paintings and statues found around the city, was covered by an assortment of golden accessories that jingled and clattered as he waddled through the door.

Vyrga tightly gripped the right stand on his chair hard, labouring to conceal any signs of irritation at his guest's arrival.

"What brings you here, Bodobert?"

"A small matter, my liege. I only wished to inform you that our speech has swayed more citizens to our side. After your heroic efforts during battle and the funeral, I believe that our misguided rivals no longer stand a chance."

The balding wretch's words gave Vyrga a bad taste in his mouth. *Our side, huh? And who saved the city? You and your ilk hid away while our 'misguided rivals' and I fought the invaders off.* The longer Vyrga gazed at Bodobert, the more his eyes filled with disgust. *It wasn't just Rak, either. Even Gerwyn and Hiltrude performed excellently. But you—*

With herculean effort, Vyrga pushed his thoughts away. "While giving the speech was a good move, antagonising the competition was not. You went too far."

"Hmph! Did I lie? All Gerwyn did was shoot some spells from the backline. And Hiltrude? Gave the poor sods food and blankets. That's it."

And you did nothing but crawl out of hiding after the fighting finished, Vyrga wanted to hiss.

Bodobert continued. "Yes, Gerwyn heroically rode your son's coattails while Hiltrude provided for the worthless needy. While we did most of the work, their actions were mere excuses to cut their own losses."

"Then why did you antagonise Lev? Did you forget about the elections?"

Bodobert sneered. "Don't remind me. I almost had my head smashed in by his pet giant. Add to that the humiliation of being pinned down like some slave!"

You assaulted the guards first. Who brings a mace to an election?

Vyrga leaned both his arms on the table to partially cover his scowl. "So you should understand how volatile the situation is. Why would you insult him? in front of his men, no less."

"I only spoke the truth. While Lev's dogs did participate in the battle, he should have been here to command them." Bodobort flashed a placating smile that only annoyed Vyrga further. "Though he is no match for you, his abilities cannot be underestimated. Alas," Bodobert said with a faux flourish, "it seems Lev cares more about his petty projects than his duty as a chief"

Vyrga pinched his nose, trying his best to hide his ever-burgeoning irritation. "Lev and I may not agree on some issues, but even I have to admit that many of his projects are of great help to our community."

"As true as they may be, does he need to oversee each of them himself? If he truly cared about our people and his duty as a pillar of this community, he would have stayed in the city and left his projects to his men."

"And what of your duties? Where were you during the battle?" Vyrga mused.

Bodobert bowed. Vyrga could see the edges of his lips contorting into an apologetic smile. "I'm merely a man who lives up to his nature. Everyone has talents—mine are simply better suited to the civil than the martial front."

And yet you insult the others for exercising theirs, Vyrga again wanted to reply. "Well then, would you care to explain what the other matter is?"

"Nothing, my liege. Just that I managed to sway another council member to our side. One of Gerwyn's."

"I see. Well done." Vyrga slowly clapped his hands. "That must have been difficult."

Bodobert beamed with joy, his puffed chest threatening the buttons of his shirt. "I am honoured to hear you appreciate my talents, my liege."

Vyrga rolled his eyes, but Bodobert didn't appear to notice.

"Then again, it was inevitable," Bodobert continued. "Great leaders like you have a natural ability to amass great followings. Together, we shall carve our names in the great history of goblinkind!"

Yes, yes, Vyrga dryly thought.

"After we've corrected some misrepresentations of past events, that is."

Vyrga nodded. "Indeed. Nothing wrong with a clean slate."

Bodobert chuckled. "I am happy you agree. Now, when will you get rid of... What was his name again? Bobo? With Lud... with the other gone, it would be better to take the opportunity to clean house, as my mother would say."

Hearing no reply, Bodobert's smile turned stiff. He could practically feel the temperature drop.

"What did you just say?" Vyrga calmly asked.

Aside from his stomach dropping, his breath turning shallow, and his blue knuckles going pale, Bodobert offered no reply.

"I agree that my story could use some proofreading," Vyrga said, "but would you happen to have some misgivings about my sons?"

"I-I meant no disrespect, my lord. I only believe that someone of your stature should have better company. Surely you understand your image will suffer from any past associations with lowly thugs."

"Lowly thugs. You're calling the greatest of my men, the ones I myself trained and mentored, lowly thugs?" Vyrga rose from his seat with a soft chuckle. His giant form towered over the garishly-attired councilman. "I was born in the darkest regions of the slums, and now I reign supreme. They played a valuable part in that and Bolo will stay by my side till the end of my days. I won't allow more of my sons to be erased from this world."

"I-I— but Heimo—"

"Died for what he believed was best for our kind. You have delivered your report. You may leave."

"My liege—"

Bodobert's stuttering was interrupted by a small jug, which hit the wall near him and smashed into pieces. He felt a few drops of liquid splash onto the back of his head.

With an audible gulp, Bodobort hastily bowed and scurried to open the door. He turned one more time towards Vyrga. "As you wish, my lord. Just remember that I meant no offence."

"Duly noted. Get out."

Bodobert nodded and proceeded halfway through the door. "I'll take my leave then. Though I recommend you work on your temper. It would not be wise to ruin your relationship with your partners. After all, we put you on that seat—"

Bodobert quickly closed the door just before another jug slammed into its wooden frame. Soon enough, Vyrga was comforted by panicked footsteps, or perhaps foot-stomps, down the hall.

Vyrga inhaled deeply, counted to three, and exhaled.

His usefulness may not be worth his attitude, Vyrga thought. He opened a drawer and withdrew a finely-crafted flute with floral embellishments carved into its exterior.

With a gentle smile, he caressed its wooden frame and brought it to his lips, but just as he was to begin, he heard chatter outside his office door. *Don't tell me he's back*, he quietly seethed. He slipped the flute back into his drawer and sat straight back up, facing the door right as it opened.

It was Lev.

I really should hire better guards, Vyrga noted.

Each eyed the other for a moment, then Vyrga gestured Lev towards an empty chair.

Lev sat down and wasted no breath. "What have we extracted from the attackers?"

"Where should I start? How informed are you?"

"Our lands were pillaged by an unknown force and you dealt with them, though why you didn't intercept them *before* they reached the city is a mystery to me."

Vyrga's eyes narrowed. "It's not like they warned us of their movements before they struck. If it weren't for Kathaga, we would have been caught with our pants down. Could you have done any better, given the circumstances?"

"Who knows?" Lev replied incredulously, with clenched fists. "Then again, I wouldn't have antagonised my fellow chiefs when what my people need most is at least a semblance of unity."

Vyrga grit his teeth. *Damn you, Bodobert.* He uncharacteristically rubbed his temples, a pained expression on his face. "I issued no orders to antagonise you. I should have kept a better eye on that idiotic snake. I'm sorry."

Lev raised an eyebrow at Vyrga's apology.

Vyrga straightened his posture. "Anyway, the berekes are still under interrogation."

"I'm aware. Have they cracked?"

Vyrga shook his head. "They're tough, even by bereke standards. Or so I've heard."

"From the dargs, I presume?"

Vyrga leaned forward. "The darg nation of Edoros trades with every corner of the continent. Moreover, Brizilum shares their borders with the bereke nation, and fought with them. Considering they had many bereke slaves, you can guess who won that conflict."

"What's the difference between our berekes and the ones Brizilum fought?"

"Ours are more aggressive while the latter are now better known for their role in Brizilum's entertainment industry. One would assume we're facing the ones belonging to the aforementioned bereke nation, but clearly, the ones we met are... different."

Lev crossed his arms over his chest. "Different environments breed different cultures. The conclusions they've drawn about their berekes may not apply to ours."

"It's more than culture. Their berekes don't look like ours."

Lev paused. "How so?" he asked with a raised eyebrow.

"Their berekes are taller than goblins but shorter than pinkskins, with tan skin and lean builds. Have you seen ours?"

Lev closed his eyes and recalled the carnage. "Their heads were mostly coated in crimson paint, but the naked bits were pale white."

"Indeed. Also, according to our experts, the invaders, both men and women, are at least a head or two taller than your average Brizilum male. And that's not even the most surprising part."

Lev nodded expectantly at Vyrga.

"Their bodies can store tremendous amounts of magical energy."

Lev tilted his head. "So their shamans might be a pain. How is that surprising?"

"They can cast spells without using foci. If they forgo safety, they can do it practically instantaneously."

Lev's eyes widened. "That's absurd."

Vyrga let out a mirthless chuckle. "They're also not limited to offensive magic. Their elites can strengthen their muscles and bones with magic, too."

Lev held his head in his hands. "Of course. Let me guess: they also shoot beams from their eyes."

"Goodness, no," Vyrga replied, "but their eyes do glow when they store enough energy. Takes three days after death for the glow to go dark."

"Ah, whatever would we do with such useful information?" Lev said sardonically.

"Pray we learn more through further interrogation."

"Not just that. We need to examine the corpses."

Vyrga's eyes gleamed in intrigue. "Inside and out?"

"Wasn't that obvious?"

"I did admire what you did with the hivelings. I look forward to working with you—for this little ceasefire, at least." Vyrga extended his right hand. "I am pleased that our ambitions do not blind us to what really matters."

Lev firmly shook Vyrga's hand with a toothy smile. "As am I."

CHAPTER 21

THE OUTLANDERS

In the days following the battle, the leaders of the frontier managed to calm the citizens and provide shelter for the settlement survivors west of Pàrras. However, some tension still lingered in the air, enough for Eleric to wear a long cloak and baggy clothing whenever he went out.

After all, aside from the long ears, berekes looked awfully similar to humans.

Thankfully, Eleric's skill as steward had proven invaluable to both Lev and the community—or at least had kept the scornful stares to a minimum. Though he continued to take precautions, he now felt safe enough to run errands in the market alleys.

He sat on a newly installed bench near a crossroads leading to the northern district and idly watched the passersby go about their day. He reflected upon how far he had come—from the betrayal of his retainers, to his escape from slavery, to his current position as a well-respected steward in what could only be described as a goblinoid democracy.

Bards and poets would get a kick out of my story, he softly chuckled to himself. *Or maybe they'd be sufficiently amused at this one.*

Eleric had never imagined that these supposedly "barbarian" races from the "wild" lands would come together to revive an ancient city, much less rebuild some of it. Even if their work wasn't quite on par with what Eleric imagined the ruins once looked like.

He took in the local soundscape. The children chattered about games and friendship; the elderly mused about their struggles in the caverns.

His nose twitched. Someone was cooking. Was it an old classic from the cavern days, or was it an experiment to use up the salvaged crop yield? Eleric wished there were more spices used in goblinoid cuisine, but at least he had never fallen sick from eating it, bland as it was.

His merriment didn't last long. *Will I ever return home? Even if by some miracle I return, what would stop those traitors from finishing me off? Could I enlist the bogeys' help to reclaim my birthright?*

Eleric chuckled. *Fat chance that'd happen. More likely, I'd be branded a traitor for conspiring with foreign powers, especially with these so-called undesirables.*

Eleric's brooding was cut short. Approaching him were four greyborns and a green bogey wearing a focus amulet.

He jumped off the bench and was ready to flee when he recognized the leader. "Hey, Bolo. I've been waiting for you."

The approaching greyborn forced a smile and returned his warmth. "Sorry. Had to get changed. After yesterday, I don't think the birdfolk would take kindly to those in guard garb."

"Yesterday? What happened yesterday?"

Bolo nervously scratched his neck. "A brawl between some of the guards and the birdfolk. It happened in the middle of the night."

"Another one? They've been here for a week and there's already been three brawls. Who was in command this time?"

Bolo avoided the second question. "The guards were drunk. Thought our avian friends would make some sort of fun exhibit. Thankfully, nobody died."

Eleric shook his head. "So the guards can't even behave themselves enough not to drink on the job, huh? Why don't you train them like you train your soldiers?"

"That seems excessive," Bolo replied.

"No. What's excessive is the size of your dedicated army. Most nations' armies consist of a small elite force. In times of war, they hire mercenaries and assemble levies from volunteers to supplement that army. And conscripts, if they have to."

"So they throw a bunch of newbies at the enemy?"

"No. The mercenaries train the new recruits."

"Is that how Brizilum does things?"

"Basically, but without conscripts. Many of the volunteers tend to stay even after their term of service is done."

Bolo was briefly speechless. "Why in the world would they do such a thing? We fight not because we want to, but rather because no one else will protect our loved ones. Do these volunteers actually want to risk death day in and day out?"

Eleric silently gestured for Bolo to continue. It didn't take long for Bolo's eyes to widen in realisation.

"Wait. Brizilum is the biggest superpower in its immediate region."

Eleric nodded. "Indeed. Few, if any, dare to challenge the status quo."

Bolo scratched his chin. "Then why stay in the army, idle as it is?"

"Benefits," Eleric revealed with a cheeky grin. "Land. Wealth. Glory in battle. Exceptional soldiers get council seats, and foreigners who excel enough can get citizenship."

Bolo's expression visibly shifted from shock to intrigue. "With morale like that, it sounds like Brizilum might as well have an army of killigs."

Bolo's comparison piqued Eleric's interest. "Killigs? I only know it as the measurement system you goblinoids use."

"The term is derived from powerful sentinels who served Ainshard. It's said they were nearly unstoppable on the battlefield."

"I wouldn't say Brizilum's army is on the level of your folklore." Eleric admitted. "Sure, we learned a thing or two fending off constant barbarian invasions, but our maps are crude at best. We know too little about the western parts of this continent, especially the northwest. Brizilum's currently focusing most of its war effort on dealing with the barbarian tribes in the southwest."

Bolo looked slightly peeved.

Eleric did his best to preserve relations. "Your society has also made admirable progress!" He commended. "Some of your war techniques are peculiar, but effective. I'm no general, but even I can tell the way you dealt with the berekes could be considered a work of—" Eleric paused.

Crap. I reminded him of his brother, he cursed when he noticed the shift in Bolo's mood.

"We do our best. Sadly, it's not enough to save everyone." Bolo sighed. "All we want is to mind our own business with no one over our shoulders. I wish we didn't have to fight for it."

"How naïve," Eleric blurted out. He instinctively took a step back.

Bolo's followers shot Eleric intense glares, but Bolo stopped them with a wave of his hand. "Can't a man dream?" he asked.

"You're right. My apologies." Eleric cleared his throat. "Now, as I was asking earlier, does Lev plan to train the guards the way he's trained the soldiers?"

"Why don't you ask him yourself? You're his steward, you hear everything that comes in and out of his office."

Eleric cleared his throat. "He isn't very talkative after work. I don't know what to expect from him. So please, do tell me."

"Lev had a different idea for the guards. It's... well, it's so insane that none of the other chiefs were willing to entertain it."

"What was his idea?"

Bolo huffed. "He wanted to establish a disciplinary school for guards and future law enforcement personnel."

Eleric tilted his head. "Where's the insanity?"

"The duration of training," Bolo said with a small chuckle. "Two years, paid, for doing nothing but learning."

Eleric's expression turned blank. It took a while before he could form a reply. "Brizilum only trains soldiers for six months. Guards, even less.

All guards do is recite simple laws, stop criminals, and monitor the borders. Two years? What is Lev thinking?"

Bolo shrugged. "You're asking the wrong bogey. Educating the soldiers makes sense. The rest of his ideas baffle me."

"Tell me about it!" Eleric complained. "The moment I started working here, I had to read scroll after scroll about how much saltpetre, limestone, and coal Lev had wasted for his experiments. All to make a powder that does nothing!"

Bolo's companions couldn't help but erupt in laughter. None liked Eleric's insensitivity, but whether Lev's wild projects were successful or not, any steward who had to deal with the associated paperwork deserved some leniency.

"I'm sorry I brought it up," Bolo said. "That must've been a nightmare for you."

Eleric got up, brushed his clothes clean, and faced the others. "I'm just glad it's over. And I might be overstepping here, but cheer up. I'm no bogey priest, but I'm sure your brother is by your war goddess' side. He's likely pissed off that you're moping around."

Bolo let out a listless chuckle. "You might be right. Let's get going."

The six of them went on their way down the northern city road, with Bolo in front and Eleric following closely behind.

A clunking sound drew Eleric's attention. He glanced at the ancient buildings and the shoddy repairs being made. "I wouldn't be surprised if the bird folk aren't enjoying their stay here."

Bolo let out an audible groan. "It's not like we wanted to put them here. The avians will have to make do with what we've got."

Eleric kept his eyes on the buildings. He caught sight of a few startled birds flying out of a frameless window with a bird-masked fellow chasing after them with a stick. "I know. I'm just saying we need to be wary of unrest. With conditions like this, I'd be surprised if there weren't any."

He took a sharp turn, and almost tripped over Bolo. "Why did you stop? I almost fell."

Bolo pointed in front of him. "You were right."

Eleric looked ahead and saw a couple of birdfolk beating each other while nearby guards desperately tried to stop them.

Bolo approached the crowd. Amid the larger scuffle, down on the ground were two large birdfolk swiping at each other with shivs. One wore a mottled blue mask, while the other sported a striped yellow one.

Bolo whistled shrilly and loudly, drawing the crowd's attention and distracting the scuffling birdfolk just enough for the guards to force apart the two opposing factions. The peeved fighters squawked indignantly and incessantly as they were separated from their leaders.

And yet the two giant avians kept swiping furiously at each other.

Bolo slowly advanced towards what remained of the scuffle, keeping his posse close. "That's enough," he declared.

The green bogey, a shaman, translated Bolo's words, but the avians ignored him, still engrossed in their fight.

"Hey. I'm talking to you," Bolo barked, prompting the shaman to translate again, but more loudly.

Nothing happened.

Bolo grabbed his mace and smashed apart a nearby stone post, sending dust and debris hurtling towards the remaining belligerents.

This finally caught the attention of the two birdfolk. The blue-masked one gave him a glance before hesitantly backing away from his rival.

"Thoir sùil ort a 'dèanamh mar a thèid innse dhut mar chù. Nì mi cinnteach gum bàsaich thu mar aon!" the yellow-masked one jeered. He swung his shiv at his opponent's throat.

The blue one leapt back to avoid the attack, but didn't need to. Bolo had grabbed the yellow-masked one's arm mid-swing.

"Don't say I didn't warn you, yellow turd," Bolo grumbled before letting go. He then smashed his mace into the bird-creature's face, knocking it to the ground.

Eleric winced. *Right on the beak. Maybe Bolo needs to get some of that bottled rage out of his system.*

The avian let out a deep, agonising cry as it clutched its fractured yellow mask. Blood leaked from the cracks. It reached for its shiv, but Bolo stepped on its arm.

"Don't even think about it," Bolo said. He kicked his downed opponent in the gut.

Eleric gulped and turned to his companions. "Bolo's pretty efficient, isn't he?"

The shaman said nothing; the oldest of the three greyborns shook his head. "He doesn't often show this side of him much. Sometimes it's easy to forget where he came from."

"Was life in the cavern that rough?" Eleric replied.

The oldest greyborn looked back at him quizzically for a moment. "Oh. Yeah," he said with a laugh, "but it wasn't just the cavern that hardened him."

"I guess. He did lose his brother after all."

The greyborn shook his head. "May Ludger rest in the cycle. But it's not that. It's Vyrga. Bolo is one of his protégés. Vyrga specially trained him to be a leader. A brutal, decisive one at that."

"I-I see."

The old bogey turned back to the skirmish. "So. Be careful whom you call naïve," he quipped.

"Feuch an stad thu! Bheir mi seachad!" the battered avian shrieked. His hands shivered and his chest heaved.

Only then did Bolo let up. "I'd rather not kill you. You get one last chance to comply."

The yellow-masked creature slowly rolled into a grovelling position. "Tapadh leat. Tapadh leat."

Right then, the blue-masked avian grabbed his shiv.

"Cha dìochuimhnich mi gu bràth do amaideas!" he cried, with a spirited lunge at Bolo—only to kiss the bludgeoning end of his mace.

The blue-masked creature staggered. Blood dripped onto the ground from the cracks in his mask. "Dè thachair—" he protested before Bolo's forehead collided with the avain's left temple, shattering his mask. The creature collapsed onto the cobblestone road.

"Same goes for you," Bolo spat. He turned to face the dumbfounded, gawking crowd. "He's alive. Barely. Let's make this the last incident on my watch."

The remaining birdfolk dropped their weapons.

Bolo sighed in relief before ordering the group's shaman to heal the wounded avians. "Eleric, note this event down. As for the others," he looked at his men with determination, "Let's get this shift over with. I want to go home."

Eleric gave a look at the unconscious avian before letting out an audible gulp. *I better watch my words when I'm around him.*

CHAPTER 22

DARG DEALINGS

"Hurry, Thorst. We need to get there early," Ghorza yelled from atop a stairway leading towards the market square. Rays of sunlight graced her silhouette, which in contrast to her small frame, cast an overwhelming shadow over Thorst.

"This wasn't how I had planned to spend our day off," Thorst grumbled. "It's not like the plaza's going to disappear."

"But the good stuff will! I haven't had a fresh mushroom since we left the caverns. We also need to buy some cooking utensils. Now hurry up, you're just a few stairs away," Ghorza urged as she walked further ahead, disappearing from his sight.

Thorst shook his head as he climbed towards the rays of sunlight at the end of the staircase.

Once Thorst conquered the final step, he was met by a sight he'd never thought possible in his cavern days.

Instead of filthy draps of old cloth on top of rotting poles in the market tunnels of the bogey caverns, he saw an explosion of vibrant colours. Ebony poles supported chequered patterns of cloth with royal colours. Instead of tattered clothes, the merchants wore flamboyant costumes reminiscent of the deprecated blue bogey nobility.

There was an impressive assortment of stands, ranging from those marketing exotic wares to those serving everyday commodities. Thorst found Ghorza taking in the sights a few steps ahead of him. Now that the plaza's restorations were finally finished, even a regular like herself was taken aback by its beauty.

Despite all the hardship they'd recently faced, the people had found the time and wherewithal to decorate the market square. Thorst smiled as he imagined that the market square must have looked like this in its Ainshardian heyday.

"Can you believe this used to be a campsite?" Ghorza marvelled.

"No wonder it became the market square. Everyone loves a landmark," Thorst answered when he noticed the massive fountain, which had once been a pile of rubble, at the centre of the plaza. Its marble foundation and intricate design had finally gotten the justice it deserved.

The diversity within the frontier city had brought great strife, but also a much needed diversity of expertise. The fountain couldn't have been restored this close to its Ainshardian glory without the dargs. With them they brought the techniques and wares of the pinkskins. Their wares were one of the major attractions of the market.

What surprised Thorst most about the fountain, however, wasn't its stature. The fountain consisted of three layers, each having a pool of water. Within each body of water stood four bronze statues at an equal distance. Whether the statues were originally half submerged by the water was unknown. The dargs had simply installed them in the same fashion they'd seen in the grand cities of Brizilum.

"I don't remember the fountain having those," Ghorza said as she, too, had noticed the statues. They were mostly obscured by the water, but upon closer inspection, figures of races they'd never seen before popped into existence from behind the continuous streams of water coming from various faucets of different shapes at the bottom of each layer's pool.

"What are those anyway?" Thorst thought aloud but before he had the chance to theorise about them, his market companion had already traded his presence for a mushroom stand close to the fountain.

"You can't be serious!" Thorst let out an obligatory sigh, tightened his grip around his empty bags, and chased towards Ghorza. "I'm going to miss this feeling," he said as the empty cloth bags dangled around his wrists.

It only took Ghorza five minutes in the market to fill one of Thorst's bags halfway.

"Did you really have to buy this many dried mushrooms? Are you planning on eating nothing but mushrooms for the coming week?" Thorst complained as he inspected his now much heavier bag.

"Weeks, Thorst. And I'm not here just for the mushrooms," Ghorza answered cheerily.

"Good. Where do you want to go next then?"

"I've said it and I'll say it again!" a deep voice growled from behind the fountain.

Ghorza and Thorst turned around and were met by a purple and blue figure with scowls plastered on their faces.

"I've paid to reserve this spot for the entire week. Get lost!" a darg shouted at a short blue bogey.

"Paid? Who?" the blue bogey spat. Thorst recognized the look on his face all too well. He'd seen the same condescending visage back in the cavern time and time again. He turned towards Ghorza, whose expression mirrored his.

"Why should you care? So you can bribe them to get the spot for a month, huh?" the darg stepped closer, his frame shadowing the blue bogey.

The bogey's face contorted in anger. He had to look up in order to meet his competitor's eyes. "D-Don't come any closer!"

The darg crossed his arms. "Or what?"

"Or I'll have your fancy stand removed," the blue bogey threatened as he pointed at a nearby guard patrolling the square, proudly sporting a piece of cloth around his upper left arm. "Everyone in the frontier knows what the red eye means. Don't you?"

The darg's determination didn't falter. "Don't make me repeat myself, twerp."

Despite his shaking knees, the blue bogey stayed firm. "I paid Lev's office for this spot. I can either show you the papers again or call one of the guards. Your choice."

Thorst saw a nearby darg accompanied by a bugbear and burga step in between the two. The muscleheads formed a wall in front of the bogey whilst the newcomer darg whispered something into the other darg's ear. After a short discussion, they turned from the blue bogey and began moving their wares away from the fountain.

The bugbear and burga moved their backs towards the bogey and accompanied the dargs back to their tent. They effortlessly lifted large crates of their wares and moved it to less hostile territory. After most had been cleared out, the blue bogey signalled for one of his own bugbears to move his wares to the fountain.

Thorst let out his breath. "Well that was resolved faster than I thought." If the situation had gotten any worse, he would've had to intervene. He was a guard too, after all. He turned to where Ghorza was standing—there was no trace of her.

"Really? Did you buy the last batch of dried mushrooms?"

He heard what could only have been Abelarda's voice bantering away nearby.

This has to be some cruel joke, he cursed. He could feel a shiver running down his arms as he took out another bag just in case. *No need to worry. Hopefully, it won't end like last time we met her in the market. Hope the other two aren't around.*

"That's right, they're with Thorst," Ghorza replied in the distance. "Oh, look who's finally coming!" She waved towards him.

"Can you stay still for one minute, Ghorza?"

"To watch scum fight scum? No thanks, I'd rather buy stuff. We're at a market, Thorst."

"Hey, moss-skin, aren't you going to greet me?" Abelarda asked as she twirled her blonde locks between her index finger and thumb.

"O' Lady Abelarda, I greet thee," Thorst said, forcing a smile.

"Don't forget us!" shouted two girls approaching the trio from behind a poultry stand.

Thorst's heart skipped a beat. "Lore? Reeza? What are you two doing here?" he asked, knowing full well why they were here and what was about to happen.

"Obviously the same thing I'm doing, Thorst," Ghorza reproached. Her frown quickly turned into a smile once she faced the two girls.

"Well, she's a piece of work isn't she," Abelarda said under her breath.

"She sure is." Thorst smiled. "By the way, how's Volker doing?"

"Heck if I know. Fine, I guess? Haven't seen him ever since he left with Lev."

"It's as if he lives with Lev, huh."

"Exactly! He's always following him around like a loyal dog. Gul's death only made it worse. I can't stand to see him like that."

Thorst patted Abelarda's shoulder. "Hey, don't talk about him like that. Sure, Lev's methods are... odd at best, but Volker's grown up a lot."

"Guard boy's right, Abel. Volker's better off than he ever was before," Lore commented.

"I know, but I can't help but worry, Lore. Lev's a target. Volker might be one, too."

"Have some faith in Small-Eyes and his master and let's get a move on," Reeza grumbled. "It's getting crowded here."

"Good idea," Ghorza replied, "I want to buy some pots before the good ones are gone."

"My dad's got you covered, Ghorza," Abelarda replied. "Unlike those cowards sulking in the alleys, he has no problem fighting Hiltrude on the main stage."

"What about the dargs and blues?" Thorst asked, raising an inquisitive brow. "Them and Hiltrude are making life in the city feel like it was in the cavern. Everyone's at each other's throats once again."

Abelarda grinned. "Let's see them try to play their games with us. If they go overboard, they have a lot more people to deal with here than in the cavern."

"Can we get going already!" Reeza growled. Sweat fell down the girl's brows as another horde of excited customers, rushing to buy birdfolk-made masks from a darg, jostled her about.

Abelarda whistled. "Those purple-skinned corpse-eaters act fast. It's only been a few days and they've already baited some avians to work for them."

Thorst nodded. "Dekas told me a darg's tongue is deadlier than a pink-ear's sword, whatever that means. Not that it's our problem."

Reeza pointed at the sun. "At this rate, we'll stay here forever. We've been talking for a while."

Thanks, Reeza, Thorst wanted to say. The weight of his cargo had numbed his arm.

To his and Reeza's relief, it didn't take long for the others to finally start moving.

Relief quickly turned to dismay, at least on Thorst's part. Pots, jars, spices, herbs, vegetables, and meats filled the last of his bags. With the sun at its zenith, he believed his suffering was over at last. Lady fate had another idea on her mind, however.

"I just remembered something. There's a deal we can't miss," Reeza exclaimed.

Please don't, Thorst pleaded in his heart.

Ghorza's eyes lit up with newfound desire. "What is it?"

"Since it's the cold season, a few dargs are selling their stock of thin clothes they got from Brizillum dirt-cheap. Not the best of their stock, but there should still be plenty of quality on the market."

"Then what are we waiting for? Let's march!" Abelarda announced in a whimsical tune. And thus, Thorst's continued anguish was writ.

Thorst had expected the shopping trip to conclude when the last bag was filled. When the time came, though, Ghorza and the others simply bought more bags. Given the weight and how long he'd been carrying them, the net bags were cutting into his skin, straining the muscles in his shoulders and neck.

After shopping for clothes, Ghorza led the group to a furniture merchant. Much to Thorst's relief, he wouldn't need to carry them for her—Ghorza paid extra for the sellers to deliver them. With the extensive shopping spree, however, Ghorza's sack quickly ran out of gold coins and haze. Seeing this, Thorst sighed to himself and offered up his month's pay.

She took me in after all, after my damn house burned down. He acknowledged with a gentle smile. *Lev was right. I should have claimed a house on the outskirts instead of right next to a smithy.* He shook the bad thoughts away and trudged his feet forward to keep up with the girls.

Luckily, by the late hours of dusk, the market had finally died down, and most merchants had packed their wares.

"Are you sure you don't want to go with them?" Thorst asked.

"For the third time, my house is on the same block as Ghorza's," Lore insisted.

Thorst let out a long-winded groan. *All I wanted was to enjoy myself on a day off.*

"Why the long face? Thanks to yours truly, you won't have to deliver Abel and Reeza's stuff to them. I would've helped you out earlier but carts and wagons only really become affordable at night," Ghorza said as she proudly tapped the frame of the moving carriage next to her.

Don't make it seem like you paid for them, Thorst seethed, placing his heavier bags down on the carriage.

Thorst nodded begrudgingly as he looked at the moving vehicle. Suddenly, Abelarda, who'd taken the only available seat, got up wide-eyed and lunged at her luggage. After a few moments of vicious rummaging, she promptly dug up a small blue box.

What is it this time?

"Hey, boogers! Got something for ya!" Abelarda yelled before throwing the box at Thorst.

With a mere flick of his wrist, Thorst caught and opened the blue box. His eyes widened. "Is this—"

"Do you like it?" Ghorza asked with a beaming smile. "I noticed you were looking at this knife earlier when we went by the darg stands, so the girls and I thought to get it for you. See it as a thank you gift."

He unsheathed the knife and observed it in all its glory, from the owl-shaped handle with two small sapphires for eyes, to the gleaming iron blade.

Lore grinned. "Ainshardian relic. Cost a small fortune. Could've cost even more if that merchant had known that it doesn't rust." Lore's chest puffed up with pride. "Poor bastard barely passes as a darg."

"I—I don't know what to say."

Ghorza giggled. "No need to say anything. You deserve it."

He put the knife away and grabbed the two girls' bags from the carriage. "Alright, we're at your stop. Got everything?"

Abelarde let out a yawn. "You bet we do. That was enough fun for one day."

"It's getting dark. Let's take a shortcut," Lore added.

Great. Maybe this day wasn't so bad after all. All that's left now is to get home and offer my captains some complimentary... Thorst stopped dead in his tracks.

"Thorst? What's wrong? Why did you stop?" Ghorza asked.

That's right. I covered transport. "It's... nothing. Let's just go home." *So much for a good day*, he thought to himself before turning into one of Pàrras's many alleyways.

* * *

As dusk became night, the bustle of the city died down. It was the perfect time for rats to roam the streets, and for guards to catch them.

"It's good to see you're back from retirement. The greenhorns will do great under your hands," a middle-aged green bogey cheered. He wore an unkempt uniform of the Pàrras' guards, Unlike Lev's expedition uniforms, the guards wore simple grey tunics, accompanied by armbands sporting Pàrras' blazon.

Kul chuckled. "What can I say? Retirement just wasn't for me."

"Still, wouldn't you be better off with the day shift or an office job in administration? You're not as young as you used to be, Kul."

Kul shook his head. "Lev and Thorst offered me the position of council guard captain. But I've had enough of uptight buffoons and I don't want to be tethered down there." He took a deep breath, sampling the nighttime air, and looked around.

A few stragglers stumbled from pub to pub in the dim light of haze lamps, while others passed beneath the shadows, hoping to not to draw attention to themselves. "This type of work fits me better. It's funny how the more things change, the more they stay the same,"

"Tell me about it. New homes, but the same shitty troublemakers we had from back in the cavern. Except now our gangs are merchant groups and we can arrest blues and goblins. Never thought the day would come."

Kul grinned. "That's a step forward if I've ever seen one."

"Preach to the gods, my friend. Maybe one day we'll have the ability to arrest those infamous pinkskins."

"That might be sooner than you think."

"And what a day it'll be. Anyway, I'll be heading to the market. I got lucky on my shift assignment." The green bogey started on his way. "Happy hunting, Kul."

Kul waved goodbye. "You too."

Once the guard was gone, Kul turned and made his way forward in the opposite direction. His eyes darted around, studying the shadows; his ears twitched at the slightest of sounds.

Either there are no misfits tonight or they're getting good at hiding from me. He shook his head. *Who am I kidding? It's definitely the latter.*

A sudden screech caught his ears. He looked up to find two corpse eaters attacking a crow with large crimson eyes.

It's weird for the damn pests to be hunting something. They're usually content with rubbish and dead husks.

Kul ignored the critters and headed to the warehouse district, which was pretty active at night.

His eyes made out a multitude of banners, flags, and insignias, each signifying which faction owned which warehouse. Most of them belonged to dargs, blues, and Hiltrude's union. A few belonged to independent merchants and craftsmen.

He moved aside to make way for a covered cart bearing the city's emblem.

Likely transferring reminted gold coins. It was a good thing the old owners of this city left much of their wealth behind. Must've left in a hurry or something.

His presence in the district brought with it an array of reactions. Some dargs eyed him suspiciously. A few blues smiled uncannily warmly, handing out coins to artisans who had lined up in front of a warehouse.

I'm sure they're getting a fair cut, he scoffed.

To him, the best reactions came from the deka and the few remaining bugbears and burga. They weren't very talkative, but cared more about the drinks in their hands than the old guard patrolling the area.

Unlike the nights before, there seemed to be no issues—until Kul noticed swift movement out of the corner of his eye. Two hooded figures disappeared into an alleyway leading to one of the entrances to the market square.

Finally some action. Time to earn my living.

He cautiously made his way towards the square, stepping softly to make sure they wouldn't hear him.

That sloppy bastard better be patrolling the market. It'll be a fool's end if I end up facing them off alone.

The figures had slowed down considerably by the time he slipped within earshot.

"C'mon. Hurry. We can't mess up with these wares. Not if we want to leave the Heart of Edorai Inn alive."

So that's where they're heading. Interesting. Close to the square stood an inn owned by a group of dargs with a monopoly on Brizilum imports. There was a rumour about that the group purchased more than just luxury goods from the pinkskins.

They'd better not be trafficking what I think they are.

Had he been ten years younger he'd have followed them further, but the ache in his old bones was a poignant reminder that it would be unwise of him to rush in like a hotblooded youth.

And still no sign of help. Where are the guards?

His wary mind halted its rambling thoughts when he heard the figures move again. He decided to follow them a bit further before heading back to report his findings.

Suddenly, they stopped, presumably to catch their breath. Kul detected specks of a blue powder shimmering in the moonlight. He felt like he'd seen it before, but not in Pàrras.

Night dust. I haven't gone a day without hearing about it. Is this where the chatter came from?.

Kul didn't know of the drug's exact composition, but he had noticed a faint trail of blue specks whenever dargs arrived with hauls from Brizilum. Back when it was legal, it sold out minutes after the market opened every morning. When mixed with water and taken orally, it provided great magical and physical enhancements in short but powerful bursts. After Lev banned the substance, suspecting it to be the same concoction Heimo had taken before going berserk, the dargs simply moved their business underground.

"Ah, took you long enough!" chuckled a familiar voice behind a corner, out of Kul's line of sight. "You bastards sure know how to make me wait."

"Listen, I know I usually ask for twenty coins, but you're gonna have to cough up more now. We've got some... overachieving guards in our midst."

Kul leaned in closer. He saw one of the figures pass a clinking bag of coins around the corner.

Lucky me, witnessing that bastard of a guard in the act.

"The dargs told us our heads will roll if something happens to this load," a hooded figure gruffly said. "Yours, too."

The guard around the corner chuckled hard enough to cough up phlegm before spitting it out. "Do you think I care? Scram!"

The figures soon disappeared out of Kul's sight, into a nearby alley.

Kul had seen enough. *Someone needs to handle this before the situation spirals out of control. You're too busy for this, so it looks like you'll have to owe me one, Lev.*

CHAPTER 23

THE CONTRACT

Lev wished he could relax, but there was still much to be done.

From his patio, he glanced at the small garden behind his house. He had planted medicinal herbs there to further his research of the frontier, but the proliferation of weeds admonished him for his neglect. He resolved to clear the garden later that day and returned indoors.

On the dining table was a black envelope.

A chief trying to blackmail me again? Give me a break, Lev thought. He crumpled the envelope in frustration. *I've been back for barely a week and all I've done is bicker with the other chiefs about the damn berekes. I even shared all the intel we got from the prisoners. Why aren't they happy?*

Lev caught a reflection of himself in the window. Donning an ornate grey tunic that signified his position as a public official, it was almost as if he'd returned to his previous life. *Bureaucracy as usual, I guess.*

He sighed and retired to his bedroom.

His bedroom was quite spartan—a bed, a desk, some closets, and a wardrobe. He didn't need anything more.

"This place is still pretty barebones. Maybe I should decorate it after all," Lev mumbled aloud.

His followers had told him so many times. A few had even scouted out other homes they thought to be more befitting of his status, but he had always refused. Never could he show the mental exhaustion of communing with Gherm or his glaive. He wanted—needed—to be alone, whether it was his tent during an operation or inside his house here in Pàrras.

From his bedroom balcony, he could see every district in the city. The buildings seemed to glow in the light of the setting sun, hinting at the prosperity of the civilization upon which his people had built theirs.

He surveyed the area and studied the choke points and barricades that had been set up under his direction. To him, the view was almost perfect.. The only thing left was to check the additional hidden tunnels he'd ordered to be built. A precaution in case of a successful siege on the city.

He closed the balcony's curtains, turned around, and opened the small door to his bathroom.

Personal bathrooms were a luxury rarely found in the city. Many wondered why such a small place had what many mansions did not. Whatever the reason, Lev found it a blessing.

He decided to prepare for bed after bathing and tackle the bereke issue the next day with a clear mind. With some lethargy in his movements, he undressed and headed to the pump to fill his barrel with water.

A number of creaky, laboured pumps later, the barrel was three-quarters full. Lev dipped a finger into the water, then turned around and walked back to his clothes. He rummaged through his pockets until he felt the edges of his focus amulet.

What a pain, Lev thought. *We need to fix the city's heating system as soon as possible.* If only that orb was still here, we could have used it to power the city's network of runes.

Lev took a deep breath and closed his eyes. The world faded away and not even the dripping pump could distract him. He could only sense one thing: the flow of magical energies throughout the void.

He raised the crystal and willed the wild energies to heed his call and they gladly obliged. They swirled around his hand and formed a furious spiral, from which sparks flickered forth.

Too fast. His brows knitted together in irritation. He slowly lowered the amulet and cancelled the spell. *Why does magic have to be so finicky?*

With another deep breath, Lev tried again. He gently called the energies to gather once more and they did. If the first time was a raging torrent, this time it was a calm stream.

There were no sparks, no crackles, and no fires this time around; only the gentle warmth of dissipating heat upon his hand.

Lev carefully opened his eyes and the flickering waves of heat brought a smile on his lips. *Success.*

With that thought, the energies tried to run amok. With great effort, Lev managed to regain a semblance of control. *One wrong move and I could've burned the house down. How are shamans able to control this?* he wondered.

Once he retained a proper hold over the energies, he slowly approached the barrel.

Gingerly submerging his hand in the water, he felt the icy chill radiate from his fingers up his arm, and the energies once again tried to break free. *Ah, this again?* Lev silently whined. *I hate magic.*

He found it unsettling to feel the hot magic and cold liquid clash and mingle, but it took only a few minutes to heat the water to the perfect temperature: gently steaming.

Lev eagerly grabbed a nearby bucket, dunked it into the water, and dumped the contents over his head. Warmth swiftly yet gently cascaded down his shivering body, dripping into the drain beneath his feet, taking away his sweat and grime with it.

He picked up a block of ash soap. *The dargs taught us that fat and lye make something useful, yet so... ugly. We need to develop a safer and more appealing soap.* Lev wished he, or Gherm, had learned more about soapmaking.

The soap slipped out of his hand, and when he bent down to retrieve it, he lost his footing on the wet floor. *I need a tub,* he seethed.

He opened the drain and reheated the water with a little more effort. Having grasped the soap anew, he scrubbed, lathered, washed, and repeated the cycle until he was satisfied. At last he put on clean clothes and chucked his dirty ones into a chest.

Satisfied and refreshed, Lev stretched his back and groaned. He almost felt like he could deal with the council the next day. *After that*, he thought to Gherm, *how about we visit Ghorza?*

Lev waited for a reply.

Gherm? Lev called again.

There was no reply.

Lev drew a dagger from his pocket and quickly scanned his surroundings. To his relief, his glaive was leaning on a stand near his bed, exactly where he had left it.

He looked out his bedroom window. The locks hung as endearingly open as before, off the frames and rattling in the chilly wind. He'd forgotten to close them. *I was careless. Still, there's no sign of trespassing and everything looks normal*, he thought, *unless—*

Lev felt something like a brush upon the back of his neck. In an instant, he leapt forward, rolled towards the glaive, and threw his dagger upwards.

The dagger bounced off the purple shell of a slender-looking hiveling. With a short series of taps and thuds, the hiveling hopped off the top of the door frame and landed directly in front of Lev, studying him with its compound eyes.

He rushed to grab his glaive with his dominant hand, a horn from his belt with the other, and ran for the balcony. As he connected the horn to his lips, a sticky thread covered his hand and the horn and yanked him onto the floor. The hiveling made a clicking noise that Lev assumed expressed amusement.

"Two can play at that game," Lev spat. He yanked on the thread, jerking the hiveling towards him. With its face within an arm's reach, Lev swung and lodged the blade of his glaive in the hiveling's eyes."

The hiveling, still tethered to Lev by the thread, thrashed about in an attempt to dislodge the glaive. Lev tried to grab something—furniture, ceiling fixtures, whatever would keep him from flying—and managed to grab hold of the glaive's handle.

The hiveling's continuous thrashing finally wiggled the glaive out. Lev was flung foot-first into a wall and heard a snapping noise on impact before he fell back onto the floor.

Lev tried to stand back up, but his foot had gone soft. From a prone position, he pointed his glaive at his purple foe, ignoring the growing, radiating pain from his foot and wondering whether he could safely eke out a fireball despite the short distance.

He suddenly felt the magic in the room gathering around the hiveling's damaged eye.

What the hell? Since when can bugs cast magic! Lev wanted to scream. *Is it healing itself?*

The hiveling began to emit a bright purple glow. A cloud of tiny scales materialised in the air.

As the pain from his foot grew stronger, Lev felt his consciousness slipping. He covered his nose with his free hand but it was too late.

He thought he heard the glaive screaming something like *Master* or *I'm right here*, but whatever it was, he was too weak to respond.

* * *

For a moment, Lev could neither move nor sense anything.

All of that changed when the smell of gunpowder filled the air. His nose wrinkled from the acrid smell. His ears rang each time a shot was fired.

He felt the cold, hard ground again, and his vision slowly returned. He was greeted by a familiar visage from his past life.

A gruff man helped him up his feet and greeted him with a smile. "Welcome back, buddy."

Brutus? Lev silently looked around and found himself in what seemed to be a bunker. He saw Maria, Eric, and some of his old comrades positioned at the windows. They were desperately shooting at what seemed to be a blinding white light encroaching upon the bunker.

Maria threw a grenade out the window. In unison, all of them ducked, opened their mouths, and covered their ears. Lev instinctively followed suit just before a loud bang vibrated through their bodies.

As the ringing subsided, Lev uncupped his ears. "What a great way to start a dream. What's next? War machines? Imperial shocktroopers?"

Maria loaded a new clip into her magazine. "This isn't how I wanted us to meet, either, but someone decided to butt into our reunion. Still, it's good to see you the way I remember you."

Maria's words caught Lev's attention. He looked at his hands, then to the side. As if it'd been created by his mind, a mirror materialised to reflect his form—human.

"Indeed," Lev replied amusedly. "Too bad it's just a dream."

Maria smiled wryly. "Even so, you must be glad to be *adult* height now."

"Of course I am! I can finally go on the big kid rides at the imperial amusement parks again," Lev joked. "Wish you could join me, though. You got banned from them all after your last stunt!"

Brutus joined in. "You mean the time she drank too much and—ogh!" Just before he could finish his sentence, Maria hit him in the guts using her rifle.

"Never mention that again," Maria warned.

"I can agree to that. Anyway, the threat?"

For a brief moment, the white light flickered, and with it, the building rumbled.

Lev didn't waste time being surprised. He grabbed a rifle off of an arisen gun rack and, with deft hands, cleared and disassembled it before reassembling it and performing the mandatory checks. All in thirty seconds.

Upon finishing, he loaded the weapon and turned to his companions. "What's the situation?"

Suddenly, the light shined aggressively, and everyone who had failed to take cover disintegrated.

Maria ran back to her position and began shooting at the light.

"Dire," Brutus answered. His expression was grim as if defeat was inevitable. "It seems we can't hold that thing back much longer."

Lev's expression darkened as he peered out into the piercing light. "The light? Who? What's happening?"

"You'll know," Brutus replied. "Remember. Never lose yourself. Never let them influence you. Never forget your goal—"

The walls around them fell.

Lev glimpsed a hand stretched out from underneath the bloodied rubble. There was a silver ring on the ring finger. *Eric!* Lev wanted to call out.

Above the ruins of the fallen walls stood the white being. Its once-magnificent robes were now tattered, with strips torn to bandage its left arm. On its half-covered face was plastered a deep frown.

"Open fire!" Maria shouted.

The first rounds to hit the being were tracer rounds, followed by thousands of exploding and armour-piercing bullets.

"Your mind is such a pain sometimes," the being hissed.

The rapid torrent of fire further tattered the being's clothes, but barely scratched the shrouded figure beneath.

With every additional hole in its garments, its expression became more menacing. "Let's end this charade, shall we?" it boomed. The being raised its hand.

Maria immediately sought cover. Lev grabbed Brutus and they tumbled behind a column.

With a snap of his finger, the light intensified again. The ceiling disappeared; the walls and pillars shattered. Everyone, and seemingly everything, except Lev, Brutus, and Maria turned to dust.

When the light faded, Lev found himself unscathed. He reached for his gun, but it was gone. Brutus and Maria lay limp on the floor, their bodies riddled with weblike white cracks.

Lev rushed to Brutus' side. "Get up, you big oaf!"

"Thanks for your concern," Maria chimed in, propping herself up by the elbows.

To Lev's—and the being's—surprise, Maria materialised an RPG launcher.

The tube erupted and the missile flew towards the being's face at tremendous speed, slipping through the still-forming barrier. It struck its battered mask and the resulting explosion engulfed the white being in a thick cloud of dust.

A piercing scream shook Lev to his core.

After a deafening eternity, the dust settled. More pieces of the being's mask had fallen off, and a hollow void was visible from the damage to the mask.

The being sped towards Maria.

"Maria!" Lev shouted.

"Serves him right," Maria chuckled. She smiled tenderly at Lev and mouthed a farewell just before the being's left hand squashed her against the ground like a bug.

Brutus stirred. "Don't ever lose yourself..."

The being crushed Brutus with his right hand. The shock from the impact sent Lev flying backwards.

The being then showed Lev both of its palms. There was no sign that Brutus or Maria had ever existed.

The being cupped its right hand. In said hand was what Lev assumed to be a black-haired deka girl with scales instead of skin and two horns instead of one. Her battered form, ridden with violet cracks, materialised from thin air.

The being threw the girl toward Lev. "I believe this toy is yours."

"I'm sorry, master," the girl cried before melting and re-forming into a damaged glaive.

Lev was speechless, but his eyes blazed with murderous rage.

The white being, its mask now fully reformed, floated down to Lev's level. "My dear Lev, we have a contract, don't we?"

It took all of Lev's willpower to control himself. He steeled his expression, but his clenched fists were shaking in anger. "Why are you here? And how?"

"The contract connects us. Though I did need some help to reach you here."

The white being loomed closer until its face was inches from Lev's. "It seems you've been neglecting your part of the deal."

"My part? Hahaha… Hahahaha!" Lev could not conceal his contempt. "As if you've upheld yours. Where's my goddamned power?"

The being frowned. It wrapped its fingers around Lev's battered body and lifted him to eye level. The light behind the mask flickered with increasing intensity as the being's frown deepened. "It seems your barrier is stronger this time."

"Glad you noticed," Lev spat.

The being laughed dryly. "I will ask again. Tell me how long until you free my compatriots."

"And I'll repeat myself. Where's my goddamned power?" Lev replied through clenched teeth.

The being's fist tightened around Lev. "Do not play me for a fool. You have the key! Ainshard's legacy resides within you!"

"Which got me this glaive and a few unlocked doors. Nothing more."

The being's fist loosened. "What are you on about, Leonard?"

"You didn't know? The city's a wreck."

"Impossible... Pàrras' caretakers should have kept it operating. Kram was supposed to—"

"Are Pàrras' caretakers a bunch of robed and masked bird-like creatures that turn to ash when they die?"

The white being was thoroughly shocked. "Those are the servitors, who clean the city and serve its citizens. What about the workers, the operators, the sentries?"

"You mean a hologram that called itself K-35?"

"No. That's the administrator."

"Well, then," Lev scoffed. "We encountered your servitors, I guess. They tried to kill us, which was great. And K-35 was barely responsive even when we met him. When we arrived at the city the second time he was already gone, along with whatever powerful relics that could've helped develop the city."

"Impossible!"

"Your oversight makes it clear how Ainshard's empire fell so easily."

Lev expected an equally snide comeback, but to his surprise, the white being shuddered. Its grip loosened and Lev dropped back to the ground.

He quickly grabbed his damaged glaive, keeping the white being within his sights.

Its mask kept changing expressions from confusion to anger and back until the light emanating from it began to brighten again.

Lev suddenly felt goosebumps all over his body.

Master! Protect yourself! the glaive screamed with the last of its strength.

Lev poured as much energy as he could into a protective bubble right as the white being's energy exploded in a fiery wave.

Kraaaaaam! the being bellowed as it unleashed a tremendous wave of energy, shaking the entire dream world.

Web-like cracks appeared in Lev's barrier. He felt the immense heat spilling in through the cracks.

Thankfully, the wave ended before the bubble broke.

Lev quickly surveyed his surroundings. Deep white fractures had spread across everything in sight, from the pitch-black ground to the now burning sky, but fortunately—or unfortunately—the cracks were not spreading.

The white being was motionless atop the pane of what looked like glass beneath it. Its light was dim and there was a sort of coldness emanating from it.

Lev focused on re-absorbing the barrier just as Orva had taught him. He knew he was contractually barred from killing the being, but wondered whether he could seal it away.

Lev raised his left hand and closed his eyes for a few moments, gathering energy in his palm. He soon felt heavy chains materialising in each of his hands.

"What are you doing?" the white being asked.

His rage renewed, Lev advanced towards the white being.

"Leonard, stop," the white being urged. "You know not what you do."

Lev advanced within a few steps of the white being. Just then, a being in K-35's image the same size as he was appeared between them, blocking his path. The shackles that had formed in Lev's hands promptly disintegrated.

My apologies, Kram intimated, *but I had to stop you before they acted.* Kram pointed to the sky where the clouds had parted. Dozens of monstrous eyes gazed down at Lev, Kram, and the white being.

"W-What are those?" Lev stuttered.

Enforcers, Kram replied. *They care not whether you are under any influence; they simply judge whether you violate the terms of the contract.*

"That contract of yours is a mess!" Lev shouted.

From what I inferred from my brother, I can't deny that. If it makes it better, I can clear things out and answer all of your questions.

Lev paused. *As much as I want to argue about the white being's actions, I won't have a better chance to clear some of my problems.*

"What's influencing me? The key?"

In a sense. After all, the key is a fragment of Ainshard's will. It has been influencing your thoughts and actions ever since you left the cavern.

"Why would it want me to chain the white being? And why did I listen to it?"

Please, call him by his name, Farald. To answer you, Ainshard bears a grudge against my kind. The fragment capitalised on your anger.

"Can't blame him, from what I've seen," Lev grumbled.

Enough. We're short on resources to maintain contact with you. We must leave at once.

"Thanks for all your help," Lev spat.

Kram chuckled. *You're very welcome. We now understand the reason for your delay. Let me do you one last favour.*

Lev suddenly felt energy gathering in his glaive. The cracks began sealing and the chips began re-forming. He saw the same was occurring with the fissures in the world around him. Before he could say any more, an echo reverberated throughout the dreamscape.

Consider this my apology for my brother's actions.

CHAPTER 24

INTERNAL STRIFE

Shortly after the two beings departed, Lev woke up. He rolled to one side, hopped to his feet, and looked around the room in search of his horn. He couldn't find it, nor any of the spares.

Those conniving bastards played me like a fool.

Lev dug around in his pockets, and to his relief, found a short blade in his hidden pocket. Lowering his hips, he stood digitigrade, preparing for a surprise attack.

He urgently scanned every corner of his immediate vicinity, then advanced to examining every corner of his room, knife brandished all the while.

Aside from a few fallen insect scales here and there, Lev found nothing suspicious, physical or magical. Disregarding the scattered furniture, his bedroom looked the same as before. The only ones in the room were himself and his glaive, if she counted.

Lev stood still, but alert, for a few more minutes. He observed no threats.

His ears twitched at a clattering noise. He whirled around to point his knife at the window, and met eyes with a curious crow. Its crimson eyes seemed to stare into Lev's soul.

The bird cawed at him.

He looked back at his glaive. *Can you hear me?*

There was no reply.

No dice with you, huh? Lev thought. *Gherm?*

A wave of panic brushed against his mind. *Lev, are you alright?* Gherm asked. *I haven't heard from you in a while.*

Let me fill you in, Lev replied, giving Gherm access to his latest memories.

By Zeja's missing eye! How did the white being, er, Farald get in? And there were two of them? Weren't they all supposed to be sealed away, Kram included!?

I don't know, Lev conceded. *I'm afraid the contract is a higher priority than I'd expected.*

But the city's still a wreck, Gherm replied. *They can't expect us to free the other guides and spread their gospel without a home base, can they?*

They can't.

Lev felt Gherm's spirits pick up.

But they're still rather impatient.

Lev felt Gherm's panic return.

We were supposed to have help, Gherm sputtered. *They promised us power, we're supposed to have an army at our beck and call. We weren't supposed to have to build one from scratch! They're the ones who aren't delivering!*

Gherm's words earned only a hollow laugh from his companion. *They were careful not to expressly stipulate that in the contract. We're still on the hook.*

But that's not fair.

Gherm. When was life ever fair?

When Gherm failed to respond, Lev decided it was time to check on his glaive again. He tread carefully towards his main weapon and kneeled to pick it up, never lowering his guard for a moment.

Almost instantly on contact, the glaive's thoughts flooded his mind and he exhaled in relief. He had not realised he was holding his breath. As a light chuckle escaped from his mouth, the crow in the window turned tail and flew away. *Look at me, worrying about a weapon like this,* he thought. *Who am I? Brutus?*

Master, there is no entity called Brutus of which I am aware, the glaive responded.

Chipper as always, I see, Lev said.

Better, in fact, the glaive confessed. *Thanks to Kram's donation, there's plenty of magical energy for me to consume. I should be back to fully operational in a matter of days. I've been starving for centuries, and you weren't able to feed me.*

Lev looked sideways in shame. *I know my magic department is rather... lacking.*

His eyebrows shot up. *Wait, Consume?*

Yes. It appears most magical energy is not compatible, but the energy that is, I can consume.

Including Kram's energy? Lev asked.

It seems I am able to consume all the guides' energies, even that of former traitors. Their magical exploits helped produce great weapons like the killigs and myself, after all.

I'd always thought the killigs were a species, Lev replied.

I am sentient, the glaive huffed. *They were not.*

Lev was puzzled. *How were Ainshard's greatest warriors so great, then?*

They were capable of nothing but combat. Once their viscous forms latched onto their prey and moulded it into a worthy form, they ensured that it would do naught but serve the empire and crush Ainshard's enemies. Family or not.

Lev felt a chill up his spine.

That's messed up. Gherm interjected.

But necessary. The glaive countered.

I'm sure there were less disgusting ways. Gherm shot back.

Lev could feel the glaive's rage building, but this time Gherm did not back down.

Such insolence, the glaive spat. *The threats the Empire repelled are beyond the comprehension of a lowly creature such as yourself.*

Let's not lie to ourselves, Gherm responded, *Your people probably found new reasons to wage war even after the threats to the Empire were gone. I'm sure the killigs got plenty of use during the infighting after Ainshard's death. Your leaders were too important to do the fighting themselves, after all.*

You're certainly one to talk, the glaive retorted. *Every time our master is in danger you run away!*

You poor, glorified stick. Lev may be your master, but he is my partner.

Partner! the glaive scoffed. *You can't even lift a finger without the master's permission!*

Gherm hesitated to reply. Lev imagined Gherm was ready to boil over.

Let me reiterate, the glaive continued. *You are no partner. You are even more subservient to our master than I am!*

Lev felt Gherm sever his connection.

Ahahaha! The glaive gloated. *How befitting of such a lowly being—*

Lev cut the merriment short by tightening his grip on the glaive.

Oh, master, why are you so tense? I merely reminded him of his place—

Lev slammed the butt of his glaive on the ground, leaving a dent on the wooden floor. *Shall I remind you of yours? Gherm wasn't wrong about the killigs, was he?*

All of the empire's actions were for the greater good.

Lev's lips curved upwards, but not into a smile. *Greater good, you say? Necessary, you proclaim?*

Why, of course, master. I would insult your intelligence if I were to explain what that meant.

Whose good was it—the people's, the nobles', or Ainshard's alone? Whose good is greater?

Master. Is it not the same greater good you send your men to die for?

I fight for survival, the same as my men do, Lev spat. *For whose survival did Ainshard send the killigs?*

For the Empire's, the glaive replied with a tiny spark of energy across Lev's palm. *An empire that is neither growing nor prospering is on its way to collapse.*

Lev jumped on the opportunity. *And in its reckless quest for growth and prosperity, the Empire exploited slaves, experimented with anything and everything, swallowed up land and resources wherever it could, and ignored corruption and unrest back home.*

The glaive went silent.

Lev sneered. *The killigs were emblematic of a larger decay. I'm almost convinced Ainshard built the Empire intending for it to collapse.*

With all due respect, master, that would be preposterous.

Lev shrugged. *You'd think.*

The glaive hesitated. *Would you kindly elaborate?*

Perhaps at some point during his rule, he realised he'd made an irreparable mistake and wanted to wipe his slate clean.

Preposterous, the glaive replied.

Maybe he didn't want anyone to inherit it, not even his own children.

Preposterous! the glaive replied, more forcefully.

Maybe he discovered that he was being manipulated by the guides and decided to take revenge.

Pre-pos-ter-ous! the glaive enunciated as clearly as it could within Lev's mind. *The guides were benevolent beings supporting the Empire from the shadows.*

Lev's brows wrinkled in disgust. *If those beings are benevolent, I must be a saint. What kind of benevolent being would invade my dream and rough you, its own creation, up? Besides, didn't you call Kram a traitor when we first met?*

Master Kram helped in my recovery! I believe he has seen the error of his ways and seeks to redeem himself.

He just wants to maintain cordial relations with me.

And that results in having his support to help rebuild the empire. I don't see the problem.

Lev looked at the glaive with narrowed eyes. *That doesn't necessarily mean he's good at heart.*

Nor does it mean your interests do not align.

Lev's eye twitched as he listened to the glaive's drivel. *That's just it. We don't know his motives. We don't know when he'll toss us aside after all is said and done according to that accursed contract.*

After a moment of silence, Lev pinched his nose and sighed. *This discussion is over.*

Understood.

Now, Lev continued, *your punishment.*

A moment passed. Lev briefly wondered if the glaive had disconnected from him.

Master, the glaive finally said. *I do not follow.*

Insubordination. I shall seal you for two weeks and only awaken you when necessary. I invite you to contemplate your transgressions against Gherm.

Master, I question your apparent hostility to a simple truth.

Lev grit his teeth. *He is more useful than you realise. For your continued contempt, your detention is extended to a month. Goodbye.*

This is unacceptable! Master, how— Lev cut her connection off.

After taking a moment to embrace the silence, he looked outside. The sun had risen; he needed to oversee the bereke interrogations and join the council meetings afterwards.

"There's no rest for the wicked," he grumbled before heading to the stairs.

But first, Lev thought to Gherm, *let's visit Ghorza.*

Thank you, Gherm replied, having resurfaced.

Of course. Lev paused as he was going down the stairs. *We're partners, after all.*

CHAPTER 25

THE MAD ONE

Far from Pàrras, a distance away from the goblinoids' lands, was an ancient city.

Its formidable walls had withstood countless sieges since its construction, dutifully protecting the pointy-eared people who called it home. Not even the korrigal—the mighty tusked raiders of the north western tribes—could penetrate into the realm of the bereke alliance. All who had dared challenge the walls had failed.

All except one.

The howls of the cold winter wind echoed through the almost-empty streets. The civilians had holed themselves up in their houses on her arrival, leaving only the remaining city guards to greet their new mistress.

Jotul's pointy ears twitched as she entered the city. She was all too familiar by the many titles the people had hoisted upon her: the War Queen, Prophetess of the War God, Bloodbringer, and her least favourite, the Mad One.

As she rode through the gates of the city with her entourage, the trotting of her ram-like steed struck fear into the guards around her. Of all those who had annoyed her, none remained uneaten by the gigantic beast.

Jotul felt her steed tense under her, and its gait became strained. She petted the creature and spoke softly to it. "There, there, Enok. Don't let them bother you."

Her sharp eyes took in the sights of the city. *Briecka, the first major city I conquered*, she mused. *That old goat said this was the… fifth time I've been here? Twice as a princess, once as a fugitive, once as a conqueror, and now—*

She closed her eyes and inhaled deeply.

—its ruler.

To Jotul, the sweet smell of victory was as intoxicating as ever.

"What is it, sister?" a loud, guttural voice asked.

"Nothing, Vres," Jotul replied as she dismounted the beast. She kept her sights on the city, not giving a look at the large, one-eyed korrigal. "I'm just basking in the glow of having done the impossible."

The one-eyed warrior crossed his arms. "You know I hate it when you don't use my full name."

Another korrigal, with only one tusk, began to laugh. "Why in the name of Drav would she be formal with you? You're her brother, Vres."

"Shut up, Baldem. Siblings or not, you should address me correctly as well. Is it that hard to say 'Vreskiven'?"

"Honestly?" Baldem replied. "Yeah."

Vres gasped. "Oh, I'm so sorry, my dear Baldem."

"About what?" Baldem warily asked.

"I forgot not all of us were blessed with intelligence."

Baldem clenched his jaw. "You wanna fight, Vres?"

Vres grinned. "Your remaining tusk looks lonely. Don't make me finish what Father started."

"So does your single eye. Uncle should have taken them both."

Jotul chuckled. "Later, you two. We have work to do."

The two korrigal groaned.

"Come on, Jotul," Vres pleaded. "Let's have a little fun. Just like the old days."

Jotul twirled her hair. "Hmmm. A little bloodshed never hurt anyone."

Baldem smiled. "Yeah. Let's blow off some steam once this is over."

"Once this is over? Our path of conquest is progressing smoothly and the Coalition has their hands full with the rest of our forces. I thought you'd be itching to finally take my last eye," Vres commented.

"I would if there weren't more pressing matters."

Vres took a step back and exaggeratedly gasped. "What? What have you done with my brother? That mangy bastard would never turn down a fight."

"You better practise your comedy, brother, for it won't be long before I rip your remaining eye out. If you want to know why, then stop falling asleep during meetings and go ask our sister's new dog."

"Baldem," Jotul retorted, "I think you should address Vilde properly. She's proven herself very useful."

Baldem snickered. "Whatever you say."

"Baldem," Jotul repeated, "if you weren't my brother, you'd be among *them*." She pointed upwards.

Her brothers followed her finger. Up on the roofs were skewered corpses, stewing in the sun with varying degrees of maggot infestation. Some of the corpses had black veins against their pale skin; others looked in every direction with decomposed eyeballs hanging from their peeling faces.

Two crows fought over an eyeball, only for it to fall near Vres, who slunk away and groaned in disgust. "Jotul. Who's in charge here again?"

"Vilde." Jotul picked at her nails.

"Of course. Her aesthetic is unmistakable."

"What aesthetic?" Jotul scoffed. "I told her to send two simple messages: don't cross us, and if you do—"

Another eyeball fell and bounced off of Vres' shoulder. He shuddered.

"—don't let us catch you."

"Some of the dead are so small that they must have been children," Vres observed with pity. "Does Vilde not know our people's teachings?"

"You know my race can live for up to two hundred years, right? The youngest of those children is thirty years old. They're older than you."

"I'd forgotten you're as old as our father," Baldem quipped.

Jotul rolled her eyes.

"Yet you acknowledge that they're still kids," Vres shot back.

Jotul halted her steed. "I clawed my way up from nothing. By their age, I was strong."

Vres shook his head. "You're different from them, Jotul."

"Yes, I would say so. I won back my birthright, and made the whoresons who backstabbed my family pay—in blood. It's just a pity we couldn't kill all of them in one go."

"I know. You think these pale city kids have ever touched a weapon?"

Jotul raised her head. One look at the hanged children was all it took for her to scowl. "They could have accomplished so much more. They started with safety. Training grounds. Full bellies. A roof over their heads."

"That's precisely why. They've never needed to fight. For what crime did you punish them? Not being strong enough for you?"

"To them, you're not the betrayed daughter of the previous high lord, but an invader who arrived with an army of Korrigals and supposed deserters to destroy their way of life!" Vres argued.

"Admit it, sister. This is a bit much," Baldem urged to no avail. All of their nagging was grating on Jotul's nerves.

"And you two call yourselves children of the sky-horde. Stay this soft and you'll be slaves in your next lives." Jotul reprimanded the two.

"That's rich, coming from someone who worships the blood-seeker," Baldem countered.

"Recently, every time you've come back from battle," he said with increasing hesitation, "you've changed."

"In a good way, it seems. More people continue to join our cause, dedicating the scant remainder of their lives to our god. If it wasn't for him, we wouldn't have had the numbers to punish the Coalition. Even those outside of our group began fighting for his cause once they embraced the gospel."

The korrigal brothers exchanged looks. "That's not because of the blood-lord. They're trying to emulate you." Vres countered.

"You mean beating back the traitors around here, or taking back the lands from the Coalition?"

"Both!" the brothers replied in unison.

"Those were no more than chores with the blood-lord's power. Nothing more."

Baldem's couldn't help but laugh. "It's just funny how you give that god of yours so much credit."

"Funny or not," Jotul replied. "it cannot be denied that our advance would be far slower without the blood-lord's power."

Vres would have no more of it. "You inspire those around you. You fight to win. And most importantly, while it is affecting you, you still retain your identity even after repeatedly using that accursed power. That's proof that not even the gods themselves could take you down." He locked his remaining eye with Jotul's. "Give yourself some credit."

He maintained eye contact with Jotul, only satisfied when he saw a smile creep its way onto her lips.

"You know what, Vres? You're right. I clawed my way here, after all."

"Not everyone is so deserving of credit, though." Vres gestured with disdain at the corpses. "Your blood-lord made a mistake with her."

"She was broken when we found her," Jotul whispered, just loud enough for her brothers to catch on.

Vres nodded. "I know. Why keep her?"

Jotul spoke through clenched teeth. "Do not make me repeat myself. I owe Vilde far more than you can imagine. We wouldn't be here if she hadn't held back the Coalition's pawns when I was a child. She allowed me to escape their purge."

Baldem exaggeratedly stretched, subtly signalling to Vres to drop the subject. "You will, you will. This ruling stuff is boring. Let's hurry up and get back to the battlefield. Vres, what's our count right now?"

Vres rubbed his forehead. "Twelve cities, two more under siege. Are you going senile on me?"

"How I wish I went senile so I could forget your ugly face," Baldem jeered.

"If I'm ugly, you're a hideous marsh-dweller."

"Your father's a marsh-dweller!"

"He's your father as well, dimwit!"

At last their bickering achieved its intended result: a chuckle escaped from Jotul. She quickly righted herself. "Cut it out, you two. We've got work to do."

"Tch," Baldem spat. "We wouldn't have so much to do if that sneaky bastard had kept his head down and done his damn job."

"I knew he was a rat," Vres told Jotul. "I told you not to trust him."

"What do you mean?" Jotul replied mischievously. "He did his job properly."

"What?" her two korrigal brothers simultaneously turned to her in shock.

Jotul grinned. "Think about it. Why would he betray me?"

"Because he's a two-faced rodent that'd sell his mother for a few coins? I think that's enough to explain his actions," Vres answered.

"Which the Coalition would take into account, especially with his significance. Lachas and his men were among our first recruits. His silver tongue has aided greatly in helping us gather more soldiers for our cause," Jotul responded.

"Silver tongue?" Baldem chortled. "Guy was all talk and no action. I'll ask again. Knowing his character and that the Coalition would recruit him, why'd you give that conniving bastard a job?"

"Because I ordered him to betray me. Who would be better suited for executing the Coalition's rats?"

She grinned at their dumfounded expressions. "Don't be so surprised, especially when you said it yourself, Baldem. Lachas was all talk, and he was good at it. What better option was there than to have him betray me, hand Briecka over to the Coalition, request reinforcements, then lure the Coalition's soldiers and those false allies to their deaths at the hands of an unknown goblinoid threat?

"Thanks to him, Briecka was cleansed of most of its traitorous defenders and we now know more about the goblinoids in the west."

"Huh, I guess I misjudged him," Vres bashfully admitted to Jotul's amusement.

She shook her head. "You didn't. He was playing loyal for the benefits. He surely had countermeasures in case the war turned to the Coalition's favour."

Hearing that, Baldem couldn't help but laugh. "A rat will always be a rat!"

"Indeed. That's why I didn't warn him when I sent him to test the goblinoids. I only told him that there was a threat in the west and he should use the Coalition's pigs to invade the city instead of wasting our men. He likely died with the rest of his ilk, if he wasn't captured. I'll need to check later."

"Smart thinking, sister," Baldem praised.

Vres proudly rubbed his nose. "You see? This proves my earlier point. With brains like yours, you don't need the help of any gods. Are you looking for another rat to use against the Coalition?"

"We already have one," Jotul answered.

"Who?"

"Me," a raspy voice replied. A bereke woman emerged from a nearby alleyway. Her greying hair lay in short, spiky strands above the mask covering her mouth. "I'm used to smoking out rats. Been doing it since the old kingdom days."

The moment he saw her, Vres' smile turned into a sneer. "Vilde. I'd say I'm happy to see you, but I'm not known for being a liar."

Vilde eyed him as she took off her mask. "Indeed, my dear Vreskiven. Instead, you are known for being a stubborn heretic who would sooner gouge his remaining eye out than believe what is right in front of him."

Vres took great pains not to react. He wanted to pile the corpses in front of Vilde and excise her eyelids to remind her what lunacy this religion represented—but all he permitted himself was to bite his lip until it bled.

Vilde noticed Vres struggling. "No one is telling you to worship the blood-lord who so generously blessed your dear sister."

"Yes," Baldem cut in, "the same god who corrupted your mind and is now trying to corrupt Jotul's with his *blessings*. If only our father had found Jotul sooner, perhaps she could have escaped the reaches of your mad god."

"Instead of gods, you korrigal have... what? Spirits in the sky, destined to fight shadowy demons until they're reborn. What have your little dust motes done for you?"

"That's enough, Vilde," Jotul warned. "We didn't come all the way here to muse about religion."

Vilde's expression visibly softened from the moment Jotul spoke. "My sincerest apologies. I wished to inform you that the plan worked. Lachas and the rest of the rodents were wiped out by the goblinoids."

"Perfect."

Vilde laughed. "I can't believe we finally sent that false believer to his death."

Jotul smiled. "Not only that, his death brought us many benefits. Such as our conquest of this city. Only a few of Lachas's dregs and its guardians remained."

"All we need to do is wipe out the Coalition's reinforcements before they realise what happened here." Vile said with an evil grin.

"Remind me, how large are their forces?" Jotul asked.

Vilde handed her a piece of parchment. "From what my spies could infer, they're negligible. Their forces are incredibly, woefully unprepared. Enough to support Briecka in case of a siege, but not enough to pose a threat. It won't be hard to intercept them."

A savage grin worked its way to Jotul's face, matching that of Vilde's. "Wonderful. WIth this we'll have dealt a severe blow to the Coalition's forces. Perfect timing as well. We could use the exercise."

Baldem beamed. "So we're going to battle? That's great!"

The miasma intensified. Vilde donned her mask again and mentally noted to burn whatever remained of the surrounding corpses.

The four of them proceeded towards the city's castle, with their men following them from behind and their strange red-eyed birds accompanying them from above.

One of the birds, a falcon, landed on Jotul's shoulder. Jotul stopped in her tracks and lovingly scratched the bird under its beak. "What do you have for me, little one?" She placed a finger on its forehead; her eyes glowed as red as the bird's.

She felt the blood-lord's power pulling her away as her vision and surroundings were replaced with another. Instead of the lifeless streets of Briecka, she found herself on a support beam, looking down at a hall filled with quarrelling goblinoids.

Just then, a short grey goblinoid opened the hall's doors and boldly marched inside. The commotion instantly fell silent, as though the short one's mere presence had pinched out a flame.

Something inside her mind told her that if left to his own devices, the short grey one would become a threat. *But that'll never happen,* she concluded. *Once we deal with the traitors and their masters, it'll be your turn. There will never be a second Ainshard.*

Ainshard? Jotul's eyes flickered for a few seconds before she regained her composure.

If not for the longevity of her race, Ainshard would be but a legend. But Jotul knew better. The elders of the bereke race had warned—no, drilled his history into everyone's mind since childhood.

It's as if the wretched emperor's will is emanating from him—as if he's bound to it.

Surprisingly, the goblinoid turned his head towards her. As she stared into his eyes, a chill went down Jotul's spine. Behind the goblinoid's golden pupils, she could make out a faint pattern of blue-ish runes flowing around in a circular pattern.

Did he willingly accept Ainshard's influence? Jotul hungered to know.

From the edge of her vision emerged a white glow; from the other side came a purple one.

You've overstayed your welcome, a deep voice echoed throughout her mind. An immense wave of white energy engulfed her surroundings and scattered her thoughts, forcing her consciousness back to her true location.

As Jotul lost her concentration, a jolt of pain attacked her head. The pain was so great that her vision blurred. She shut her eyes and tightly grabbed her forehead trying to alleviate the pain.

"Jotul!" Baldem yelled as he rushed to her side. He caught her before she could fall and gently held her in his arms.

"What happened? Are you alright?" Vres exclaimed.

Jotul's grip loosened. She gently massaged her head until the pain subsided. "I'm alright. Give me a moment."

"What did you see?" Vilde inquired.

Baldem faced Vilde and let out a menacing growl. "She was in pain and this is the first thing you ask?!"

"It's fine, Baldem," Jotul assured. "She's right to be inquisitive. Without that vision, we'd be blind to a greater threat. The goblins in that ruined city have the potential to wield an ancient power once thought extinct."

Jotul blinked and re-oriented herself. The castle at the centre of Briecka lay a short distance away on an elevated plateau accessible by a lengthy staircase. She gestured to the castle. "I'll explain in there."

Not wasting a moment, she started ascending the staircase. The others soon followed.

I don't know who you are or what the beings guarding you were, Jotul quietly vowed, *but once I've dealt with the Coalition's forces, it'll be that Ainshardian slave's turn.*

With their departure, silence returned to the streets. Even when her guards had long left, none of the citizens dared to go outside. They could sense it.

War was on the horizon.

CHAPTER 26

CHAMPIONS

Inside a ruined temple, nestled within Sinner's Reach, stood a white-masked being and a purple hiveling. The insect's shining eyes were fixed on a large black orb.

"I'm beginning to doubt your current incarnation still retains your intelligence, Kram," Farald grumbled.

With a wave of the purple hiveling's antenna, the surface of the orb turned translucent.

"Seems you're still upset about our little game."

Rows of hiveling carcasses lay lifeless against the ruins. "Your little game has killed off our deterrent."

"I disagree." Kram glanced at the frostbitten hivelings. "There are plenty of eggs in the cavern and they still have a role to play."

When Lev escaped with the exodus group, the hivelings near the shrine's entrance had stopped moving. Having lost their only purpose—luring the goblinoids to the frontier—their connection with the manipulated queen was cut, leaving them lost in the mountains.

With no pheromones or instructions to find their way back home, they had been left to wither in the frigid weather of the mountain range, their exoskeletons frozen until not a single one remained. All that was left now of the hivelings that'd chased after the goblinoids were the corpses of the few scouts that had managed to sense their aura and follow them to this place. An undiscovered temple with an active shrine.

"As long as the queen is still under my influence, I can keep curious eyes away from the caverns," Kram said.

"As unorthodox your plan is, I understand its purpose in furthering our goals. It did lead the goblinoids to the city. But that doesn't excuse how you had me play the part of a short-sighted fool," Farald criticised. The aura surrounding the temple tensed. "And for what? Antagonising our future prodigy?"

The hiveling simply kept its focus on the orb, as if pondering something. "No. Lev needed a kick to keep him on his feet, Farald. He also likely figured out it was a ruse," Kram finally declared, hoping to ease the white being's temper.

As Farald's aura intensified to envelop more and more of the site, it suddenly halted. After a few moments, the subtle red hue surrounding Farald subsided and opted for a gentle blue.

If the hiveling Kram possessed were able to showcase emotions, an understanding smile would've accompanied this change in Farald's temper.

Farald's mask, which previously had no discernible features except for two holes serving as its eyes, briefly flashed a malicious grin. "Regardless, we've got them right where we want them. In your cradle of malice—your city of *progress*."

The gentle blue hue was swiftly conquered by a deep crimson. "Even if our plans show signs of weakness," the being continued.

The aura seeped into a scout's carcass. Its once lifeless eyes now flickered crimson.

"Even if our prodigy decides to betray us."

The reanimated scout's exoskeleton slowly crumbled as Farald's aura burnt it like paper.

"In the end, it doesn't matter if he grows suspicious," Kram answered. "He's surrounded by hostile nations who've sensed change in that once-forgotten city of mine."

The scout's exoskeleton was almost fully dissipated into the air.

"And I'm sure he'll be too busy handling them to worry about us, especially if we provide a push in the right direction," Kram continued.

Only ashes laid where the scout once did.

A disembodied chuckle filled the temple site. "You're finally making sense again. Knowing you, I'm sure you've prepared countermeasures?"

Farald's aura intensified even further; Kram's host clacked its mandibles. "Kindly avoid wasting more of my specimens. Even in death, they still have their uses."

"And of course I have," Kram continued. "but I'm still wary. Lev was surely suspicious of us from the very beginning. Your contract might have bought you some insurance with him, but that isn't real trust."

Farald's eyes glimmered. "It was a desperate move for both parties."

"A foolhardy one. If enough of our brethren are freed, the enforcers might offer Lev the opportunity to renege on the contract," Kram muttered.

Farald's mask flashed again, this time flickering between different variants of laughter. "They would, wouldn't they?"

The mask abruptly returned to its neutral look. "If that happens, we'll have to find another way to sway the outsider to our side."

"I hope so." Kram grumbled. "If our compatriots' ignorance topples our budding empire like last time, we can still rebuild it as long as we have Lev."

"Remember that if the contract fails, Lev's existence might become an issue. We'll be walking a fine line. After all, Lev isn't Ainshard," Farald warned.

"Difficult as it may be, I doubt he'd deny my help," Kram responded. "He's intelligent enough to understand that all I want is for him and his people to prosper."

Farald paused for a moment, waiting for Kram to continue. Upon seeing that Kram had resumed his task, he spoke up. "How benevolent of you to care so much for the goblinoids. I advise you limit the 'benign saviour' act, lest you isolate yourself again."

"Where's the fun in that? Life is like a soup, you need spices to complement its flavour," Kram chided as the orb began to glow.

"Don't overdo it, Kram." Farald argued back. "Lest your hubris affect our wanted results."

The hiveling gave a slight nod. "You have a point."

Placing its front legs on the orb, the hiveling's body glowed a soft purple. The translucent ball harvested Kram's energies and gradually turned red.

Once the orb's surface became completely red, the glowing hiveling knelt down; a purple beam escaped from its body and entered the orb.

"We can only hope our negotiations bear good results," Kram's voice echoed out as his insectoid vessel lost its glow and turned silent.

Without uttering a reply, Farald placed a hand atop the orb and vanished.

* * *

A crimson-caped figure clad in golden armour sat on a throne inside a cloudy red void.

He was known by many names. The Blood Lord, Bringer of War, Father of Warriors, and his favourite title, The Crimson One.

A hazy, red mist swirled around the being and the surrounding space. From the void, occasional flashes of lightning struck near the figure, who remained unperturbed.

From his eagle-like mask, two glowing red orbs fixated upon a cluster of small pools in the centre of the void. Each pool displayed a different scene.

His interests were situated in the two pools closest to his feet. One showed Jotul at the front of her army. The other showed a house within an ancient city; a grey goblinoid stood upon its balcony, gazing into the distance.

For a second, the mist stilled. The crimson figure raised his head and turned his gaze towards his left.

With a wave of his hand, the mist dispersed, revealing two masked beings.

"Seems the two of you have been busy," he uttered to Farald and Kram before turning his sight to the pool with the grey goblinoid. "Your visit is a detrimental effort, if you ask me. I know why you came and I don't want to take part in it. Outsiders cause nothing but trouble."

"Have you forgotten that they're not the only ones who don't belong to this world, Egon? Surely the local powers have ensured our understanding of that," Farald pointed out.

"We were sealed not because of our origins, but because of our actions. We were far too rash when we allowed Ainshard to utilize our power," Egon remarked.

He pointed at a pool displaying the council hall in the frontier. "To fulfil our ambitions, we disrupted the natural evolution of civilizations and challenged the local powers before properly planting our roots. I do not wish to repeat such failures."

"There will be no repeat," Kram comforted Egon. "We'd be fools to allow that to happen again."

"Then why have you chosen an outsider as your champion?" Egon asked.

"As opposed to a local?" Farald snorted. "You know as well as I what happens every time we choose someone from this world. Their minds fall prey to our influence. Their grip on sanity weakens until all we have at our disposal are berserk madmen wielding our power and a perversion of our ideologies."

Kram nodded in agreement. "Only the strongest of souls can properly wield our gifts. And no souls are stronger than those who survived the journey between worlds."

He pointed to one of Egon's pools, within which stood a desecrated statue of a bereke wearing a crown. On his epitaph was written, *In this cursed soil dwells the corpse of Havard the Mad. In his desire for bloodshed, the cultist king brought ruin upon the lands.*

"And judging by their records, all of your local champions became tyrants and berserkers. Seems you're doing a wonderful job by yourself," Kram remarked.

Though Egon couldn't see Kram's expression, he knew all too well where this conversation was headed. "Mocking me again? Don't you have anything better to do, Kram the Wise?"

"Depends on your choice. Your support would greatly expedite our plans. Be reasonable, Egon. You've continuously tried your approach and failed each time. What do you call someone who repeats his failures?" Kram asked with a chuckle.

"Why don't we place a bet? Our new champions are about to collide."

The reflections in the pools zoomed in on Jotul and the grey goblinoid respectively.

"As always, you can't help but make things unnecessarily difficult," Kram grumbled.

"I'm merely testing which one of us is right." Egon pointed at the pool showing the goblinoid. "You, who chose to put his hopes on another failure who'll likely lose his drive and indulge in his low-hanging fruits."

He waved his hands towards the pool showing Jotul. "Or I—"

"The father of all failures?" Kram chided.

Egon growled. "I, who chose a champion who understands the woes of this world and is destined to build a blossoming empire that will withstand the tides of time."

Kram shook his head. "You stubborn fool. We haven't chosen another Ainshard. I can only hope you won't regret your actions once the dust settles."

"Don't forget that Ainshard, too, was an outsider. Even if this Lev of yours is as great as you claim, Jotul is my champion for a reason. Even a berserker can kill a demon if her madness is strong enough."

"And even a lowly greyborn, a race stemming from a lost age, can reveal his worth and rise to eternal glory," Farald added.

"Only time will tell," Kram concluded as he turned his back to both Egon and Farald. "I must withdraw for now. Pressing matters are begging for my attention."

Kram's goggles reflected a bolt of lightning striking the ground in front of him. "Let the contest between heirs begin."

BONUS CHAPTER 1

INTO THE LION'S DEN

He couldn't—wouldn't—believe that buildings like the one he stood in front of were to be used only once a year. A grand banquet hall designed and built for the upper echelon of the Empire, it served as a safe haven for the most powerful class to gather and socialise. From careless banter to the latest military tech, there was a topic to discuss for every subgroup within the imperial hierarchy.

"Lev, I'm glad you made it in time."

Lev let out an audible gulp as he recognized the woman's voice. It had changed, but he could still recognize the girl he'd played, laughed, and cried with for half his life in the slums.

Maria.

She was dressed in full regalia. Her white robe looked stiff and expensive, yet beautiful. Her dress code, or rather, the imperial code, was a strange mix of the noble and military class. Even though her bottom half suggested that she was attending a wedding, her upper half showed her medals proudly pinned on her chest, as if she were attending one of those veteran reunions back in Eurasia.

Lev tucked in his modest shirt, one he'd gotten from Brutus back in the hideout, and stepped straight ahead towards Maria.

"Maria, I—" Lev wanted to say, but got interrupted by a servant droid bumping into him. Its cold eyes stared at Lev for a few fleeting seconds as it recalculated the trajectory to the nearest kitchen.

Lev took a few steps back, but just as he opened his mouth, Maria stepped in.

"Looks like this one needs a reboot. Kitchen is the other way."

The droid looked at her, presumably scanning her to identify her rank, and bowed deeply.

"Maria Von Mitternacht, welcome to the Imperial Lion Estate, home to one of the finest banquets the Empire can offer."

The droid then reversed its wheels and disappeared inside the giant mansion.

"Isn't this a bit too much?"

"It's just a servant-class droid. Can't believe they're still being used in such a prestigious place like this," Maria said before glancing at Lev.

She saw an expression on his face she'd never seen before, one of sheer surprise. Seeing this, she cleared her throat and dropped her noble charade. "Sorry, I guess I'm too used to this by now."

Lev smiled, signalling to Maria everything was still fine between them.

Lev pointed at the mansion. "I meant the giant palace. Is this really meant to host a mere fifty nobles?"

The mansion, or as Lev had put it, palace, was about eight thousand square feet. It had two grand oak doors with a mix of human and elite droid guards in front of it.

"Let's go, or we'll be late." Maria took Lev's hand and led them to the entrance hall, past the doors. Just as they were entering the hall, a security droid placed his arm right in front of Lev.

"Verifying identity..."

Damn you, Maik. You'd better have fixed that ID.

"Officer Moritz Antonius Bluthund, ex-spec ops," the droid stated as it lifted its mechanical joints, allowing both of them to enter.

Ex-spec ops? I guess that means Maik retired Moritz. I'm glad he did.

Lev briefly looked back at the droid, it was equipped with a bulletproof exoskeleton and a plasma rifle.

If the ID had been faulty, I wouldn't have stood a chance against such firepower.

He looked back at Maria. She hadn't let go of her vice-like grip on Lev's hand when the droid blocked them. He'd felt her heart skip a beat when they successfully passed through. It reminded him of old times, like when they'd run across police patrols as kids during curfew.

She's still in there. I'm glad.

The hall was lit by a beautiful cluster of silver chandeliers, with a red and white patterned carpet leading towards the dining hall. It'd been cold and silent outside, but upon entering the building, the beaming upper life of nobility instantly violated his being.

Just the expensive clothing of the surrounding nobles and the entrance hall's size would be more than enough to humble even an Eurasian council member.

"Where are the tables and chairs?" Lev asked, looking about.

Maria showed a grin, almost carrying Lev away to the past. He'd seen her with the same expression time after time as they pulled off stunts in the slums. Whether it be stealing old beggar Joel's beer or ration coupons, seeing her grin had made it all the better.

A waiter, surprisingly a human one, offered both Lev and Maria a drink as they waited for the host to announce the start of the banquet.

Once the waiter was gone and the coast seemed clear, Lev leaned close to his old friend.

"Maria, about your messages. We received them and successfully decrypted them back in Neue Berlin. Is this banquet really as important as you—"

Maria's warm eyes turned sharp as she bumped her drink against Lev, spilling it. "Look at what you did, silly. You're saying funny stuff."

Besides a few glances from bystanders and the buzzing of a cleaner droid zooming by to cleanse the expensive carpet, nothing seemed out of the ordinary.

Right. Not the time or place to talk about this.

As if swapping masks, Maria's expression quickly returned to its previous form. With pouted lips she grabbed another drink and joined Lev shortly after.

"I can't wait to taste the exotic menu," she said as she took a sip from her wine.

"Exotic?"

"As in foreign, Moritz," Maria said as she rolled her eyes.

She's too good at this. No wonder she managed to slither up their ranks.

"Oh, right," Lev replied as he took another sip from his glass.

As Lev tried to imagine the strange foods he was about to eat, Maria emptied her glass. A droid immediately rolled by to collect it, placing it with the others on the metal tray that had been integrated into its design.

"There's something you should know before the banquet starts, Moritz."

Lev lowered his half-empty glass. "You're gonna tell me which assets are important to the mission, and which aren't?"

Maria chuckled, "Don't be so cold. They're still humans. Is that what they call important people back home these days? Assets?"

"You see Moritz, there's a way of conduct in the higher circles of the Imperial court. Without the proper etiquette in place, they'll see right through you," Maria said as she grabbed a new glass filled with a strange orange substance.

"Let's start with the people that matter here," Maria looked into Lev's eyes before turning towards the back of the entrance hall, near the banquet's entrance.

"That man right there is our ticket to the Emperor's private sphere. His name is Lucian, from the house of Ruxgan, he's one of the dukes enforcing the emperor's wishes in the capital," Lev took a brief glance at Lucian. He was modestly dressed for a noble, a simple black vest with an eagle emblem pinned onto it.

"You see that? That's the imperial eagle, also known as the court eagle."

Lev gave a puzzled look at Maria. "Are they the emperor's right hand or something close to that?"

"No, they're not. The Imperial court has two levels. The lowest one, the emperor's eyes, simply enforces the wishes of the Emperor and the laws of the Empire upon its citizens."

Maria took a shrimp from a nearby platter filled with seafood. "They're powerful, yet fragile when higher powers are in play."

She crushed the shrimp's exoskeleton, extracting its tender flesh underneath it. "But in reality, they don't have the power to change anything, much like this shrimp. Its shell may be strong enough to hunt worms, but outside of its habitat, it's merely food to those above in the food chain," she said before eating the shrimp.

"So the right hand is the second level, I presume?" Lev replied.

"That's correct, they're the ones influencing the Emperor's wishes, indirectly creating their own laws."

Lev's eyes turned sharp. "So the emperor's wishes can be dictated as long as you get close enough?"

"Yes. Which is why we need to get in touch with one of them at this banquet. Our ticket to an audience with one of them is Lucian Ruxgan."

"I must ask. Why him?"

Maria hid her laugh behind her glass. "Moritz, look at the poor bastard. He doesn't even have the funds to get a proper dress for this venue."

She's right, I did find that odd. Most nobles here are dressed in hand crafted dresses and formal shirts.

"The Ruxgan family has been in the Imperial court for many generations, but that's about to come to an end, it's all thanks to supporting the wrong heir during the last imperial feud."

Lev rubbed his chin. Multiple calculations ran through his head but in the end his response was a mere shrug. "I don't get it. If they're going to collapse, why are they our target?"

"It's simple. Though they lost most of their profits, the family managed to retain their title but that won't last long once they fall into ruin. Unless we pull some strings."

"So we're bribing them?"

Maria's eyes turned cold for a moment. "In a way, yes. To make their matters worse, their family has been losing even more face ever since Lucian represented the family in court. He's a nonchalant pig, one of the worst. If he weren't needed for our plan, I'd rather see him lose his title along with what little pride he has left."

She held Lev's right hand firmly. "I need to be sure you're ready for this. Moritz, do you care about his fate in the grander scheme of things? Even if it gets worse than merely losing his title?"

Lev nodded. "No, I don't. If he gets us closer to our objective, then I'm fine with whatever happens to him after all has been said and done."

"Good, I'm glad we're on the same frequency."

Lev's eyes glinted. *Like in the good old days.*

Maria loosened her grip. "We'll be assigned to a table soon, but I'm pretty sure they won't seat us next to him."

She nervously looked at her watch. "It's almost time, stay here. I'll find a way to secure seats at his table."

As Maria walked into the crowd, Lev observed the splendid interior of the hall. His eyes fixated on one of the many paintings decorating the hall. It was a painting of an elderly man sitting on an impressive throne. Judging from his attire, Lev concluded that it must've been painted recently.

"A magnificent piece isn't it?" a woman next to Lev commented.

"Uh, yes. It's beautiful. I've never seen something as detailed as this."

"Oh? Are you from the vassal states then? If I may ask, of course."

"Oh no, I'm from the capital," Lev said as he made eye contact with the woman. She was dressed appropriately in an impressive waist dress sporting the imperial colours. She had a strange air to her, one that reminded Lev of Maria.

Yellow, red, white. Lev recounted as he visualised the Imperial flag in his mind.

Her eyes sharpened. "Everything alright?"

"I'm fine. I was just appraising your fine dress."

"Oh, I love this one. My husband bought it just for this occasion. As the pinnacle of the Empire, we should represent its glory in any way possible. Don't you agree?"

"Certainly."

A man dressed in black approached the woman, and gently tapped on her left shoulder. "Lady Webfield, the banquet will start any time now."

"Oh right." She looked at Lev with pouty lips. "I'm sorry our conversation ended so abruptly. Anyhow, I hope you'll enjoy the food! The calamari is exquisite here."

As the woman disappeared into the crowd, a clink on an empty wine glass announced the host's speech had begun.

Lev looked in the general direction, trying to make out who looked rich enough to host such an event. Alas, his definition of rich couldn't be applied to that of the imperial aristocracy. For him, having clean clothes and a meal three times a day was enough to qualify as rich.

He looked behind him, waiting for Maria to come back, but couldn't see her. The crowd gathered closer towards the stairs leading to the banquet's entrance doors, and soon, a chubby man climbed the stairs and faced the crowd.

He cleared his throat and quickly wiped leftover appetisers from the corners of his mouth on his napkin, before neatly tucking it back into his chest pocket.

"I'm glad all of you could make it," the man said with glittering eyes. "As you know, the menu tonight will consist of foods from various parts of the Empire. From the sweet fruits of the south, to the delicious meat from the northern hunting zones.

The North, huh. So their hunting grounds are near the great wall. Lev thought as he visualised a squad of starving Eurasian soldiers hunting a deer near the wall—only for a fat Imperial noble to swoop the tasty creature right under their noses, throw away the meat, and preserve the hide. A nice addition to his ever growing collection.

"Oh dear, you're finally here," the host announced. A woman joined the host, standing next to him with a wide grin spread on her face.

Lev immediately recognized the imperial colours woven into her dress.

It can't be.

"Could you take over, dear. I need to check if everything's ready for our guests." The host continued, still talking directly into the microphone.

"Of course dear. After all, a Webfield's banquet is nothing without the host's final touches," she said as her grin turned into a smile.

A smile that scared Lev, as he realised how wrong his initial comparison of her to Maria was. *She isn't wearing a mask like Maria, she's just being herself.*

Lev couldn't help but feel disgusted by the couple. They hadn't done anything wrong—at least not yet—but their demeanour ticked off the wrong boxes in his mind.

"Well, whilst we await my husband's final assessment, I'll bring you the latest news from the frontlines."

The crowd cheered, with some of them taking another glass in preparation.

Are they expecting good news?

"As you all probably already know, our frontline has pushed forward yet again!"

The crowd fell silent, waiting for more.

"We've almost conquered the entirety of the neutral zone. The last vestiges of Eurasian scum are fleeing away to central Europe."

Impossible.

Lev had been in the neutral zone a few months ago. It was true the Empire had been pushing Eurasia back in certain areas, but Eurasia had been responding in kind. Like they'd always done, year after year.

Lev shook his head. *I guess Imperial propaganda is as strong as Eurasian, if not stronger.*

"And with that said," Lady Webfield looked behind her, checking if her husband was still busy, "this feast shall honour our sons and daughters as they slaughter those pigs."

On the opposite side of the hall, a record player blasted the Imperial anthem on queue with Lady Webfield's last words.

She turned around, facing the doors leading to the banquet, and walked in. The doors slowly opened wider with each step she took until a vast assortment of food and drinks became visible.

"Let the festivities begin!"

The crowd formed pairs and entered the banquet following Webfield's tracks.

"Moritz!" a female voice shouted.

Lev turned around and saw Maria approaching from behind a thick layer of people. "Follow me, I've got us a table!"

It's time I put on my mask, like Maria.

BONUS CHAPTER 2

THE MASKED MAN

The entrance hall, once filled with an audience of hungry imperial nobles, now lay vacant as cleaning droids diligently cleansed off the dust and crumbs on the patterned carpet leading to the banquet.

"Where are we going Maria," Lev struggled against her firm grip. "My table is this way. You can't just drag me along to someone else's place."

"I told you I was going to secure us a table, and I will."

"You did, but I didn't know that meant stealing a spot from another table you somehow secured yourself a seat to!"

Maria stopped in front of a big round table near the centre of the room. "This is it," she noticed the seats were already taken with some utensils missing. "They're probably grabbing food. Let's wait for them here."

"What about the guy I'm replacing? This table seems way out of my league."

Maria looked at Lev with a strange smile. "We'll be just fine. I've been through this multiple times."

"Been through what?" Lev was about to say before feeling a hand on his shoulder.

"Mister, that's my place."

Without as much as resisting, Lev stood up, tidied his suit and looked at Maria with a hint of hesitation in his eyes.

"You're staying right where you are, Moritz."

The old noble tightened his grip on Lev. "What are you on about? This is my spot. Do you even realise who you're talking to?"

"I do. Do you?"

The man's face contorted in anger. "No, enlighten me."

"I'm Maria Von Mitternacht, and I think you should find another spot since I reserved this place for myself and my compatriot."

"Von Mitternacht? You mean you're—"

"That's right." Maria smirked. "Now get a move on or I'll get security here."

"B-but that's preposterous! You might hold a higher position than me, but what does this compatriot of yours hold against me?"

Maria lowered her head. "Moritz Antonius, former bluthund and decorated veteran of the Imperial army. I'm sure you understand how important it is to pay your respects to those who've given their best years to the army."

The noble let out an audible gulp as he tried forming a counter-argument. "I understand, but—"

"And I'm sure if your son were still here, he'd say the same," she added.

The man's brow furrowed further. "Don't you involve him in this. He has nothing to do with this banquet!"

"Then at least give your place away to someone more valuable than yourself. I heard they declined your application when you tried to join the army back in the day."

"Why did they deny you again?" Maria placed her index finger on her chin. "Oh... was it your height?"

The noble's forehead turned red as he opened his mouth to protest, but once Maria lifted her chin, looking down her nose at him with an icy stare in her blue eyes, he knew he had to back down and cut his losses.

He grumbled as he moved to another table, putting on a pleading smile as he went table by table to secure a new spot with his plate still filled with a slowly cooling meal.

"Well, let's wait for the others then, shall we?" Maria declared in a totally indifferent tone. She had a different air about her after scaring off that noble. It was as if she'd turned into an entirely different person.

I'll have to secure my mask as tight as hers, then.

"So Maria, who's this fella," another noble said with a peculiar accent.

"This here, Gabriel, is Moritz Antonius," Maria announced as Gabriel carefully observed the foe who had just stolen the seat of one of his closest friends.

"I see. And how did you end up in this horrible place, Moritz?"

"Horrible place?" Lev answered with a raised eyebrow.

"He's a Bluthund, or rather, he was."

"Oh, I see," Gabriel replied as he focused his attention on his plate of steaming vegetables. "Well, that's nice I suppose. Glad you're here instead of my stubborn friend over there."

Gabriel glanced at the noble Maria had scared away a few moments prior. He'd finally found himself a seat near the entrance.

Maria giggled behind her hand as she looked at the poor bastard. He was seated next to a few idle butler droids who were staring at the man with their dead eyes as they recharged.

"I hope his meal isn't as cold as his new friends by now," Gabriel added with a slight hint of mockery in his voice.

"Moritz, huh. Maria told me about you."

Lev looked at Gabriel with an expressionless face, trying his best to hide behind Moritz's cold mask. "I've been hired for a lot, sir. Word must've spread."

"Yeah, I figured. Well, she told me you're one hell of an agent." Gabriel took a sip from his wine.

"You were and still are a fine asset to the empire, Moritz, I'll be awaiting great things from you during the selection."

Lev cleared his throat. "The selection, sir?"

"You don't know? Why else would you be here," Gabriel said with an uncomfortable chuckle.

Lev felt Maria's leg bumping against his as she looked at him with a forced smile. "Yes, sorry. I thought you meant something else."

"Like what?"

The jolt of the last empty chair at their table broke the tension.

"I'm sorry I'm late," another male voice announced.

"If it isn't Lucian. I heard the Ruxgan house is still competing this year?" Gabriel took a bite from a decorated cabbage in the centre of his platter.

"I don't believe you're supposed to eat that, Gabriel," Lucian said as he eyed Gabriel, who was still peacefully consuming his cabbage.

"Now don't be silly, Lucian. It's bad manners to waste food. I'm sure the emperor would agree."

Lev noticed Lucian clenching his fork with his left hand. "And what's that supposed to mean?"

Maria swiftly glanced at Lev. Her expression made it abundantly clear to him that things were about to swiftly turn for the worse if they didn't intervene.

"I'm just saying your family is like this piece of cabbage. A fine decoration, to be sure. But when compared to the juicy oysters surrounding it, it's nothing special," Gabriel calmly said whilst squeezing out a slice of lemon onto an oyster.

"What's gotten into you, Gabriel. Let the man be," Maria said softly, trying to de-escalate the forming storm between the two nobles.

"My apologies. I only meant it as a joke. Now, Lucian, I would like to introduce you to our unexpected guest."

Lucian cast his eyes over Lev. His eyes quickly scrutinised Lev's entire being, inspecting every single detail. Lev could practically hear the mental workings inside Lucian's head, listing his every trait, calculating his worth.

But in the end, Lucian merely looked down at his plate and sighed. "I see. So Count Fritz isn't accompanying us tonight."

"Well he was, until," Gabriel said as he looked at Maria, who hid behind her glass.

"Anyway, this here is Moritz, Moritz Antonius. He's a man of renown. Don't underestimate him because of his attire or manners. He was one of the Empire's best spies."

Lucian kept his gaze focused on his food, still uninterested. "I see. So what does he have to do with me, I wonder?"

"He's participating, shouldn't you show some respect to your retainer, Lucian?"

Lucian's eyes went wide. "My retainer? Don't be ridiculous!"

That last part Lucian had said a bit too loud. He felt the eyes of nearby guests scanning him.

"Oh, I'm sorry. I was under the impression that the Ruxgan household didn't have a participant for the upcoming event."

"We don't, but I never agreed to sign on Moritz. I don't trust him. If he was such a great spy, what's stopping him from spying on me for the other families."

Gabriel chuckled as he wiped off a piece of sauce from the corners of his mouth. "You should be grateful, boy. Your family is dead meat if you don't find a good retainer to defend their prestige."

Lucian silently contemplated for a moment before speaking again. "The selection has nothing to do with upholding my family's prestige."

"It has *everything* to do with it," Maria interjected.

Lev kept his silence. He felt they'd finally caught Lucian in a downward spiral. *He knows how important the selection is, but whatever is left of his pride is holding him back.*

"Lucian," Lev interrupted their discussion, "If I may, I'd be a fine asset in the selection."

The three went silent as they focused on Lev. "But it's like you said earlier. If your family doesn't require me, then I'll just offer my services to another."

"Le—Moritz!" Maria shouted, quickly biting her lip as she realised the mask she had so desperately tried to perfect had almost cracked.

Lucian looked around him, at the countless nobles chatting about. He couldn't hear any individual conversation over the general din, but he knew that most of the drivel in the room was at a surface level, a paltry attempt to appear civilised and amicable before they returned to their mansions to plot the downfalls of the very "friends" they'd just broken bread with.

"Fine," he finally said. "I'll take you in as my family's retainer."

"Then we will seal the deal after dinner," Maria said as she returned to her platter.

"So, anyway. How's your wife, Gabriel?" Maria asked. Contrary to her previously calculating and cold countenance, she now exuded warmth and integrity—though Lev wasn't sure about the latter being true.

"She's a bit under the weather these days. I've had her examined by one of the best Imperial doctors, but to no avail."

As their chatter continued, Lev's mind wandered elsewhere. He'd never understood this kind of meaningless talk. It felt as fake as his Imperial identity.

I guess Eurasia's too pragmatic, but I don't mind that. I'd rather have the hard truth shoved into my face than parade around it like a damn fool.

"Moritz, don't you agree? This salmon is delicious. I heard they're cultivated locally."

Lev merely nodded in response. He didn't know what salmon was, and to provide some much needed honesty to the situation, he didn't really care. All he cared for was the end this charade and to gain full citizenship.

* * *

The comfort of their bunk was enough to satisfy an Eurasian's needs.

"Finally, a break," Lev huffed as he sat in one of the few decent chairs in the hideout's living quarters. He gazed at the four occupants of the quarters. Maik was sketching schematics on a blackboard whilst Brutus played poker against himself.

Maria had left a few hours ago, after escorting Lev back. He still wasn't used to the capital's metro system, let alone the hundreds of small alleys leading to the hideout.

"We'll meet again in two months when the selection starts," she'd said moments before she disappeared into the night. "I'm counting on you." Her words had echoed in the streets a few seconds longer.

In front of Lev, on the other side of the room, was an Imperial propaganda poster. It depicted an imperial soldier strangling a snake over the Mediterranean sea. *I guess the snake's supposed to be the Eurasian army. Or perhaps, its council?*

He'd seen posters like this back home, though most were simple recruitment posters and spared no space mocking their Imperial opponents. *I wonder which beast the Imperials would be.*

"Why do we have these posters here? Aren't we fighting them?" Lev blurted out a bit too loud.

Both Maik and Brutus gave him a confused look. *If only the walls could hear.*

Maik looked back at Lev, laying down his marker on a nearby table. "That's true, but we're still in the lion's den. Moreover, as I'm sure you're aware, this is still supposedly an Imperial warehouse."

"That's true," Lev agreed.

"Well, I can't focus like this," Brutus huffed. He threw his cards on the table and went for Maik's markers. It took only a few seconds for Brutus to scribble something on the poster.

"Brutus what in the hell are you doing!" Maik shouted as he grabbed a smirking Brutus by the arms.

The marker dropped on the floor. "The deed has already been done, Your Highness," Brutus said with a wide smile plastered on his face.

The snake, previously victimised by the Imperial soldier, now had an extra pair of arms. Its left arm held a glass of pale ale, whilst its right arm smashed the soldier right in the crown jewels. The childish emotions added to the soldier's face sealed Brutus' magnum opus.

"Well, that's... definitely something new," Maik whispered under his breath whilst rolling his eyes.

"Thousands of miles away from home, a new name, yet still the same." Lev added.

Brutus walked back to his table and rearranged the cards into his left hand. "You bet. Though I've gotten better at poker while you were gone."

"Dare to say that again?" Maik said just as he picked up the marker again.

"Hell yes! I've gotten better. Possibly better than you. Prove me wrong if you got the balls!"

It didn't take more for the two to embroil themselves in a heated match of poker.

"Lev, you joining us?" Brutus said as he took another card from the staple.

"No, I think I'm gonna head to my bunk if you don't mind."

"You do you," Maik said whilst waving his free hand. "Don't forget to train your imperial etiquette tomorrow, Lev. Maria's orders."

Right... Almost forgot about that.

Lev turned on his bunk's light as he grabbed for a stash of documents. His eyes paused on an aged yellow page. "Imperial Etiquette for Administration," it read.

I bet those noble kids grow up on this kind of stuff. At least I had a childhood.

He flipped to the next document. "The Imperial draft and the honour of serving one's nation."

This sounds more familiar. It's similar to the levy system if I recall correctly.

He shoved the document from under its plastic binder and inspected the first page.

"How to prepare for your children's application to the royal imperial officers' academy," the first line read.

Lev had gotten quite interested in Imperial society since arriving. It wasn't like he'd had a choice in the matter, but he was happy to find he enjoyed the material he had to go through for the selection.

If most of the right hand are nobles, they must've gone through the academy as well. Seems like it's a must for the higher class here.

His eyes stopped at the end of the following paragraph and briefly re-read the last sentence.

"The Imperial System allows commoners to rise up the social ladder whilst demoting noble families whose performance has fallen below the minimum."

They're swapping the incompetent ones for fresh families. If only Eurasia had something like this for its council.

"The system revolves around a healthy competition between families. Promotion or demotion is based on several factors, including but not limited to: loyalty, military service, donations to the state..."

A smile formed on Lev's lips. *Donations to the state. That's a nice way of saying 'pay lots of taxes.' The old world had a system like this, though it had nothing to do with improving one's social rank.*

"...and above all, a royal degree at one of the many prestigious academies of the Empire."

That's what I'm missing. Moritz has one—at least I think he has—but I don't.

He slid the document back into the binder and grabbed another one. This time, his smile faded quickly.

"Imperial Economics."

Time to dig in.

AFTERWORD

Well, where do we start? This volume was a wild ride for (hopefully) you, the reader, but also for us. It's taken us more time than we'd like to admit to get this book out. We've been busy with the webtoon production whilst trying to keep up our writing pace but it hasn't been easy.

Having said that, this book was a major leap forward for the lord of goblins series. New foes appeared, mysteries were uncovered, and Lev's still not done with his rise to power just yet.

As we and our quills jump into the next issue's manuscript, we hope you'll wait for us a tad longer. I'm sure that'll be another task us authors and editors will slave on in the coming months. Speaking of our editors, without them, this book would've never reached its current polished state. They have battled through various paragraphs, slain the punctuation dragon and climbed the grammar mountain. Truly commendable work from the MoonQuill team yet again!

Stay tuned for Vol. 4!

About Michiel Werbrouck

Michiel Werbrouck was born in Oxford, UK but grew up in the Belgian city of Leuven. He is currently studying Applied Computer Science while working as a freelance Graphic Designer and Marketing Assistant.

Aside from his studies, Michiel is an up-and-coming author, having started out writing short Sci-Fi stories on various online platforms before finally taking the next step. Since then he has improved his craft, honing his writing skills.

In his free time, Michiel enjoys playing grand strategy games, hanging out with friends and reading fantasy novels. As a tech fan, he spends lots of time developing apps and games of his own.

In the future Michiel sees himself developing games about his books, working on software/web IT solutions, writing more books and travelling the world.

About Hadi Y. Bendakji

Hadi Bendakji has always been a fan of fantasy and science fiction, whether they be games or books. Since childhood, these interests spurred a desire to create his own works.

Hadi was born and raised in Beirut, Lebanon and graduated in Bir Hassan's Technical College, graduating as an IT-Software Developer.

Due to his studies and family life, he'd been unable to spend time on creative pursuits until after his graduation.

He now pushes himself to constantly improve his skills in order to achieve his dreams.

On top of his passion for creative writing and gaming, Hadi likes listening to metal, reading books, and watching historical documentaries.

Please consider leaving a
review on the book's
Amazon page.

Thank you very much for
enjoying our work.

Thank you for reading a MoonQuill original novel. To experience more exciting stories, visit us at moonquill.com

To know when we release new books, join our mailing list from our site and receive three books for free!

We will never spam you!

To talk with other members of the MoonQuill community, check out our community Discord.

Finally, we would really appreciate it if you could take a moment to review the book. Every review greatly helps the author and supports their ability to continue writing fantastic books for us to enjoy.